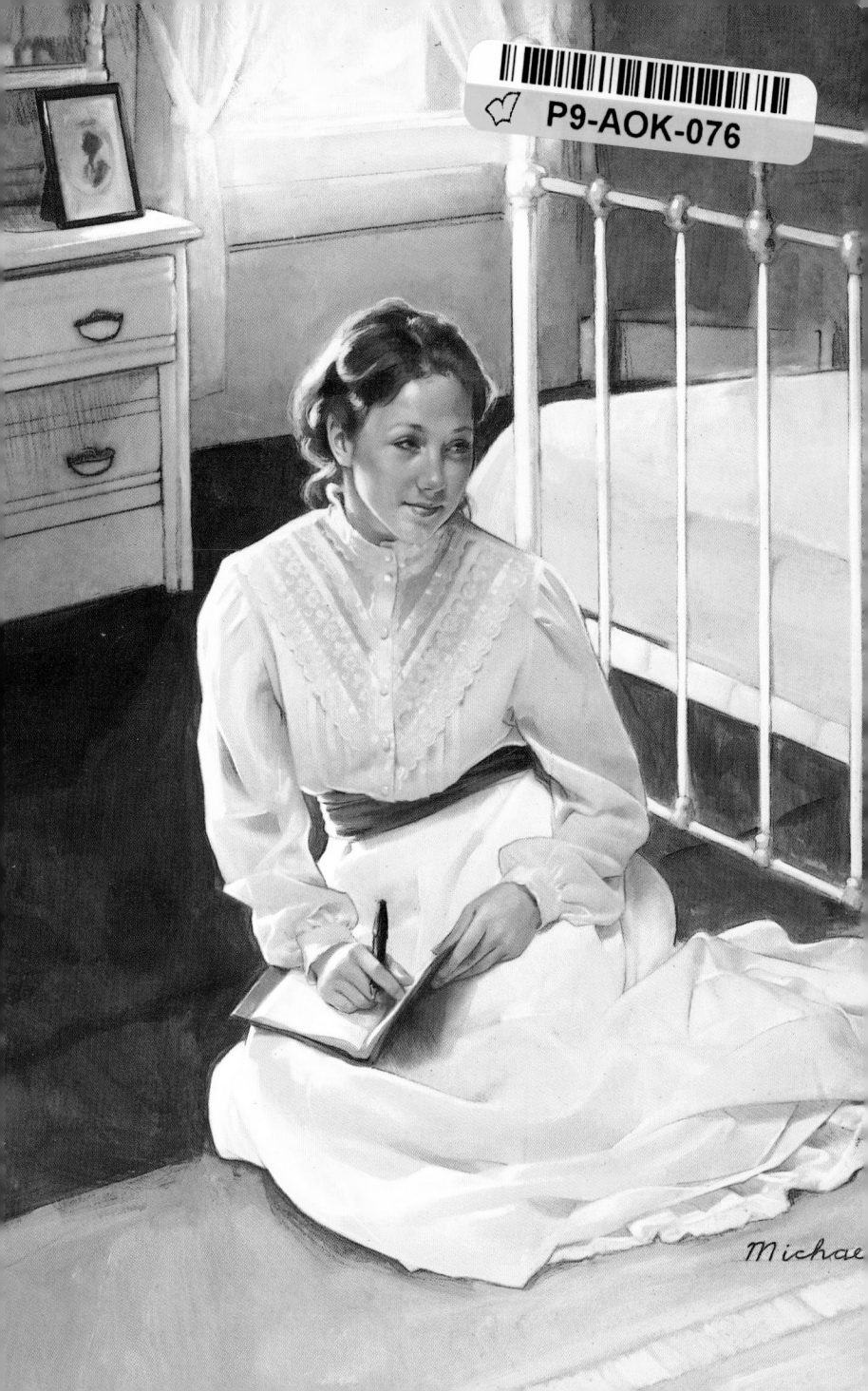

Michae[l]

Betsy in Spite of Herself

Betsy in Spite of Herself

Maud Hart Lovelace

Illustrated by Vera Neville

HarperTrophy®
An Imprint of HarperCollinsPublishers

LC Number 46-11995
ISBN 0-06-440111-1 (pbk.)
First published by Thomas Y. Crowell Company in 1946.
First Harper Trophy edition, 1979.
❖
Visit us on the World Wide Web!
www.harperchildrens.com

For
ROSEMOND *and* ROMIE LUNDQUIST

Contents

Foreword

When I was first asked to speak about Maud Hart Lovelace I had to reread all ten of my Betsy-Tacy books. I would like to make this sound like a hardship, but most of you know better. There are three authors whose body of work I have reread more than once over my adult life: Charles Dickens, Jane Austen, and Maud Hart Lovelace. It was, as always, a pleasure and delight.

And the truth is that I have been preparing for this speech, in a variety of ways, for thirty years, and especially for the last ten. That was the decade in which I began to examine most closely what it meant to be a feminist in America, as I am, and why I felt so strongly that the women's movement and what I believe it stands for has changed my life.

Many of those issues have been explored in my column in *The New York Times*, and over and over again I have tried to reinforce a simple message that I believe has been distorted, muddled, misunderstood, and just plain lied about in recent years by those who want women to go, not forward, but backward.

And that is that feminism is about choices. It is about women choosing for themselves which life roles they wish to pursue. It is about deciding who does and gets and merits and earns and succeeds in what by smarts, capabilities, and heart—not by gender. It is about honoring individuals because of their humanity, not their physiology.

And that is why my theme today is: Betsy Ray, Feminist Icon.

Could there be better books, and could there be a better girl, adolescent, young woman, to teach us all those things about choices than the Betsy-Tacy books and Betsy herself, along with her widely disparate circle of Tacy and Tib, Julia and Margaret, Mrs. Ray and Anna the hired girl, Mrs. Poppy and Miss Mix, Carney and Winona, Miss Bangeter and Miss Clarke? All these different women, who go so many different ways, with false starts and stops, with disappointments and limitations, and yet a sense that they can find a place for themselves in the world.

Do you realize that not once, in any book, does any individual, male or female, suggest to Betsy that she cannot, as she so hopes to do, become a writer? Can anyone possibly appreciate the impact that made on a child like me, wanting it too but seeing all around me on the bookshelves the names of men and seeing all around me in my house the domesticated ways of women?

In the early books, of course, this is not what we see. We see prototypes, really, as surely as Snow White and Rose Red, or Cinderella and her stepsisters. We see three little girls who begin as types: the shy and earnest one; the no-nonsense and literal one; and the ringleader, the storyteller, the adventurer, the center—Elizabeth Warrington Ray. Then the adventures and, more important, the traditions begin—the picnics on the Big Hill, the forays to little Syria, the shopping trips at Christmastime, and Betsy's sheets of foolscap piling up in her Uncle Keith's old trunk.

The books are simply stories of small town life and enduring friendship among little girls, and so it is easy to overlook their importance as teaching tools. But consider the alternatives to children in the early grades. The images of girls tend, overwhelmingly, to be of fairy princesses spinning straw into gold or sleeping until they are awakened by a prince.

Even the best ones usually show us caricatures instead of characters. Recently, for example, I wrote an introduction for a fiftieth anniversary edition of *Madeline* (Viking, 1989). It is one of my favorite picture books for children, has been since I myself was a child, mostly because of one line which sums up the rest of it: "To the tiger in the zoo Madeline just said 'Pooh, pooh.'"

Madeline, unlike the straw-spinning princesses, has attitude. She is nobody's fool.

But attitude, truth to tell, is a surface, two-dimensional characteristic, attractive as it may be. The stories of Betsy, Tacy, and Tib transcend attitude just as the simplistic drawings of the early books give way to the more realistic (albeit, to my mind, slightly oversweet) pictures. They are ultimately books about character, and especially about the character of one girl whose greatest sin, throughout the books, is to undervalue herself.

For those are the mistakes Betsy finds she cannot forgive, when she sells herself short, when she is not all she can be. As opposed to the shy, retiring, and respectful girl who became so valued in girl's fiction, Betsy does best when she serves herself, when she is true to herself. In this she most resembles two other fictional heroines who, not surprisingly, also long to be writers and take their work very seriously indeed. One is Anne Shirley of the *Anne of Green Gables* books, and the other is Jo March of *Little Women*.

But the key difference, I think, is a critical one. Both Anne and Jo are implicitly made to pay in those books for the fact that they do not conform to feminine norms. Anne begins life as an orphan and never is permitted to forget that she must work for a living—in fact, you might call her the Joe Willard of girls, although she is far less prickly and far more easy to like than Joe Willard. Jo March of *Little Women* habitually reminds herself how unattractive she is and settles down, in one of the most unconvincing matches in fiction, with the older, most unromantic Professor Bhaer. It is her beautiful sister Amy who gets the real guy, the rich and romantic Laurie.

* * *

Betsy, by contrast, never had to pay for the sin of being herself; in fact, she only finds herself under a cloud when she is less than herself. At base, she is a charmed soul from beginning to end because she can laugh at herself and take herself seriously at the same time, because she is serious but never a prig, and interested in boys but never a flirt. Can anyone forget the moment when, returning from the sophomore dance at Schiller Hall with that absolute poop Phil Brandish trying to worm his fist into her pocket, she turns to him with desperation and blurts out, "You might as well know. I don't hold hands."

In fact it's probably in that book, *Betsy in Spite of Herself*, that we see Betsy most the way I think we were always meant to see her, as a girl who will do what is right for her, not necessarily what the world wants her to do. But first, like most of us, she has to do what is wrong for her to find out what is right. She decides to nab Phil just for the fun of it, and to that end she adds the letter E to the end of her perfectly good name, sprays herself with Jockey Club perfume, and uses green stationery to write notes instead of her poetry or stories. It's inevitable— when the real Betsy sneaks out, in the form of a song parody she and Tacy invented before the Phil/Betsy affair began, they break up. But instead of a sore heart, Betsy is left with Shakespeare: "This above all: to thine own self be true."

Betsy already knows, as do we, that that self varies widely from girl to girl, that there is no little box that will fit them all. In *Heaven to Betsy*, she says, in the passage that made the future so clear and yet so mysterious for me:

> She had been almost appalled, when she started going around with Carney and Bonnie, to discover how fixed and definite their ideas of marriage were. They both had cedar hope chests and took pleasure in embroidering their initials on towels to lay away. Each one had picked out a silver pattern and they were planning to give each other spoons in these patterns for Christmases and birthdays. When Betsy and Tacy and Tib talked about their future they planned to be writers, dancers, circus acrobats.

Betsy never looks down on those aspirations of Carney and Bonnie's. But she never looks away from her own aspirations. She follows a sensible progression from writing, to dreaming of being a writer, to actually saying she is going to be one, to sending her stories (when she is a mere senior in high school) to various women's magazines. She makes the mistake so many of us make—like Jo in *Little Women*, she learns early on that writing about debutantes in Park Avenue penthouses is doomed to failure if you've neither debuted nor visited Park Avenue—but her gumption carries her through.

And there are, interestingly, no naysayers among her

family members. While the Rays have three daughters, early on two of them are already committed to having careers outside the home, Julia as an opera singer, Betsy as a writer. Betsy's parents are totally committed to this idea for them both, sending Julia to the Twin Cities and even to Europe to further her training as a singer, and arguing vociferously that Betsy's work is as good as any that appears in popular magazines.

The idea of something that is yours to do became narrower and narrower as my mother grew up. As Betty Friedan wrote in *The Feminine Mystique* (Dell, 1963), by the time my mother was ready to enter what Julia always called The Great World, it had narrowed to one role and one role alone, that of wife and mother.

I don't know when exactly I knew that that was never going to be enough for me. But I know where I got the idea that more was possible. It wasn't from career women or role models—when I was a girl, there really weren't any.

I learned it from books, and none more than from the stories about Betsy, Tacy, and Tib. Because the most important thing about Betsy Ray is that she has a profound sense of confidence and her own worth.

Of course, if this had been wrapped in a sanctimonious, plaster saint package, Betsy would have been—perish the thought—Elsie Dinsmore, the perfect, boring little girl of popular fiction who Betsy herself once mocks. And, if there had been no boys in the books, I, for one, wouldn't have read them.

But we did read them, many of us, for so many reasons: because Maud Hart Lovelace had a real gift for adapting the prose to the appropriate age level, and the themes, too; because we fell in love, not only with Betsy but with Tacy and Tib and all the others, and wanted to know from year to year what was happening to them; because of Magic Wavers and Sunday night sandwiches and smoky coffee brewed out of doors and all the other little ordinary things that, in some fashion, became our ordinary things.

And because they were just like us.

But we know there are many us's, with many different goals and aspirations. For many years those goals and aspirations were truncated by one simple fact: our sex. Everything around us reflected that, from who sat on the Supreme Court, to who listened to our chests when we were sick, to who oversaw services when we went to church on Sunday.

But from time to time we encountered a teacher, or a parent, or even a book that told us that we should let our ambitions fly, that we should believe in ourselves, that the only limits we should put on what we tried for were the limits of our desires and our talents. When I told people I was going to give this speech, most had never heard of

Betsy-Tacy, and I had to describe them as a series of books for girls. But they were so much more than that to one little girl who grew up to be a woman writer and who, perhaps, learned that she *could* by the example given inside these books.

—ANNA QUINDLEN
(*Adapted from a speech given to the Twin Cities Chapter of the Betsy-Tacy Society on June 12, 1993*)

This above all: to thine own self be true,
And it must follow, as the night the day,
Thou canst not then be false to any man.

—WM. SHAKESPEARE

1

The Winding Hall of Fate

"JUST A FEW LINES to open the record of my sophomore year. Isn't it mysterious to begin a new journal like this? I can run my fingers through the fresh clean pages but I cannot guess what the writing on them will be. It is almost as though I were ushered into the Winding Hall of Fate, but next day's destiny was hidden behind a turning."

❧ 1 ❧

Betsy paused, and read what she had written with a dreamy self-satisfied smile.

She was curled up on a pillow beside her Uncle Keith's trunk which she used as a desk. It stood in her bedroom, a large blue and white room with two windows in which white curtains were blowing. The time was September, 1907, and next day she would be a sophomore in the Deep Valley, Minnesota, High School.

"My ambition," she continued, *"is to be an author some day, and therefore I'll describe myself and some of my friends. My name is Elizabeth Warrington Ray but most people call me Betsy. My sister Julia always calls me Bettina.*

"I am tall, and thin as a willow sapling with a droop which my mother calls a stoop but I hope isn't too homely. Some benighted people, boys mostly, even think it is pretty. I have dark brown hair, put up in a pompadour over a rat, perfectly beautiful skin but just ordinary hazel eyes, and my teeth are parted in the middle.

"My hair is wavy most of the time, but to manage that I have to put it up on Wavers at night, which I despise, because what am I going to do when I get married? But on the other

hand if I don't put it up on Wavers, I probably never will get married. That's the way I look at it. Not that I care about getting married. But I certainly want to be asked.

"I don't see why Edison and these people who go around inventing autos and things can't concentrate on something important like how to make a girl's hair stay curled without Wavers. Of course, I adore autos, though.

"And speaking of autos . . ." Betsy paused, and gave her diary a look. *"Speaking of autos, we are just back from two months at the lake and the whole town is agog, simply agog, about a new boy with a bright red auto. He's the grandson of the rich old Brandish who lives across the slough. His name is Phil . . ."*

"Hoo, hoo, Betsy," came a masculine voice outside the house. Betsy slammed her journal shut, crammed it into her trunk and ran to the window.

In the street below, a black-haired boy with a bright humorous face sat on a bare-backed brown nag. Cab Edwards was riding the family horse down to the watering trough at the foot of High Street.

"Hello," called Betsy.

"Hello. Heard you got back last night. Have a good time?"

"Swell. Any fun around here?"

"Dead as a doornail. Seen anyone yet?"

"Just talked on the 'phone to a few of the kids."

"What are you doing today?"

"Picnic with Tacy."

"Well, I'll be in tonight." He slapped the horse's rump, then changed his mind and "whoa'ed" her to a stop. "Say: Read *Ivanhoe*?"

"Sure," said Betsy. "Why?"

"Don't you remember? Gaston told us to read it over the summer. We have to pass a test on it, second day of school."

"I remember. Just like one of Gaston's ideas! It doesn't bother me, though. I read *Ivanhoe* in the cradle practically."

"Gosh, I wish I had," said Cab, and slapped his horse again, and rode on down the hill.

Betsy looked after him, and up the hill beyond where trees made a thick green fringe against the sky. High Street itself ran horizontally, halfway up a hill which was criss-crossed by streets and had a German Catholic College on the crest. Off at another angle rose the cluster of hills where she had lived as a child, where Tacy still lived, and where they would picnic today. All were bathed in an early morning freshness.

Betsy went back to her trunk and the journal.

"Where was I? Oh yes, Phil."

"It's a good thing there's a new boy on the scene for last year's Crowd is shattered, simply shattered. Larry and Herbert Humphreys have gone to California to live. Their going was tragic because they're boys. Two perfectly good boys snatched by Fate out of Deep Valley High School.

"There's a new girl named Irma coming into our Crowd, but there always seem to be plenty of girls. I wonder why that is???? She's nice; she's very sweet, with a figure like Lillian Russell's. The boys are crazy about her . . . none of us can see why exactly. She and Winona are thick as thieves.

"Winona is tall and thin with black eyes that are positively snapping. She's full of the D. . . . Carney, (Caroline Sibley), is very pretty, neat as a pin, with eye glasses perched on her nose, and one dimple. The boys like her, girls like her, too. She always says just what she thinks, and she wouldn't know how to be catty. It's hard to describe Carney without making her sound sissy. But she isn't. Not a bit. She's full of the D . . . too.

"The other girls in our Crowd are Alice, who lives up near Tacy and is very full of fun, but her parents are strict. And Tacy who is . . .

well, there's nobody like Tacy. She's been my chum since we were five years old, and you couldn't have a better one. Tacy's bashful but full of the D . . . She likes to imagine things the same as I do and make adventurous plans about when we grow up. Most of the girls just plan on getting married but Tacy and I want to see the Taj Mahal by moonlight, and go to the Passion Play, *and live in Paris with French maids to draw our baths. The funny thing about Tacy is that she's perfectly indifferent to boys. She's the only girl I know who doesn't think that Boys are the Center of the Universe.*

"Tib is my chum, too, but she moved to Milwaukee. She's little and blonde and very pretty. At least she used to be. I wonder whether she's changed as much as I have in the last two years? I've certainly changed.

"As for boys, the most interesting boy in school isn't in our Crowd. He isn't in any crowd. His name is Joe Willard, and he's blond and terribly handsome. He hasn't any family, but lives in a room somewhere and works at the Creamery afternoons and Saturdays. Last year he won the Freshman points in the Essay Contest. Away from Elizabeth Warrington Ray! The aforementioned Miss Ray is

going to have REE—VENGE *this year. (There's an Essay Contest every year.)*

"Cab just about lives at our house, and so does Tony. I used to be in love with Tony last year. Doesn't that seem funny? Tom comes here a lot when he's in town. He goes away to school though. Cox Military!

"These boys are nice. They're perfectly dandy. But they're just neighbors. There's nothing romantic about them. Where is Romance, anyway, I wonder? Is it in these unwritten pages?"

Betsy flipped them thoughtfully through her fingers. A gong sounded downstairs, and she put her journal away a second time. Going to the mirror she turned her self-styled willowy figure slowly for inspection. Her blue sailor suit was old, chosen because of the planned picnic, but the belt encircled a waist gratifyingly slim. Betsy's face, however, was anxious. She usually gave a mirror an anxious face.

The door opened, and her mother's red head ducked in.

"Dressed? I'm glad. Get Julia up; will you?"

"I'll try," said Betsy. She crossed the hall to her older sister's room.

Getting Julia up was harder than it looked to be

when one saw her. Slender, almost fragile, in a thin white nightgown, she was flung lightly across the bed, face down, her dark hair fanning out.

Betsy shook her vigorously. "Julia! The gong! There it goes again!"

"Let it go gallager."

"But breakfast's on the table." Betsy shook her again.

Julia sat upright, her violet eyes flashing.

"But *why* do I have to get up? Just because Papa was born on a farm and all ten children always came to meals on time . . ."

The door swung open and Margaret, the nine-year-old sister, came in, her hair ribbon spreading white wings above her shining English bob. Her black-lashed eyes, always large and serious, widened in surprise.

"Why, that's *just* what Papa was saying. All *ten* of them used to be on time, and he sent me up to . . ."

"I know. I know. Well, *I* don't live on a farm. And I'm going to be an opera singer." But Julia was good natured now. She jumped out of bed, smiling. "Opera singers," she continued, dressing under her nightgown, "have sense enough to work at night and sleep all morning. They *invariably* sleep until noon. And that's what I'm going to do . . ."

"Come on, Margaret," said Betsy and they ran downstairs.

Sunshine was pouring into the dining room which was papered with pears and grapes above a plate rail full of Mrs. Ray's best china. Here, too, the curtains were blowing, full of autumnal zest. Mr. and Mrs. Ray were already seated, and Mr. Ray looked up sternly as Betsy and Margaret slipped quietly into their chairs. Tall, large, dark-haired and hazel-eyed like Betsy, his usual expression was one of calm benevolence, but he lost it when the girls were late to breakfast.

Mrs. Ray had already poured a soothing first cup of coffee, and now Anna, the hired girl, brought in eggs and bacon, raw fried potatoes, buttered toast, and cocoa for the children. Mrs. Ray made conversation briskly. "The girls go back to school tomorrow."

"If Julia gets up in time." Mr. Ray turned to look through the music room, up the still empty stairs.

"Cab came by this morning, Papa," Betsy said talking very fast. "He's having a fit because he hasn't read *Ivanhoe*, and Gaston said we had to read it over the summer vacation. Do you think that's fair, Papa?"

"Reading *Ivanhoe* isn't exactly punishment," Mr. Ray replied.

"Of course not. But it's the principle of the thing."

Julia slid into her chair, shook out her napkin. "It's the principle of the thing, Papa," she repeated.

Mr. Ray gave her a look to show she hadn't fooled him.

"There's a principle involved in getting down to breakfast, too," he said. But as his gaze swept the now completed circle, his brow cleared. "Reading *Ivanhoe* won't kill any of you," he decided cheerfully. "How about another cup of coffee, Jule?"

When the coffee was drunk, he walked around the table, kissing his womenfolk. Mrs. Ray jumped up, ran her arm through his and walked with him out to the porch.

"It's good to be going back to the store," Mr. Ray said. "The lake's fine, but it isn't like 400 High Street."

"This house is a year old, and I love it as much as I ever did. I'm going to have fun cleaning it," Mrs. Ray replied.

The morning was busy. Anna started scrubbing while Mrs. Ray at the telephone ordered meat and groceries. Then Mrs. Ray wound her red head in a towel and started scrubbing, too. Julia and Betsy unpacked the trunk, settled drawers and closets. Margaret went out to pick greens for the fireplace and a bouquet of nasturtiums.

After noon dinner Tony, without knocking, poked his head in at the door.

"Hello, folks! Glad you're back."

The girls hailed him joyfully, and accompanied him

to the kitchen to greet Anna. He persuaded Mrs. Ray to come down from a step ladder, picked up Washington, the cat, and they all sat down to talk.

Tony's black hair stood up in a curly bush. He had black eyes, bold and laughing, and a lazy teasing air.

"Last year I was in love with him. Now he's almost like a brother. Life is strange," thought Betsy.

"What did you do at the lake?" Tony was asking.

"I learned to swim," said Margaret.

"Julia forgot about Hugh, got a new beau, and then bounced him before we came home. Not a nice thing to do," Betsy said.

"I didn't have any piano," Julia explained plaintively. "And Bettina wrote all summer . . . a novel, I guess."

"Speaking of novels," said Tony, "what about this *Ivanhoe* Gaston said we had to read?"

"I read it years ago. But I think it was beastly of him to assign it. Have you read it?"

"How could I? I've been delivering groceries all summer. And by the way, I'm supposed to be doing it now." He lounged to his feet. "I'm late, but I'll be a little later if Julia will pound the ivories just to prove you're home."

So Julia went to the piano and started one of last year's songs. Mrs. Ray and Margaret, Betsy and Tony stood behind her and sang:

"Dreaming, dreaming,
 Of you sweetheart I am dreaming,
 Dreaming of days when you loved me best,
 Dreaming of hours that have gone to rest . . ."

Then Tony hurried off to his delivery wagon and Mrs. Ray to her step ladder, and Margaret went out to play. Julia stayed at the piano.

"I'm going to have a lesson today. Better warm up," she said, opening an opera score.

Julia spent all her allowance on opera scores; spent it before she received it, usually, for she had an ill-advised charge account with a music store in St. Paul. She got her money's worth, though. She sang the operas from cover to cover, all the parts and all the choruses. The newest one was called *La Boheme*: it was about Bohemians.

Bohemians, like Tib's grandparents? Betsy had asked. No, Julia had explained, artists and writers. The poet, Rudolph, was writing when a little seamstress came to his door asking a light for her candle. She told him her name, and then came the aria which Julia started now. *"Mi chiamano Mimi,"* it began, and it meant, Julia said, that people called her Mimi, although her name was Lucia; and it went on to say that the flowers she embroidered in her work made her think of distant flowery fields.

"*Mi chiamano Mimi*," Betsy hummed softly and found a shoe box and went to pack a picnic lunch.

A Betsy-Tacy picnic, she thought as she foraged, was just about the nicest thing in the world.

When the box was packed and firmly tied with a string, she put on her hat and set off for Hill Street, up side streets that climbed gently at first, then more and more steeply. Children were playing in the streets, but tomorrow they would be in school.

"Tomorrow," thought Betsy, "I start down the Winding Hall of Fate."

And just at that moment, with what seemed prophetic timing, an automobile horn wailed behind her. Turning, she saw a red automobile. It was passing with almost meteorlike swiftness, fifteen or twenty miles an hour. Yet Betsy had a good view of a large boy, wearing a visored tan cap and a brown linen dust coat, behind the steering wheel.

2

Dree-eee-eaming

WHEN SHE ENTERED the familiar block in which she
had lived for the first fourteen years of her life, Tacy
came running to meet her. Tacy was tall, with red hair
bound in Grecian braids, blue eyes that were both shy
and merry, tender red lips, a slender freckled face. She
and Betsy embraced and kissed.

Tacy carried a copy of *Ivanhoe*.

"That fiend of a Gaston!" Betsy said.

Tacy groaned. "I only started it yesterday. Gee, it's long!"

"Take it along on the picnic."

"Not much! I'm not going to mix up any old crusades with Mamma's devil's food cake."

"Devil's food cake?" cried Betsy. "Really?"

"This is a celebration," Tacy said, "because you're home."

At the Kellys' white house, Betsy lingered to talk to Tacy's large gentle mother, with rosy efficient Katie, the sister Julia's age, and the other sisters and brothers. It was midafternoon when she and Tacy at last started up the Big Hill. This rose behind the former Ray cottage, across the street from Tacy's, a slope which Betsy and Tacy had climbed uncounted times.

They climbed contentedly now with the shoe box, a wicker basket spread with a red and white cloth, newspapers with which to start a fire and the tin pail in which they proposed to make cocoa. Sumac was reddening on either side of the rough rutted road.

At the top of the hill they paused to look out over the town. Then they turned right and entered a double line of beech trees which in their childhood they had called the Secret Lane. Leaving that deep shade behind, they came out on another crest of hill where low trees were widely spaced and there was a sweeping valley view. But this valley was empty except for the clustered rooftops of Little Syria. Beyond that settlement stretched the slough, and the wooded river bluffs.

"We can see almost to Page Park," Betsy said.

"Let's take a picnic out there sometime," Tacy suggested. "Maybe the whole Crowd will go."

"What's left of it," Betsy amended. "It isn't much of a Crowd with the Humphreys gone."

"Have you heard from Herbert?" asked Tacy as they sank into the grass.

"A letter every week. He loves to write letters, and so do I. So we're still Confidential Friends."

It was warm in the grass. The sunshine hit the hill full on, glittering over the goldenrod which rolled in a green-gold flood to the depths of the valley. The sky hung like a painting full of clouds.

"Those clouds make steps," said Tacy staring upward.

"I wish we could climb them," Betsy answered dreamily. "Walk up and up, and out into the air."

"Just keep on going. See where we got to."

"The clouds were beautiful out at the lake."

They talked about Murmuring Lake. Tacy and Katie had visited at the cottage which stood with its feet in the water not far from Pleasant Park, Mrs. Ray's girlhood home.

"I used to go out alone in the boat," said Betsy. "Row over to the bay where the water lilies are, take along a notebook and pencil, and write."

"What did you write?"

"Poems. And I worked on that novel you said reminded you of *Graustark*. I'm not going to neglect my writing the way I did last year. Joe Willard isn't going to win the Essay Contest again."

"I should say he isn't," Tacy answered indignantly. "Lightning doesn't strike twice."

"It wasn't lightning," Betsy answered slowly. "He's good. Do you know, Tacy, I wish he was in our Crowd."

"I remember you liked him," said Tacy, "when you met him at Butternut Center."

That had been in summer, a year ago. Betsy was returning from a visit with the Taggarts, farm friends of her father's. Waiting for her train in the hamlet of Butternut Center, she had gone into the general store . . . Willard's Emporium . . . to buy presents for the family.

Joe had waited on her. He was a nephew of the Emporium Willards. He had helped her pick out the presents, and they had had fun. But they hadn't hit it off at school, somehow.

The sun slipped behind Tacy's cloud-built stairs, and at once the air took on a premonitory chill.

"Better get our fire going," Tacy said briskly. She always took charge of the fire, being better at it than Betsy which didn't, however, signify much.

She twisted the papers into a heap on the rock

while Betsy brought twigs and branches. Smoke billowed generously, blackening the pail which was set precariously atop a nest of branches. It filled the air with its smell so fraught with promise, and Betsy and Tacy grinned at each other across the checkered cloth.

"I wish Tib was here," Betsy said.

"Have you heard from her?" asked Tacy somewhat later when the cocoa had thumped in its pail, and she had poured a cup for each of them.

"Yes," answered Betsy, spooning beans. "She's taking dancing lessons from a very good teacher."

"Is she going to that Browner Seminary again?"

"Yes. I wonder what a girls' school is like? It must be peaceful. No boys around."

"I thought you liked boys," said Tacy, surprised.

"I do. But they're an awful worry. At the lake, there weren't any boys my age living near us and it made life so peaceful. When there are boys you have to worry about how you look, and whether they like you, and why they like another girl better, and whether they're going to ask you to something or other. It's a strain."

"That's why I don't bother with them," said Tacy. She leaned back on her arms and looked up at the sky where her stairs had dissolved into glistening gold-rimmed clouds. "I'm peaceful all the time like you were at the lake."

"I'm not in love this year at least."

"You soon will be," Tacy prophesied.

Betsy too leaned on her arms, and they both stared upward while color flooded up behind the clouds as though from a geyser gushing rose. The clouds were tinged with pink, as the sky behind them paled. At last scattered clouds were pink all over the bowl of the sky.

"I saw that Phil Brandish on my way up to your house today," Betsy volunteered at last. "How does it happen he's coming here to school?"

"Kicked out of Cox Military."

"How thrilling!" Betsy sat upright. "What did he do?"

"He just wouldn't toe the mark, Tom says."

"I remember when he and his sister used to come visiting. Don't you? Aren't they twins?"

"Yes. Phyllis is in a girls' school somewhere. They sent Phil here to see if Grandpa Brandish couldn't straighten him out. But you might as well not feel romantic about Phil Brandish, Betsy."

"Why not? Has Irma got him?"

"No. But he's older than we are."

"Oh, fudge!"

"He's going with a senior crowd," said Tacy contentedly.

"Well, we can dream about him anyway," said Betsy. And beginning to feel silly, as she usually did at the end of a picnic with Tacy, she started to warble "Dreaming," inventing suitable words.

"Dreaming, dreaming,
Of your red auto I'm dreaming."

Tacy chimed in, inventing too.

"Dreaming of days when we went to ride,
Dreaming of hours spent by your side."

They composed joyfully.

"Dreaming, dreaming,
Of your red auto I'm dreaming,
Love will not change,
While the auto ree-mains,
Dree-ee-eaming."

"You fake an alto," said Betsy, and they sang their masterpiece again. They fell into the grass and laughed until echoes rolled over the hill.

But the grass was wet. It was drenched with dew.

"Golly!" said Betsy. "It's getting late. And cold!"

They put out their fire, which wasn't difficult and piled the empty plates and cups hurriedly into the basket. The tender pink was suddenly gone from the sky. It was gray with a star or two, and the crickets were singing.

The Secret Lane was already broodingly dim.

"This lane reminds me," said Betsy, "of something

I wrote in my journal this morning."

"What?"

"That starting a new journal, and our sophomore year was like being ushered into the Winding Hall of Fate. This lane doesn't wind, but it's certainly like a hall."

"What do I see ahead?" asked Tacy dramatically. "Methinks I see Betsy Ray in a bright red auto!" And that was a signal for them to burst again into song. Arms bound around each other's waists, for it was both scarily dark and frostily cold by now, they began to sing. They sang all the way through the Secret Lane, and when they came out to a light-sprinkled view of the town, and down the rough bumpy road that led to Tacy's house.

> *"Dreaming, dreaming,*
> *Of your red auto I'm dreaming. . . ."*

At the end Tacy changed from alto to tenor with a stunning dramatic effect:

> *"Love will not change,*
> *While the auto REE-mains,*
> *DREE-EE-EAMING."*

3
Ivanhoe

WHEN BETSY AND TACY reached the Kelly house they saw Old Mag hitched out in front and Julia, Hugh, Tom and Cab sitting with Katie and Leo in the front parlor.

"They drove up to get you," Tacy hazarded. "It got so dark."

"Let's go in the back way; we look like frights," Betsy said. They stole up to Tacy's room, washed their faces, brushed and braided their hair. Betsy borrowed a little powder from one of Tacy's grown-up sisters, and they entered the parlor with good effect.

"We're discussing the noble work of *Ivanhoe*," said Cab. He was short but springy and vigorous with a dark Welsh face full of fun and sparkle. His suits were always meticulously pressed, his shoes well polished. Tom, on the other hand, was burly and carelessly dressed.

"I'm about halfway through," said Tacy.

"I haven't started it," said Cab. "Don't ask me in when we get home, Betsy. Don't suggest fudge or singing or anything else. I have to read *Ivanhoe*."

"Hully gee, I'm glad I go to Cox!" said Tom. "They never heard of the thing."

"Did we read *Ivanhoe* when we were young?" Julia asked Katie.

"I have a faint recollection of it," Katie answered. "Isn't there a tea kettle boiling in the first chapter?"

"That's *Cricket on the Hearth*," said Hugh who was studious and serious.

When the Rays started home Tom wanted to stay, but Tacy would have none of him.

"I have to read *Ivanhoe*. GOOD NIGHT."

Back on High Street, Betsy did not mention fudge but when Cab saw Tony and Carney in the lighted parlor, he went in.

"I can't stay, I can't stay," he kept repeating. "I

have to read the noble work of *Ivanhoe*."

"You can't read it on an empty stomach," Tony said.

"Cab told me not to mention fudge," said Betsy. "But there's chocolate and sugar in the kitchen."

So they all went to the kitchen, except for Julia and Hugh who remained in the parlor, and Tony put on an apron. Just as the fudge reached a boil, Winona and Irma, and Pin, a senior boy, dropped in.

Winona inquired at once, "Say, who's read *Ivanhoe*?"

"What's *Ivanhoe*? Sounds like a cigar," said Tony, stirring.

"It's a noble work which I propose to read as soon as Betsy will let me go home," said Cab.

"I'm simply struggling with it," said Irma, and at once all the boys looked sympathetic and as though they wished they could be helpful.

"What *is* it about Irma?" Betsy thought.

She had, as Betsy had told her journal, a beautiful figure, and round soft eyes and a round soft mouth. And she was sweet. The girls liked her usually, but when boys were around she was exasperating.

"Betsy's read it," Cab remarked.

"But not this summer," Betsy hastened to explain. "I just happened to read it when I was a child. Had a sore throat, or something."

"Well, gosh! When are we going to read it?" asked

Winona who was perched on the kitchen table swinging her long legs.

Tony poured the rich dark mass he had been stirring into a buttered pan. "While the fudge cools?"

"Here! Let me lick that spoon!" Winona hopped off the table.

"Not much! I lick the spoons around here."

The long sticky spoon waved wildly above wildly bobbing heads.

As soon as Winona arrived at any gathering, a scuffle ensued. Winona loved scuffles. Her black eyes and white teeth gleamed, her long black braids came loose, fudge streaked her face as she scuffled with Cab and Tony. Pin watched her, grinning, and Irma giggled, a soft alluring giggle.

"It makes me lonesome for the Humphreys to have the Crowd together," Carney said to Betsy. She meant "for Larry," Betsy knew.

It made Betsy wish for Herbert too, although she and Herbert had not "gone together" as Carney and Larry had. But it would have been nice to have Herbert around. Especially since Cab now looked at Irma with such admiring eyes.

"What's going on out here?" Julia demanded, appearing in the doorway.

She wanted to get away from Hugh, Betsy suspected. Julia was growing bored with Hugh, as she did with all her beaus. She cast off beaus with the utmost callousness, and kept Betsy busy comforting them.

"Come on in and sing while the fudge cools," Julia suggested now.

"I can't stay, I can't stay," Cab kept murmuring, but he stayed. Arms locked, the Crowd sang around the piano. When Julia started "Waltz Me Around Again, Willie," Tony flipped back the rug and asked Betsy to dance. Mrs. Ray's curly head popped over the banisters.

"Pardon me for mentioning it, but isn't tomorrow a school day?"

"We'll go home," Tony said. "But it isn't a school day, really. We just go over to register. Cab can read *Ivanhoe* all afternoon."

"The noble work!" said Cab. "We've made fudge, Mrs. Ray. May we stay to eat it?"

"Eat it in a hurry, and go home," said Mrs. Ray, and smiled, and disappeared.

The fudge was brought out hastily and cut.

"Darn your *Ivanhoe*!" said Carney who was a junior. "I thought we could go to the Majestic tomorrow afternoon."

"It's a grand idea," Betsy cried.

"Why, we can read *Ivanhoe* in the evening, can't we, Cab?" Tony asked.

Cab looked gloomy. "There are five hundred and thirty-four pages in the noble work," he said.

"I wish that Gaston was boiling in oil," remarked Winona, munching fudge.

As Tony had said, there were to be no classes the following day, but it was officially the first day of school so Anna made muffins for breakfast.

"The McCloskeys always had muffins for breakfast on the first day of school," she said when she brought them to the table around which, to Mr. Ray's satisfaction, the entire family was gathered . . . Mrs. Ray tall and slim in a starched yellow morning dress, Julia and Betsy in new shirt waists and skirts, Margaret in a new striped gingham with a big striped bow atop her head. Tacy, too, was present, having called for Betsy early.

The McCloskeys were a family for which Anna had worked in a legendary past. She never told where the McCloskeys had lived nor whither they had gone, but she held them over the Rays' heads. New members of the family turned up in her talk whenever she needed them to make a point. The Rays found it hard sometimes to live up to the McCloskeys. But again, as now, they were true friends.

"Why did the McCloskeys have muffins on the first day of school, Anna?" Betsy asked.

"Maybe the little McCloskey girl didn't like new

teachers," offered Margaret. She looked sober.

"Why, Button," said her father. "You wouldn't like to stay in Miss Parry's room forever."

"Yes, I would. After a while I could help her teach."

"Have some plum jam on your muffin, lovey," Anna said. "I bet you'll have a puny teacher." Puny, which Anna thought meant handsome, was her word of highest praise.

"*I* certainly need muffins," Mrs. Ray remarked. "This is the last fall Julia will be starting off to high school. Isn't that perfectly awful, Bob? Did you dream when she started kindergarten that such a day would ever come?"

"I suspected it," said Mr. Ray.

"And Betsy and Tacy are sophomores!"

"Just think," said Betsy, "how old we'll seem to the freshies. Remember how old the sophomores seemed to us last year?"

"Old and know-it-all," said Tacy.

"Remember how we hurried over early to get those back seats? This year we're not in any hurry at all. Have another muffin, Tacy."

"This year," said Tacy, "I'm positively nonchalant."

"I'll stifle a yawn as I stroll in."

"Ho hum! High school! What a bore!"

"Aren't they bright, Papa?" Julia asked.

"Teachers are underpaid," said Mr. Ray. "I'm going to speak to a friend on the school board and get raises for the lot."

"Not for Gaston, Mr. Ray!" cried Tacy. "Not after he made us read *Ivanhoe* this summer!"

"That Gaston!" said Betsy. "He doesn't appreciate my flowery style of writing!"

"No wonder!" said Julia scornfully. "He came to Deep Valley to teach science. He's a science teacher, really."

"Maybe he won't be teaching English this year. Maybe he'll be teaching his beloved biology, and we'll have a new English teacher. Oh, wouldn't that be wonderful?" Tacy cried.

She made this heartening suggestion to Cab who joined them on High Street. High school–bound boys and girls crowded the sidewalk, filling the golden morning with noise and excitement. But Cab was still gloomy.

"Naw, we'd have heard. And I'm in a heck of a spot. My father asked me if I'd finished *Ivanhoe*, and I said I had. I'm not a liar. I read the last page. But what about the other five hundred and thirty-three?"

The wide-flung doors of the turreted red-brick high school sucked them all in. On the landing as they clattered upstairs, Mercury welcomed them with up-flung arm. In the large upper hall they separated,

Betsy and Tacy going to the girls' cloak room to hang up their hats and look in the mirror. For all their boasted unconcern Tacy's cheeks were scarlet, and Betsy's pink.

They passed on into the assembly room, which was large, with a turret-alcove. Betsy and Tacy found adjoining seats about halfway along the second of the sophomore rows. Leaving tablets and pencils to prove ownership of their desks, they strolled back to the hall.

Here they paused before a glass-covered case in which three silver trophy cups were displayed. These were the cups . . . for athletics, debating and essay writing . . . for which the two high school societies annually competed. The athletics cup bore the turquoise blue of the Zetamathian Society to which Betsy and Tacy belonged. The bows on the other two cups were Philomathian orange.

Betsy stared at the Essay Cup and something of the self-condemnation she had felt last spring when she lost the freshmen points flooded into her heart. Tacy read her thoughts.

"Not this year, Joe Willard!" she said, shaking her fist at the cup.

Betsy laughed. "Let's go into the Social Room. Impress the freshies."

No written law barred freshmen from the Social Room. It was merely a classroom, designated as a gathering place during school intermissions. But sophomores, juniors and seniors claimed it as their own. Betsy and Tacy, sailing in, threw condescending glances at the freshmen in the hall.

Betsy looked for Joe Willard, but she did not see him. Carney approached with junior sangfroid.

"Just think!" she said to Betsy. "The Humphreys are registering out in San Diego."

"It must seem funny," Betsy said.

She tried to imagine not living in Deep Valley. She tried to imagine graduating as Julia would do this year . . . not coming back to the high school when September touched the leaves with gold. Julia, she knew, was longing to be free of it. She didn't even want to go to the state university. She wanted to be studying acting and singing out in the Great World. That was what she always called it, "the Great World." Betsy planned to see the Great World too, of course. Oh, yes, she and Tacy planned to circle the globe. But they weren't in a hurry to start.

"I love it here," Betsy said abruptly. "I just love it."

Carney flashed the lone dimple which changed her face from demure reserve to mischief. "There's Phil Brandish, the red auto boy."

Betsy looked around. He was in a corner with a noisy crowd. He stood out from the rest both because he was better dressed and because he was taller. He had straight light brown hair that fell down over his forehead.

"Tacy says he's in with a senior crowd."

"Yes, he's just a junior, though. But he doesn't interest me. He's too sophisticated. I don't like sophisticated boys."

The first gong clanged, and out in the hall freshmen scrambled. The sophomores in the Social Room smiled tolerantly. They strolled into the assembly room just as the second gong sounded.

Up on the platform Carney, who played the piano, was already at her place. Miss Bangeter, the principal, rose from her arm chair and walked to the reading desk. She was a tall, queenly woman with a mass of slippery black hair, and piercing eyes. Speaking with a Boston accent she announced the opening hymn.

The school rose, and boys and girls released pent-up excitement in song that shook the rafters.

"Mine eyes have seen the glory,
Of the coming of the lord . . ."

The school sat, and Miss Bangeter read a Psalm. She read from the Bible every morning, and Betsy looked forward to this moment, to Miss Bangeter's grave voice intoning the majestic poetry. Today's psalm was one she liked especially, because it had hills in it:

"I will lift up mine eyes unto the hills."

The school joined in repeating the Lord's Prayer.

After opening exercises Betsy and Tacy made the rounds of the classrooms to register for Latin, geometry, modern history and rhetoric and find out what books they were to buy.

Mr. Morse who taught Latin was impassive; he seemed never to have seen them before although he had taught them Latin grammar last year . . . or hoped he had. He told them to buy the *Commentaries of Caesar*.

Miss O'Rourke who had suffered them through algebra welcomed them to geometry with breezy friendliness. She was curly-haired, merry-eyed, pretty, but strict. Betsy and Tacy, well aware of their deficiencies, shuddered under her genial gaze.

Miss Clarke who taught history was anything but strict. The students hailed her with affectionate condescension. She was Zetamathian faculty adviser, and relied on Betsy a great deal in society affairs. If Mr. Gaston, as Betsy had claimed, did not appreciate her talents, Miss Clarke more than made up for the lack. Even Mrs. Ray, even Tacy, was no more generous with praise.

They passed on to Mr. Gaston's room. He had not yet come in, but shortly Joe Willard came in. He held his head at a challenging angle which matched the swing of his walk and the confident almost defiant slant of his red lower lip.

Joe Willard was the only boy in high school without a home. He was different from the other boys, but he didn't seem to mind it. He was even dressed differently, Betsy noticed. All last year he had worn a blue serge suit. This year he wore blue serge trousers, but his coat was light brown. No boys wore coats and pants that did not match, but Joe Willard did, today.

And they looked all right. Perhaps because they were so carefully pressed, or perhaps because he was so handsome. His summer tan made his blond pompadour look even blonder, and his blue eyes bluer below his thick light brows.

He did not glance at Betsy, but when she went over to him he smiled.

"How come you didn't show up in Butternut Center?" he asked.

"I didn't visit the Taggarts this year. We went to the lake."

"You shouldn't have missed Butternut Center," he said. "There was a runaway on the Fourth of July and a funeral on August the second."

"Wasn't there a church social?"

"Come to think of it, there was. Cocoanut cake. If you'd been there I'd have bought you a piece."

To her annoyance Betsy blushed. She was given to

blushing, especially with Joe Willard. The pink ran down to her high, white, lace-edged collar.

"Read *Ivanhoe*?" she asked hastily.

"Of course. Why?" He sounded puzzled.

"Don't you remember? Gaston told us to read it over the summer. None of the kids have read it. They're having fits."

"You've read it, haven't you?"

"Yes. But I'm not admitting it."

He looked at her keenly.

"You wouldn't!" he said.

Now what did he mean by that? Betsy wondered, blushing again. Did he know she was so dissatisfied with herself that she was always pretending to be different? Probably he did, and despised her for it. More than anyone she knew, Joe Willard was always, fearlessly, himself.

Tacy interrupted, hissing tragically. "There he comes, the brute."

Mr. Gaston entered and strode to his desk. He was a dark, sardonic-looking young man with thick, unrimmed glasses. He took the roll call briskly, announced the list of books to buy. Then he looked around and grinned.

"You remember, of course, that tomorrow you take a test on *Ivanhoe*?"

Cab and Tony conferred in whispers, with more

and frantic whispers interjected by Tacy, Alice, Irma and Winona. Then Cab rose. He took a jaunty stance, his hands in his pockets.

"You're joking, aren't you, Mr. Gaston. You didn't seriously mean that we were to read five hundred and thirty-four pages . . . over *vacation*?"

Mr. Gaston looked more sardonic than ever.

"Why, Cab, reading *Ivanhoe*'s a pleasure."

"Yes, sir, but don't you think it might be a good idea to give the test next week? In case some of us haven't had time to finish the book?"

Mr. Gaston gazed at him coldly.

"I'm teaching this class, young man. The test will be given tomorrow. I hope *you've* finished it?"

"I read page five hundred and thirty-four last night," said Cab, and winked at Betsy and sat down.

"Class dismissed. *Ivanhoe* tomorrow." Mr. Gaston said.

4
More Ivanhoe

IVANHOE AND MR. GASTON notwithstanding, the Crowd went to the Majestic that afternoon.

Alice had finished the novel, and Tacy had only a hundred pages left. Winona was cheerfully resigned to flunking. "I'll flunk plenty of tests before the year's over."

"I've read parts of it," said Irma. She didn't seem too worried. Perhaps she thought that even Mr. Gaston was not impervious to her soft-eyed charm.

Tony didn't seem too worried either, but Cab's air was reckless. It troubled Betsy.

"Really, Cab, I think you'd better stay at home and read."

"Can't. My father thinks I've finished the noble work."

"Then come over to our house and read."

"While the rest of you see *Raffles*? Not much!"

So after dinner the Crowd went together to Cook's Book Store to buy books and then proceeded to that other store which, not many years before, by means of red and yellow paint and a flamboyant sign had become the Majestic Theatre, a High Class Place of Amusement, with Up to Date Moving Picture Entertainment, Especially for Ladies and Children. Admission 10¢.

In the afternoon, to the satisfaction of the Crowd, admission was only five cents. Paying their nickels they filed in to one of the rows of hard seats. On the screen up front, flickering, silent figures acted out the adventures of *Raffles, the Amateur Cracksman*. Afterwards a girl played the piano and sang. The verses were illustrated by garishly colored slides.

> *"Shine, little glow worm, glimmer,*
> *Shine, little glow worm, glimmer . . ."*

The Crowd hummed under its collective breath.

Repairing to Heinz's, to the small mirror-walled room in back of the bakery which was labelled Ice Cream Parlor, it did more than hum. It sang, banged, whistled, shouted from one small table to another as though across a football field. Mr. Heinz was indulgent. He appreciated the devotion . . . and the nickels . . . of high school boys and girls. *Ivanhoe* was forgotten in Banana Splits and Deep Valley Specials, and at parting Cab said to Betsy:

"See you tonight."

"You will not see me tonight. You read *Ivanhoe* tonight."

"I'll read it after I get home. Midnight oil, you know. The family will be in bed, and I'll pore over the noble work beside my shaded lamp . . ."

He was fooling, but he was anxious. Betsy knew it; Cab's father could be stern.

She wanted to turn him out when he came that evening, but Hugh had dropped in, and Tony, and Tom with his violin. And they all had to leave at ten o'clock sharp. Mrs. Ray said so.

Julia kept them all around the piano, somewhat to Hugh's annoyance. He could see that her feeling for him had cooled and wanted to find out why, but Julia couldn't tell him, not knowing herself, and so she avoided a tête-a-tête.

"Now go home and read *Ivanhoe*," Betsy hissed to Cab at ten o'clock.

"Maybe," put in Tony, "he'd do better in the morning not knowing a lick of *Ivanhoe* but having his wits about him."

"Maybe in the morning I'll have an inspired idea."

"You're dippy," Betsy said, shutting the door.

She dreamed about *Ivanhoe* that night. She woke dreaming about it, and went to the bookcase for her well-worn copy and brought it back to bed. She had not admitted it, but she loved the book. She had read it countless times.

She grew so interested now that she read past the breakfast gong. She dressed like a flash then, but when she reached the table even Julia was there and Mr. Ray was almost ready to leave for the store.

"I'm sorry, Papa. I was looking over *Ivanhoe*."

"*Ivanhoe! Ivanhoe!*" said Mr. Ray. "The way the Deep Valley High School treats the classics!" He went around the table stiffly, kissing good-by.

But he unbent before departing for Tacy came in and her opening cry made him smile.

"I've finished *Ivanhoe*!"

"Tacy," said Mr. Ray, "how is your father bearing up under this?"

"He says he wishes Sir Walter Scott had never been born," Tacy replied.

A burst of song sounded from the porch. Tony and Cab were ascending, their arms across each other's shoulders, singing in harmony to the tune of "Tammany."

> *"Ivanhoe,*
> *Ivanhoe . . ."*

"Let me out of here," said Mr. Ray, and made a dash for the street.

Tony and Cab came in smiling.

"Nothing like a good night's sleep," said Cab, rubbing his hands.

"We had that inspired idea," Tony said. "Both of us. Same idea."

"What is it, for goodness' sake?"

Tony searched though his pockets for a pad of paper and a pencil, and Cab too brought out writing materials with a businesslike air.

"We thought," Cab explained, "we might sit here and take notes. We thought that while you were finishing breakfast you might chat a little about the noble work."

"Just give us the high points," Tony said.

Betsy stared at them and began to laugh. Everyone laughed.

"Stars in the sky!" cried Anna. "This *Ivanhoe*! What is it, anyway?"

"It's a story, Anna. Betsy's going to tell it to us in a few well chosen words."

"Well, I'm going to listen," said Anna, and sat down, dish towel in hand.

Betsy gulped her cocoa and put the cup aside. She folded her hands on the table then, and Cab and Tony took chairs opposite and stared hard, as though by looking at that curly beribboned head they could absorb its precious knowledge of Scott's masterpiece.

"Well," began Betsy, and paused. She thought of Joe Willard and took a deep breath and started again. "I have to say something that will shock you. It's a perfectly grand book."

"What?" Cab and Tony cried together.

"Perfectly grand. If you don't say so, Gaston will know you haven't read it, because you couldn't read it without liking it."

Tony looked at her sharply. "You're not fooling?"

Cab wrote down on his pad of paper, "Perfectly grand."

Betsy decided to begin where Scott had.

"It begins," she said, "in that pleasant district of merry England which is watered by the River Don."

Tony put down his pencil. "You *are* fooling!"

"No really. That's the first sentence. It opens in a forest with a swineherd named Gurth, and Wamba, son of Witless. . . ."

"See here, Betsy! In ten minutes we can only hit the high spots."

"All right," said Betsy, yielding. It saddened her that Cab and Tony should not know about Gurth and Wamba, and the meeting with the Pryor. She felt she was cheating them, but it couldn't be helped.

"The important characters," she said, "are Wilfred of Ivanhoe, a knight, returned from the Crusades; Rowena, the girl he's in love with; Cedric, her guardian, who disapproves; Rebecca, a girl who's in love with Ivanhoe; and some assorted villains."

"Fine!" said Tony. "Now we're getting somewhere."

"King Richard's in it, too. He went to the Crusades, and left England in charge of his brother Prince John, who's a crook. Richard comes back to see what's going on, disguised as the Black Knight. He comes to the tournament and on the second day when Ivanhoe is fighting three men at once. . . ."

"A good fight?" asked Cab, leaning forward.

"Just the best one ever written, that's all." Betsy's cheeks flamed. She told the story of the tournament and told it so well that Anna leaned across the table, breathing hard, Tacy's eyes sparkled and the boys forgot to scribble notes.

"Betsy," said her mother. "You'll be late for school."

They went out to an almost empty High Street with Betsy still talking, Tacy, Cab, and Tony now hanging on every word.

"Does Prince John give in, and admit that Ivanhoe won?"

"Yes, and Ivanhoe chooses Rowena to be Queen of Beauty."

"Do they live happily ever after, then?"

"Heavens, no! She's kidnapped, and so is Rebecca. They're held captive in a castle, with Ivanhoe, and the Black Knight storms it."

They dropped down on the school steps, and Betsy kept on talking. The first gong rang and they moved slowly toward the upper hall where Betsy continued to talk until the second gong clanged.

"Anything else?"

"Remember the bad feeling between the Normans and Saxons."

"What happens to Rebecca?"

"She goes into a convent."

"Sounds like quite a tale," drawled Tony, returning his notes to his pocket.

"Wilfred of Ivanhoe, Rowena, Cedric, Rebecca . . ." muttered Cab.

Tacy took Betsy's arm. "It was wonderful the way you told it, Betsy." And then Tacy too started muttering, "Wilfred of Ivanhoe, Rowena, Cedric, Rebecca . . ."

All through the morning, whenever Betsy looked toward Tacy, Tony or Cab she saw them muttering.

Mr. Gaston greeted the rhetoric class with a glance derisively bland. He gave the next day's assignment, ignored the frantic whispering going on all over the room, and said casually: "Now I want each one of you to write me an essay on *Ivanhoe*."

He leaned back in his chair and unfolded a scientific journal.

Betsy swept a glance around the room. Tony, Cab and Tacy were all muttering. Joe Willard looked as he had looked before he set to work on the Essay Contest last year. His paper, ink, and pen were ready and he was brushing his fingers thoughtfully over his yellow hair.

Betsy smiled at her paper. What a delightful assignment! What fun to write an essay on her beloved *Ivanhoe*! She dipped her pen in ink.

She began where she had tried to begin before, and now there were no Tony or Cab to cry, "Just give us the high spots, Betsy!" She told all about Gurth and Wamba and descibed the Lady Rowena's beauty and Ivanhoe's mysterious coming and the arrival of Rebecca and her father.

The clock said that half the allotted time was gone, so she hurried on to the tournament. She tried to make spears ring in her prose as they rang in Sir Walter's.

Now and then she almost thought she succeeded.

Looking up dreamily, she saw that Tony and Cab had already finished. Joe Willard still had his pen in his hand, but he was reading what he had written. Mr. Gaston had closed his magazine. He was tapping the desk and looking at the clock, obviously impatient.

Betsy rushed for the finish, scattering blots. But Rowena and Rebecca were still captive, the story hung in the air like a bright banner, when the gong sounded and Mr. Gaston said:

"You may leave your papers on my desk as you go out."

Betsy was sorry she had not finished, but after all, she reflected, panting and warm from her attempt, Mr. Gaston would certainly see that she knew her *Ivanhoe*. It was nice what she had said about those silvery spears: and the part about Rowena's hair. Even Sir Walter Scott hadn't thought to compare it to maple syrup.

"How did you get along?" she asked Cab anxiously.

"I think I did the noble work justice."

"Mine was a masterpiece," said Tony.

"Mine was all right, too," said Tacy.

Betsy sighed in proud relief.

It was two days before Mr. Gaston returned the

papers. And during those two days *Ivanhoe* continued to possess the Ray household.

"If Washington should have kittens . . . but he won't, because he's a boy . . . I'd name one Ivanhoe and one Rowena," Margaret said.

Mr. Ray heard about Betsy's fifteen-minute condensation of the masterpiece with a chuckle.

"I wonder how Cab and Tony will come out?"

"I think they will get Fair at least," Betsy said. Mr. Gaston marked his papers Excellent, Good, Fair and Poor.

When the class filed in on the third morning the papers were piled on his desk. After roll call he tapped them condescendingly.

"These essays on *Ivanhoe* weren't bad," he said. "Really, they weren't bad at all! Three of them are marked 'Excellent,' and from a class of the mentality of this one, that's pretty good." Mr. Gaston liked to make that sort of joke.

Three "Excellents!" Betsy, without thinking, flashed Joe Willard a glance. She intercepted one from him, and they both smiled. Both felt sure where two Excellents had gone, but what about the third one?

"None of you," Mr. Gaston continued, "will be surprised to hear that one 'Excellent' went to Joe. But the other two may startle you. They did me."

He smiled mockingly.

"Tony and Cab," he said, "drew 'Excellents,' too."

To say that the class was startled was putting it mildly. Tony and Cab grinned from ear to ear. Tacy threw up her hands in pantomime to Betsy.

"Tony and Cab," Mr. Gaston continued, "turned in essays that showed they had read the book. I must admit, Cab, that when you told me you had finished it, I had my doubts. But you and Tony obviously had not only read *Ivanhoe*. You had digested it. Therefore, your papers are brief, concise. You just . . ." Mr. Gaston's smile for once was genuinely approving, "you just hit the high spots."

Tony slipped down until the desk almost hid his face. Cab's ears were red.

"Your admirably organized papers," Mr. Gaston went on, "were in contrast to some I received. Some writers who, perhaps, had not even finished the book tried to show off their so-called literary skill at Scott's expense."

At that Betsy turned crimson. Mr. Gaston had spoken in the plural, but no one in the class would doubt that he meant her alone. For just a moment she was appalled. Then the joke in the situation struck her, and she smiled around at Cab, Tony and Tacy. Joe Willard was looking at her with a puzzled expression.

Tony and Cab after football practise, headed for the Ray house. They paused on the hill to pick a bouquet of sumac, goldenrod, asters and prickly thistles, and presented it to Betsy with sweeping bows. There was much joking and when Mr. Ray heard the story, he laughed until he shook.

But saying good-by to Betsy, Cab turned serious. He was, after all, Welsh Calvinistic Methodist.

"Betsy!" he said. He looked around to make sure that no one was listening. "Betsy, I just want you to know. . . . I'm going to read the noble work. The whole five hundred and thirty-four pages. Darned if I don't!"

And he did.

5

Septemberish

SEPTEMBER WAS VERY Septemberish that year. It was Septemberish in the excitement of the opening days of school. These were so busy that soon the quiet summer at the lake seemed like a remote and peaceful dream. But a dream . . . Betsy thought . . . it was good to have had. She liked to remember the faintly rocking boat, the smell of water lilies, and her novel.

School was demanding. It came at her from all sides.

During the first week sophomores, juniors, and seniors, with ostentatious politeness invited the freshmen into the Social Room. There they talked up the merits of the two school societies. The freshmen must choose their societies, and rivalry was keen.

"Just look at the trophy cups. You'll find orange bows on two of them," Betsy heard Philos everywhere saying, and every time she heard it, she writhed. If she had not lost the freshmen points to Joe Willard, the Zetamathians might have had the Essay Cup.

Teaming up with Tacy, she worked frantically, telling freshmen boys that the Zets had all the pretty girls; freshmen girls that the Zets had all the nicest boys. It seemed to work.

They saw Phil Brandish surrounded by Philo girls. As a newcomer, he too would join a society today.

"*Dreaming, dreaming,*" hummed Tacy mischievously. "You'll never have a better chance."

"I'll think of the red auto and plunge," Betsy said.

But she didn't, and Tacy had known that she wouldn't speak to Phil Brandish. He was too old, too big, too worldly. They continued to court the freshmen.

At the afternoon assembly Miss Bangeter and the presidents of the two societies spoke.

"Philo, Philo, Philo!" "Zet! Zet! Zet!" shrieked the

opposing clans. Lists were passed, and after the signing Phil Brandish wore an orange bow.

Early in September, also, came class elections. Betsy felt a thrill when she was elected secretary of her class. The family at supper was pleased, too.

"I'm not a bit surprised, though," her mother said.

"Na, neither am I," said Anna, passing biscuits. "The McCloskey girl was secretary."

"Bettina is a natural leader," said Julia, whose opinion of Betsy was so good that it kept Betsy busy living up to it. Margaret's eyes were awed.

Mr. Ray always laughed at Mrs. Ray for being proud of their daughters, but his face had a special look when one brought home news like this. He was anxious that Betsy should be a good secretary.

"Go to every meeting, Betsy. And write up the minutes carefully in a notebook you keep for that purpose."

"I'll buy one tomorrow," Betsy said, happily. She had a weakness for fresh new notebooks and finely sharpened pencils.

September brought plenty of these, along with new books, and the impact of new studies. Some of these jarred all too heavily.

"Geometry is awful, simply awful," Betsy wailed.

Julia couldn't understand this. "I love geometry. It's like music."

"Like *music*?"

"Yes. It's exact, like music."

"Stop! Stop! I've always liked music. Don't you go comparing it with something hideous. . . ."

"Poor Bettina!" said Julia, and that night she tried to help. She placed the ruler carefully with her slender white fingers, drew lines with fastidious precision, and explained that when two straight lines intersected, the vertical angles formed were equal. She spoke with such a glowing face that Betsy tried not to scowl.

"Do you understand now, Bettina? Isn't it fascinating?"

"I'd never call it fascinating. But perhaps I begin to see . . ."

She didn't. When she was called to the blackboard next day she went on dragging feet. Chalk in an icy hand, she turned to look pleadingly at Tacy who was suffering with her, just as Betsy suffered when Tacy was called to the board.

"Don't look at Tacy. Look at the blackboard," said Miss O'Rourke, good naturedly but crisply.

Betsy looked. She tried despairingly to remember what Julia had said. What was that about vertical angles? It had all fled.

"Betsy," said Miss O'Rourke. "I think you've made up your mind that you can't understand geometry. Well, you'll have to unmake it. You understood algebra, and you can understand geometry."

She marked Betsy's card with a firm unmistakable zero, and Betsy went back to her seat.

It was good to escape from school after such a session, to pile into the surrey behind Old Mag or the Sibleys' Dandy, and roam country roads in the lazy sunshine. The woods were still green except, here and there, for an old tree turning yellow. But September was in the smoky air.

Only girls went on these expeditions, for the boys were busy with football practise. Joe Willard didn't play. Betsy saw him sometimes after school streaking toward the Creamery while the other boys streaked toward the field. Tom had left for Cox, and on these feminine rambles the shortage of boys in the Crowd was a favorite topic.

"There are plenty of boys in school. They just have to be lured into our Crowd."

"Irma could lure a few," someone would say if Irma happened not to be along.

"Yes, but when Irma lures them, she keeps them. What good would that do us?"

"What about that good looking Joe Willard?"

"He's a woman hater," said Winona who had tried vainly to inveigle him.

"I think we get along fine without boys. I love hen parties," Tacy said. But no one thought this even worth answering.

"Why the heck the Humphreys had to go to California!" someone always groaned, and Carney always looked sober.

Everyone in the Crowd missed the Humphreys but not as Carney did. The letters which passed steadily between Deep Valley and San Diego did not fill Larry's place. Neither did any of the many boys who were attentive to her.

As happened every September Chauncey Olcott came to the Opera House and Mr. Ray took the family to hear him. Anna went with Charley, her beau. They sat in the balcony, and between acts she came to the railing to wave to the Rays sitting below. She wore such a big hat, such a fluffy boa, so much perfume and jewelry of every sort that she attracted considerable attention. There was much craning of necks. But the Rays waved loyally back.

This year's play was called *O'Neill of Derry*. But the name didn't matter much. The play was always like last year's play, and probably next year's too. They were all laid in Ireland, they were full of plumed hats, high boots, laced bodices; and the Irish tenor, still handsome although stoutish, always sang the ballad he had earlier made famous:

> *"My wild Irish rose,*
> *The sweetest flower that grows . . ."*

When he began Mr. Ray always took Mrs. Ray's hand, and the girls sat very still, not to miss a note or quaver. Even Julia enjoyed it, although she infuriated Betsy later with condescending remarks.

"Chauncey Olcott," she said, "should really have done something with his voice."

"*Done* something!" Betsy repeated. "*Done* something! He's made himself famous with it. What do you call *doing* something?"

"He might have sung real music. Oh, Bettina, you must hear Mrs. Poppy's records! You must hear the really great ones . . . Caruso, Scotti, Melba, Geraldine Farrar. . . ."

"Chauncey Olcott," said Betsy stubbornly, "is good enough for me."

When not irritated by slurs on Chauncey Olcott, however, she was a sympathetic repository for Julia's talk of the Great World.

Julia took singing lessons from Mrs. Poppy, a large blond former actress whose husband managed the Melborn Hotel. They lived at the Hotel. Julia had been studying for a long time now, but she still came home from every lesson with burning cheeks and a faraway look in her eyes. She went straight to the piano, usually, and started to sing one of her opera scores. And after supper she often called Betsy into her room. She would talk and talk about pitch and resonance and breath control, illustrating with a *"Ni-po-tu-la-he,"* followed by another *"Ni-po-tu-la-he"* which to Betsy sounded just the same.

"Do you hear the difference?" Julia would demand, and rush on without waiting for an answer. "Isn't it marvelous?"

She would dart across to Betsy, comfortably ensconced in the window seat, grasp Betsy's hand and press it over her own diaphragm while she sang the *"Ni-po-tu-la-he"* again.

"Do you feel that? Here! That's the way to produce a tone."

Betsy felt as bewildered as she did by geometry, but she pretended to understand.

Above Julia's dressing table was a large picture cut from a magazine of Miss Geraldine Farrar, the American singer who was scoring such triumphs in Europe and New York. Her long glittering train coiled about her feet; her head was high; her smile, triumphant. Julia used to gaze at this picture thoughtfully.

"I think I look like her."

"You do."

"She seems taller. But it's just that train."

Julia, standing on tiptoe, pushed down her slender hips.

Julia was soloist in the girls' vested choir at St. John's Episcopal Church. The choir too started in

September after a summer recess. Betsy also was a member and she liked marching down the aisle and singing, in a long black robe and a black four-cornered hat. But she liked even better going alone to the early Sunday morning service.

She could usually waken herself by planning to do so. She slipped out of the house while the rest of the family was sleeping. The world was misty, cool, the lawns frosted with dew and filled with great numbers of blackbirds feeding busily.

The attendance at this service was small. There were usually just a few old ladies and Betsy. The Rev. Mr. Lewis knelt and rose, read the prayers, moved about the snowy candlelit altar, in a sort of reverent abstraction which Betsy shared.

"Ye who do truly and earnestly repent you of your sins . . . and intend to lead a new life . . ."

Every Sunday morning Betsy resolved dreamily to lead a new life.

She always got back for breakfast very hungry and as for the new life . . . usually it didn't last very long. But every Sunday morning she could start one again.

As September moved on there was a fire in the grate for Sunday night lunch. It was cozy; it was re-mindful of last winter to have a fire again. Mr. Ray made the sandwiches as usual. He was famous for his Sunday evening sandwiches. And after these were eaten, along with coffee, and cocoa, and a big layer cake, the family and the ever-present guests sat around the fire and sang.

But the grand climax of the month was, of course, Julia's birthday. She was eighteen this year. Mrs. Ray gave her a party for eighteen girls, including some of Betsy's friends. And Betsy and Carney, assigned to serve the refreshments, were hilariously inspired to wear their fathers' dress suits. The black trousers were turned up, the waistcoats were padded out with pillows. Both girls painted on mustaches and goatees of burnt cork. They were, someone said, good enough to serve at a fashionable wedding.

And that gave Winona an inspiration of her own.

"Girls! Girls! Let's have a mock wedding!"

Mock weddings were a favorite diversion in Deep Valley.

"I'll be the groom," cried Carney. "I'll act like a typical male and pick Irma for my bride." She fell to her knees at Irma's feet.

"I'll be the minister," shouted Betsy.

They all scurried about, pushing palms into a half circle in the Rays' front window, pinning a lace curtain on the giggling Irma and giving her a cabbage bouquet. Winona, in Mrs. Ray's bathrobe, acted as bridesmaid and Tacy in Mr. Ray's smoking jacket played the Best Man. Julia sang "O Promise Me" with many high falsetto trills and Mrs. Ray banged out the wedding march.

Breathless from laughter Betsy rushed to the dining room table for the remnants of birthday cake.

"We must each take a piece home and sleep on it. That's what you always do after a wedding."

"Yes," said Julia's friend Dorothy. "You put it in a box along with the names of seven boys. Every morning for seven mornings you draw out a name, and the last one will be your future husband."

"Carney will make all seven 'Larry.'"

"No, you have to name seven different boys."

"But what if you haven't met your future husband yet? I hope I haven't," Tacy said.

"Write 'A Stranger' on one of the slips."

Julia ran upstairs for pencils; paper was hurriedly torn into strips, and the girls set to work.

"Is there anyone here who isn't beginning with Phil Brandish?" Betsy asked. But everyone was too busy to answer. She wrote "Phil Brandish" with a flourish and picked up the second slip of paper. On that she wrote without hesitation "A Stranger."

Herbert had acquired a romantic aura since going to California. She licked her pencil and wrote "Herbert." Cab ought to be put down. Of course he had a crush on Irma, but everyone couldn't go with Irma. She put down "Cab." She put down "Tony" for old times' sake, and "Tom" because she had known him longer than any other boy.

"I have one slip left," she announced.

"I have five," groaned Tacy.

Everyone else was either thinking or writing.

Betsy put the end of her pencil in her teeth, and her mind's eye roved over Deep Valley High School. It paused at a challenging blond head.

"Girls!" shouted Winona. "I've put down 'Gaston.' If I draw that last I invite you to my suicide."

"I'm putting down 'Chauncey Olcott,'" said Tacy. "There's a Mrs. Olcott, I believe, but Chauncey will just have to get rid of her."

"I haven't a local boy in my list," said Julia loftily.

That caused a sensation among the seniors.

"Why, Julia! What about Hugh?"

"I'll auction off Hugh."

"Really?" "May I have him?" "I think he's cute."

Through the clatter of voices, Betsy pondered over her seventh slip.

"See here," she called out suddenly. "I'm thinking of the general good. I'm thinking of someone we could use in our Crowd."

"Who?"

"Joe Willard."

"I've told you before, and I'll tell you again, he's a woman hater," Winona declared.

"Oh, fudge!"

"If you think you can get him into the Crowd, why don't you try?"

"Ask him to a party or something?"

"I will, maybe," Betsy said. She wrote "Joe Willard" firmly on her seventh slip.

Tacy and Katie stayed all night after the wedding, and there was more hilarity about putting the wedding cake, and the names, under their pillows.

In the morning Betsy drew out Cab, and the following morning, Tony, and after that Herbert and Tom. At last she was down to A Stranger, Phil Brandish, and Joe.

But alas and alack, that morning she did not make her own bed! She was late, and left it for Anna who knew nothing about the great enterprise. Anna found some crumbs of cake and soiled papers and threw them all out. She even changed the sheets for good measure, and Betsy's plight was pitiful. She was stranded by Fate not knowing whom she would marry . . . A Stranger, Phil Brandish, or Joe.

6

The Moorish Café

THE MOCK WEDDING WAS followed shortly by a wedding anniversary, a real one . . . Mr. and Mrs. Ray's.

It came in mid-October and every year, or almost every year, the family celebrated in the same way. They went out to Murmuring Lake, had dinner at the Inn, and then visited Pleasant Park. Mr. and Mrs. Ray showed the three girls the oak tree they had been sitting under when Mr. Ray proposed; they pointed out the big bay window in which they had been married. The trip usually came at a glittering autumnal moment when Minnesota was a paradise of blue skies and lakes, with red and gold leaves overhead and underfoot.

On the year Betsy was a sophomore, however, the fifteenth of October was a rainy day.

The rain began the night before, but lazily.

"It'll clear. We won't be starting until after school," Mr. Ray said optimistically. Mr. Ray was always optimistic. He never expected things to go wrong, but if they did he was not daunted. If a plan upset he could always make another one, so pleasant that everyone was almost glad the first one could not be carried out.

In the morning it was plain that he would have to plan, and plan fast. The rain was a torrent, and the wind was lashing the shrubs to and fro.

Whistling, as he always did when troubled, Mr. Ray went to the basement and started the furnace. Heat crept comfortingly through the registers, but no one cheered up. Anna made popovers, which helped any situation. Still the breakfast table was subdued, until Mr. Ray, with his second cup of coffee, remarked:

"I have a snoggestion." "Snoggestion" was what

he always called a particularly good suggestion. Faces brightened all around the table.

"What is it, Papa?" Margaret asked eagerly.

"We'll put off the trip. But just so your mother won't think I'm sorry she hooked me twenty-one years ago today, here's what I'm going to do."

"What?" Everyone waited radiantly.

"Take her out to supper tonight. Take her down to the Melborn Hotel. Poppy has put in a new café. The Moorish Café, he calls it. Oriental decorations, lights so low you can hardly see your nose, an orchestra making hoochy koochy music. All the fellows are taking their best girls there, and I'm going to take mine . . . tonight!"

"Bob!" cried Mrs. Ray. "How dear of you!" She tried not to show that she was disappointed because their daughters weren't included.

Of the three girls, Julia rallied first.

"That's a lovely snoggestion. It's the proper thing for a bride and groom to go off all alone."

"Um-hum," said Betsy and Margaret.

"And the new café is wonderful. Just like the Twin Cities, Mrs. Poppy says. Maybe Anna will make us beef birds," added Julia, glancing at Margaret who was especially fond of beef birds.

"But Anna has the evening off," objected Mr. Ray.

Anna, replenishing popovers, spoke hastily. "Na,

I'll stay home. It does that Charley good to get left once in a while. Margaret and I'll have fun making the beef birds. Won't we, Margaret?"

"No," said Mr. Ray. "It wouldn't be right to disappoint Charley. I don't like to see anybody disappointed." He seemed not to notice the crestfallen faces around him.

"Well, I can't make beef birds, but I can make pancakes . . . Margaret can help flop them," Julia volunteered.

"Pancakes and maple syrup! You won't have anything that good at the Moorish Café." For Margaret's benefit, Betsy smacked her lips in simulated delight.

"I like pancakes," said Margaret sitting very straight. She even smiled, although glassily.

Mrs. Ray looked troubled, but she wanted Mr. Ray to know that she was appreciative so she said gaily, "I'm going to dress up. I'll wear my new tan satin dress. And you have to put on your dress suit, Bob Ray, whether you want to or not."

"It isn't back from the dry cleaners, after Julia's party."

"Yes it is. It came yesterday."

"But I haven't a clean collar."

"You have plenty of clean collars."

"I've lost my studs!" Mr. Ray wailed.

He always pretended that he didn't like to put on

his dress suit. It was a family joke, and Margaret's eyes began to shine.

"Your studs are right in my jewel case where they always are," Mrs. Ray scolded. "If we're going to the Moorish Café, we're going to do it *right*."

"Go late, Mamma," urged Julia, laughing. "Twin City people eat very late, Mrs. Poppy says."

"Of course we'll go late. Seven o'clock."

"I can't wait until seven o'clock for my supper," Mr. Ray groaned.

"Not supper. *Dinner, Dinner!*"

All the girls were laughing now.

"See how she picks on me, Anna?" Mr. Ray asked. "Don't you think I'm a wonder to have stood it for twenty-one years?" He went around the table, kissing. And when he came to Mrs. Ray he kissed her twice. "I'm even willing to stand it for twenty-one more," he said.

Julia, Betsy and Margaret in waterproof coats and rubbers braved the storm to go to school. They swam there and back, they reported at noon.

By late afternoon it had cleared a little. There were layers of turquoise between the gray clouds along the western sky.

"We could almost have gone to the lake. But I'm glad we didn't. Because Mamma is going to the Moorish Café," Margaret said.

"Let's start to make our pancakes, shall we?" Betsy asked. Anna had left. The kitchen was clean and empty.

"Wait until after we're gone," Mr. Ray suggested. "Mamma will need you to hook her dress up, probably. And Julia always ties my tie."

"All right. We'll see you off in style before we eat," said Julia.

So Mr. Ray went to the bathroom to shave, and the girls went to help their mother dress.

She was sitting at her dressing table, wearing a lacy corset cover and a bell-shaped taffeta petticoat, bright green. Her red hair was dressed in its high pompadour. She was powdered, and had darkened her reddish brows with the charred end of a match. She looked pretty, but she gazed at the mirror critically.

"I wish, I wish ladies could wear rouge, like actresses do," she said.

Betsy laughed, but Julia was sympathetic. "I like your face pale, Mamma. Your hair is so red, your eyes so blue. Just remember to bite your lips going into the Moorish Café."

She helped her mother into the tan satin dress, which was heavy with buckram lining, elaborate with high boned collar, lace-covered yoke, *soutache* braid on sleeves and flowing skirts. While Betsy hooked it, Julia went off to tie her father's tie, and Margaret sprinkled violet perfume on a fine embroidered handkerchief. Mrs. Ray was buttoning white kid gloves, when Mr. Ray came in.

Mr. Ray looked handsome in his dress suit. In spite of his jokes he really liked to wear it. He was tall and very erect; he almost bent backwards, in fact. He was beginning to get stout around his middle. But it only made him look more dignified, Mrs. Ray said. His black hair lay flat and shining on his head. He had a big nose, fresh cheeks, and hazel eyes which were full of mischief now.

"Come on. Hurry up," he said as Mrs. Ray stroked down the fingers of her gloves.

"Why, Bob! It's only six o'clock."

"I know. But I want to go for a ride before dinner, a long romantic ride in the twilight. Haven't you any sentiment?"

"I have plenty of sentiment," said Mrs. Ray and kissed him.

She turned for his inspection gaily. Mr. Ray shook his head at his daughters.

"Not one of you girls," he said, "is as good-looking as your mother."

Then he put on his top coat and got his silk hat and his gold-headed cane. He held Mrs. Ray's wrap and they all went downstairs.

Betsy whispered to Margaret who ran into the

kitchen and returned with one fist clenched.

"Good-by, darlings!" Mrs. Ray bestowed fragrant rustling kisses.

"Good-by! Have a good time."

"It's so nice for you two to go off *alone*," said Julia, and her father turned and winked at her.

"Now!" Betsy hissed in Margaret's ear.

Margaret ran through the doorway and threw a handful of rice.

"Margaret!" "You little rascal!" Mr. and Mrs. Ray shouted and dodged. The girls laughed and Julia banged the door and leaned against it.

"Bettina! Margaret! I know the most wonderful secret."

"What?"

"Are they out of sight?"

"Not yet. They're climbing into the surrey."

"Well, wait! I won't tell 'til they're gone."

After a breathless moment the sound of Old Mag's clopping hoofs died out down the street.

"It's a good thing I can act," said Julia then. "I've known for the last ten minutes. Ever since I went to fix Papa's tie."

"Known what?"

"We're going to the Moorish Café."

"*We're* going?"

"Me, too?" asked Margaret stupefied.

"Yes, baby. You, too. Mr. Thumbler's hack is calling for us at a quarter to seven. We're going to surprise Mamma. It's Papa's idea."

Betsy leaped and squealed. Margaret was sedate as always, but her eyes almost swallowed her face. Julia flung her arms around them both.

"We've got to *hurry*! For once I can't be late. Papa wants us sitting at the table when he brings Mamma in, and in our very best dresses."

"I can button everything except the middle button," Margaret said, and they made a rush for the stairs.

Julia was ready last, of course. But before beginning on herself she had dressed Betsy's pompadour and tied Margaret's hair ribbon into sculptured beauty. They kept Mr. Thumbler waiting only five minutes.

In the hack Margaret sat erect and tense. Autumn fog circled the street lamps. Lighted parlors looked cozy in the dusk.

"Most people are doing their dishes. We're going to the Moorish Café," Margaret said.

Julia squeezed her hand. "Aren't we glad we're us?"

"If we weren't us, who would we be?"

"Let's see," said Betsy. "If Mamma had married somebody else, we'd be just half ourselves."

"And if Papa had married someone else, too, there'd be another half of us goodness knows where."

"How exciting! I could pass myself on the street."

"Half of yourself could say to the other half, 'Miss Ray, your petticoat hangs.'"

Julia and Betsy were having fun but Margaret said, "Oh, dear!"

"Don't worry!" said Julia. "It couldn't possibly have happened. Papa and Mamma were meant for each other, and we were meant for them."

Mr. Thumbler deposited them grandly at the Melborn's limestone entrance, and Julia led the way inside. The Café was on the ground floor. One could enter it from the street or from the lobby. Mr. Ray had told Julia to enter from the lobby; Mr. Poppy would be waiting for them. And he was. Three hundred pounds of suave sophistication.

"Good evening, Mr. Poppy. Here are the three bears," Julia said breezily. She was as poised as though she came to the Moorish Café every day. Betsy was fervently admiring. She assumed her Ethel Barrymore droop, and attempted a bored smile, but her own smile kept coming through, excited and eager.

"Three bears indeed!" said Mr. Poppy. "Three beautiful young ladies! You're coming up to the apartment after dinner, Mamma says." He always called Mrs. Poppy, "Mamma."

Taking Margaret's hand he led them into the Moorish Café.

Music swam out to greet them, seductive and soft. The long narrow room was mysteriously dim, lighted only by small brass lamps studded with red and green and purple glass. When she grew accustomed to this colored dusk, Betsy saw rich rugs and hangings, a turbaned orchestra.

They came to a table for five bearing a sign Reserved, and a large tissue-wrapped package.

"I've had my instructions," Mr. Poppy said, and placed the three girls in a row facing the door which led to the street.

They were barely seated when the door opened. Mrs. Ray, looking tall and lovely, her red head rising above her velvet wrap, came in, followed by Mr. Ray. He gave his hat, coat, and stick to a girl who came forward to get them, and Mrs. Ray looked around graciously. She didn't look to see anything. She looked as a woman looks who knows she is being inspected . . . head high, face proud and smiling.

Julia, Betsy and Margaret squeezed hands under the table.

"Table for two, sir?"

"It's ordered. Ray is the name."

The oriental waiter almost scampered down the room.

He paused before the three girls but for an instant Mrs. Ray did not even glance down. Then she looked to see what was causing the delay, and her company expression melted into amazement and delight.

"Girls! Girls! What are you doing here?"

"Papa invited us." Margaret was almost bursting.

"Happy anniversary, Mamma!"

"Congratulations, Mamma!"

Mrs. Ray turned to Mr. Ray who smiled broadly.

"Bob," she said, "this is perfect! Absolutely perfect!"

And it was!

The Moorish Café was even more Twin Cityish than Mrs. Poppy had said. The music was very hoochy koochy, and for dinner they had oyster cocktails, and then soup, and then fish, and then turkey, and then salad, and then dessert . . . pie, ice cream or Delmonico pudding. The coffee came in small long-handled brass pots.

"Just like they have in Little Syria," Betsy cried.

Everyone had coffee, dark and very sweet, in cups the size of thimbles.

Mrs. Ray opened the tissue-wrapped package. It held a dish, gold-rimmed, hand-painted with sprays of green leaves and reddish colored berries.

"I thought it looked like October," Mr. Ray said.

The orchestra stopped its hoochy koochy music, and played "O Promise Me," which Julia had sung at the Mock Wedding. All the other diners smiled at the Rays, and Margaret sat straight and acted very dignified, as though she couldn't imagine why they were smiling.

Even when the music ended the party wasn't over, for the family went up in the elevator to the Poppys' apartment overlooking the river. In her pink and gold parlor, large, pink and gold Mrs. Poppy passed candy and grape juice and cigars and played while Julia sang.

Standing like Geraldine Farrar in the picture . . . although she lacked the glittering train . . . Julia trilled through a waltz song by Arditi. Mr. Ray listened with crossed legs, looking grave. He didn't understand much about music. Mrs. Ray looked stern, as she always did when her children performed. Betsy thought about the Moorish Café, and Margaret tried not to act sleepy.

Mrs. Poppy put her arm around Julia.

"You have a very talented little girl," she said. "I wish she could hear some grand opera. She's my star pupil—absolutely."

And that was a nice thing for parents to hear on a wedding anniversary.

Leaving the Poppys, they went down in the elevator to the big, warm, brightly lighted lobby.

"You wait here," Mr. Ray said. "I'll go out and bring around Old Mag. . . ."

He was interrupted by Margaret, still erect although very drowsy now.

"Oh, Papa! I almost forgot."

"What, dear?"

From the pocket of her dress Margaret drew out a dollar and handed it to him.

"What's this?" asked Mr. Ray looking mystified.

"It's yours," said Margaret, trying not to yawn. "You forgot and left it on the table down in the Moorish Café. I saw it just as we were leaving. I've been meaning to give it to you."

"Oh, thank you, Button," Mr. Ray said.

His lips twitched a little, and Mrs. Ray and Julia smiled at each other, but Betsy didn't see anything funny in Papa forgetting a dollar and Margaret rescuing it.

"Wasn't that killing about Margaret?" asked Julia at home, undressing while Betsy wound her hair on Magic Wavers.

"What about Margaret?"

"Her picking up the tip."

"Tip?"

"The tip Papa left for the waiter."

"Oh . . . oh . . . yes, of course. Perfectly killing," said Betsy. She laughed heartily but her expression was puzzled. A tip! A tip! What, she wondered, was a tip?

7
The Man of Mystery

WINONA DID NOT ALLOW Betsy to forget that she was going to ask Joe Willard into the Crowd.

"When are you going to do it?" she prodded.

"Whenever I give a party."

"Well, when are you going to give one?"

"Not until Papa forgets the fifty-four I got in my geometry test. Joe Willard will keep. Don't worry."

Yet she herself felt a little worried, and she couldn't see why. It was certainly all right to invite Joe into the Crowd. It was the grandest Crowd in school and he belonged in it. She looked for a chance to speak with him alone but this was not easy to find.

He was elusive around school. He went from one class to another as though shot from a gun. If a girl wanted to talk to him she had to stop him; he never waylaid anyone. He swung through the halls confidently, a little brashly, and he was fun in class. He liked to say things that would startle people . . . teachers or pupils. At such times he had an infectious grin which swept the group into his mirthful mood.

He was popular, but very little known.

"He's practically a Man of Mystery," Betsy thought. She began to look for him outside of school.

Every Saturday now there was a football game. Some were played in neighboring towns, and Julia's friends made up parties and went off on the train with the team, and Stewie, the coach. Betsy's crowd was content to meet the train when it returned with the conquering or defeated heroes.

But they attended the home games in a body. Wearing streamers of maroon and gold, they drove out behind Old Mag or Dandy, who waited patiently on the outskirts of the field.

This year there was an auto at the games, Phil

Brandish's bright red auto. When they saw it, Betsy and Tacy used to hum, "Dreaming, Dreaming." But Phil Brandish didn't know they were on earth. Big, obstreperous, noisy, he was usually with a crowd of boys. Once he brought a senior girl, alone. They sat in the auto with a big box of candy, watching the game from afar.

"The big stiff ought to go out for football," Cab said. "He doesn't care for a thing but that darn auto, takes it to pieces and puts it together again and crawls underneath it and lies there by the hour."

Cab himself was still on the scrub team, but he practised ardently.

It was the custom for spectators to watch the games from the sidelines, walking up and down the field to follow the play. They saw it as it is never seen from grandstands . . . the mud on the heroes' faces, the tears in the eyes of the boy sent out of the game, the grim concentration of the quarterback, calling signals hoarsely, the bottle of arnica, gore now and then.

Football was still puzzling to Betsy, but she enjoyed the excitement, the crisp air, the trees on the far horizon which, as the season progressed, changed from ruddy gold to russet and dry brown.

Betsy looked for Joe, but she never saw him. He worked every Saturday, football or no football. She remarked on this to Cab.

"Needs the filthy lucre, I suppose," Cab replied. "I know he likes football. Sometimes when we practise late, he drops by the field. Stewie lets him take a fling, and he's good. Darned good. Stewie'd give a lot to have him on the team. He told him so, the other night, and I thought Joe would be pleased. But he acted sort of superior about it. He said, 'Oh, I'll play in college!' And got away as quickly as he could."

"College!" said Betsy. "He's going to college!"

"Some people are gluttons for punishment," Cab replied.

This conversation proved so enlightening that Betsy sounded out Tony.

"Where does Joe Willard live?"

"With Mrs. Blair, a widow, at the north end of town. You know that little gray house, sort of under Agency Hill? My mother knows her, and she says Joe's all right. He doesn't want any mothering, though. He eats around at restaurants and he won't let Mrs. Blair give him a home-cooked meal, unless she'll let him pay her."

"I wonder why that is?"

"He's independent! But Mrs. Blair likes him. He pays his rent and keeps his room neat . . . except for books. It's all over apples and books, she says."

"He was eating an apple and reading a book the first I saw him," Betsy remarked.

"He loads up with books every night coming home from the Creamery. He just about lives at the library," Tony replied.

Betsy's heart warmed. She loved the library, too . . . the quiet, the smell of books, the fireplace in the Children's Room with a painting called "The Isle of Delos" over the mantle. And she loved Miss Sparrow, the small winsome librarian, with her curly untidy hair and merry eyes.

When Hallowe'en drew near Mrs. Ray told Betsy she might give a party, a costume party for boys and girls, and that same afternoon, after school, Betsy got out her library card.

"Isn't it late to be going to the library?" her mother asked.

"Oh, I just remembered something," Betsy replied off-handedly.

"Well, wear your heavy coat. It's turning cold."

"I will," said Betsy. She put on her red tam and mittens with her gray winter coat.

The warm well-lighted rooms were almost empty, and Miss Sparrow helped Betsy choose some books. She had known for years that Betsy planned to be a writer; they often talked about it. Tonight she suggested books by women writers . . . Jane Austen's *Pride and Prejudice*, *Wuthering Heights* by Emily Brontë.

"It will give you confidence to read them," Miss Sparrow said.

"I wish you'd give me a list of novels to read, Miss Sparrow."

"I'd love to."

"Novels that would help me learn to write."

"And you ought to read poetry, too. In fact, the poetry is more important now, in my opinion. You're at the age when poetry sinks in. . . ."

Joe Willard didn't come but Betsy didn't care. The trip had been well worth while. Smiling and full of plans, she swung out into a chilly twilight . . . and met Joe on the library steps.

Unceremoniously he seized her books and looked at the titles.

"I'm surprised," he said grinning. "I thought you'd be reading Robert W. Chambers."

"I read women writers. I think they're the best," Betsy said.

"Especially Elizabeth Warrington Ray, I suppose."

"Oh! Do you know her work? I thought it would be beyond you."

"I wade through it now and then." His blue eyes were gay above a blue woolen muffler tucked inside his coat. He handed back her books.

"Have you read these?" Betsy asked.

"Naturally. I've read everything."

"I'll bet you haven't read . . . *Hamlet*."

"Shakespeare in one volume. Take it off the parlor table and try it some time."

They were getting on famously when Betsy said with an abrupt change of tone, "Joe, I want to talk to you."

"No charge. Can I advise you about Gaston's peculiar methods?" He was still joking, but his tone had changed, too. He sounded wary.

"It's about our Crowd. We think you ought to . . . ought to . . . I mean, I want you to come to a party."

His friendly look faded.

"Thanks very much. I'm afraid I can't."

"But you don't even know when it is!" Betsy cried. "How do you know you can't come when I haven't even told you when it is?"

"I know. Thanks just the same."

"It's a Hallowe'en costume party."

"Fine, fine! Have a good time."

"Joe," said Betsy. "I think you belong with our Crowd. Everyone thinks so. And we do have the best times. We play around at each other's houses, and go to the Majestic and Heinz's together. . . ." She stopped, because his expression grew more and more hostile.

"Thanks a lot. Mind if I go now?"

"But why, why, don't you want to go with our Crowd?"

He looked trapped. After a brief pause he said, "It would just bore me, that's all."

Bore him! Betsy could hardly believe her ears. Imagine her beloved Crowd boring anyone!

Betsy didn't get angry easily; she almost never got angry. But she felt a hot flare of anger now.

"I see. I'm sorry I mentioned it."

Her tone was as cold as the wind which came sweeping down Broad Street across the library steps. It whipped at the blue muffler and pulled it loose. The muffler was so becoming, and Joe wore it with such a jaunty air, that Betsy wondered with irritation if he was going without an overcoat just to call attention to his muffler. Or maybe overcoats bored him, too.

"See you in Gaston's hangout," he said, and swaggered into the library, quickly, as though it were a refuge.

Betsy stood on the steps, and tears came into her eyes. Her feelings were mixed up. She felt hurt, humiliated, angry, and yet she was almost sorry for him . . . or would be, except that you just couldn't be sorry for Joe. He was so proud, so confident . . . it would be ridiculous.

"Bore him!" said Betsy, trying to whip up her anger, but it was fading fast.

That night she telephoned the Crowd about the

party. She told the girls that Joe Willard wouldn't come but she didn't tell anyone what he had said. She didn't want to make trouble for him . . . rude as he had been.

To Winona she said airily, "He *must* be a woman hater. He even hates me."

She couldn't settle down to study, and finally she went into Julia's room. Betsy wasn't much of a confider, but Julia's advice was invaluable sometimes.

Julia, who was buffing her nails, listened thoughtfully. After Betsy had finished she said, "I think you went at the thing wrong."

"But why? I was perfectly honest."

"Too honest."

"You can't be too honest."

Julia put down her buffer. She spoke slowly.

"Of course not. But it wouldn't have been dishonest, exactly, to have kept on talking, having fun. He'd have asked to walk home with you . . . it was getting dark. And maybe . . . who knows . . . Mamma would have kept him to supper? We had apple pie. And then we'd have asked him to Sunday night lunch, and he'd have fallen for Papa's sandwiches. And we'd have told him about the party, and started planning costumes. You could have asked him to plan one for you. The first thing he knew he'd *be* at your party, and smack in the midst of your Crowd."

"Julia," said Betsy. "You're wonderful. Why don't I know how to wangle things?"

"You'll learn."

"You didn't learn. You were born knowing how."

"Yes," said Julia, glancing up at Geraldine Farrar. "But even if you wouldn't do a thing like that instinctively as I would, you could figure it out. You're a writer. You could plan it out and do it."

Betsy was silent.

"About Joe! Wait a few days and try again, using a little finesse."

"No," Betsy interrupted firmly. "We bore him. He said so."

"Maybe he didn't mean that. Maybe he just can't afford to go with a crowd."

"Oh, fudge! We're not millionaires. Cab delivers papers; doesn't he? Tony drives a grocery wagon every summer! All of us have a terrible time managing on our allowances. No, we just bore him, like he said."

Julia didn't answer. She knew that tone . . . and look. There was no use trying to change Betsy when she was feeling stubborn.

Before Hallowe'en a curly-headed Irish boy named Dennis started going around with Cab. Cab brought him to the Ray house, and Betsy asked him to her party. And she asked a football hero named Al who had started going with Carney, and a boy nicknamed

Squirrelly who had a case on Irma.

The party was a great success, and soon the Crowd had plenty of boys.

But not one, Betsy thought sometimes, feeling hurt inside, was so nice as Joe Willard, who went his solitary way.

8

Rosy Apple Blossoms

BETSY ALWAYS HAD had the gift of getting along with people. She was like her father in that. Bob Ray had friends all up and down Front Street; he had friends all over the county. And everyone in high school liked Betsy . . . or had last year. Now, however, there was this new coolness between her and Joe Willard. She hated it, but she didn't know how to end it. Presently something even more antagonistic arose between Betsy and another person. And the person was no one less than Mr. Gaston, the rhetoric teacher.

He had liked her well enough last year. His recommendation had helped to give her the coveted chance to compete on the Essay Contest. But this year, he liked her less and less.

Mr. Gaston, as Julia had said, wished to be a science teacher. He did not enjoy teaching English. The only part of the subject that interested him was punctuation, paragraphing, spelling. He liked neat, factual papers.

Betsy punctuated and paragraphed better than most; her spelling was good, and her papers were neat. But alas, they were almost never factual! Betsy liked to invent, to create. She could not write even about Our System of Taxation without coloring it up a bit.

When at rare intervals . . . very rare, for Mr. Gaston, the scientist, disliked fiction . . . an original story was given as a class assignment, Betsy went into a delirium. She wrote and wrote, evolving hair raising plots, conjuring up romantic characters, describing Paris, Vienna, and other cities she had never seen. The class liked Betsy's stories, but the general approval only deepened Mr. Gaston's exasperation.

"Betsy, you have this miser hoarding a twenty-five

dollar gold piece and there is no such coin."

"Oh, well . . . I'll make it twenty dollars then."

But Mr. Gaston would not allow her to toss off the mistake. The story was returned with a red F for Fair, when Betsy felt fiercely sure that it was the best submitted. (Except for Joe Willard's, perhaps. He wrote good stories, too, and his gold pieces were always of a proper denomination.)

Seething, she mentioned the affair at supper.

"Really, Bob," exploded Mrs. Ray, "you ought to speak to the school board."

"Now, now, Jule! Remember you have red hair!"

"I am remembering. That's why I suggest something temperate like speaking to the school board." Mrs. Ray's blue eyes were snapping. "The very idea! Bothering Betsy about twenty-five dollar gold pieces. . . ."

"And commas," put in Margaret, remembering Betsy's most frequent complaint.

"It won't do Betsy any harm to learn about commas," Mr. Ray said. "I've noticed myself that she scatters them like grass seed."

"Who reads Shakespeare for the commas?"

"Maybe . . ." Mr. Ray's eyes twinkled. "I duck when I say it. You hold the carving knife, Margaret. . . . Maybe Betsy isn't quite in Shakespeare's class?"

That drew Julia into the fray.

"How do you know she isn't? Maybe this generation

is going to produce another Shakespeare, and maybe it's Betsy."

"It wouldn't surprise me a bit," interjected Mrs. Ray.

"What do you think, Margaret?"

Margaret looked grave. "Just who is Shakespeare, exactly?"

"*Ja,* who is this Shakespeare?" Anna burst through the swinging door. The argument had penetrated to the kitchen only faintly, but Anna knew that Betsy was being attacked.

"Who is he anyway?" she demanded, squaring her plump shoulders. "Does he ever come here? Well, he'd better not."

"He's dead," Julia said.

Anna was dashed, but only for a moment.

"Small loss, probably. If anyone picks on you, Betsy, lovey, you know who to come to. I always said the same to the McCloskey girls." She returned to the kitchen, breathing heavily.

Everyone laughed, and Julia began to tell about Miss Bangeter's Shakespeare class.

This was an institution at Deep Valley High School. It was a class of which the whole school spoke with reverence. It was open only to seniors, and was almost of college level, other teachers said. They eavesdropped when they could, on Miss Bangeter's reading of the plays.

"You'll adore it, Bettina," Julia said. "Just now we're studying *As You Like It*. How I'd love to play Rosalind!"

She read the play to Betsy that evening, and after that Betsy read all the plays right along with Julia. Julia passed on Miss Bangeter's explanations, her comments, her enthusiasm, and Betsy took to experiments in blank verse. Tacy thought they were wonderful.

"Better not show them to Gaston though," she added cautiously.

"I know. He'd think I was conceited. But I'm not. Am I, Tacy?"

"Of course not!"

"I just happen to be able to write, like Julia can sing, and Carney can sew, and Gaston . . . probably . . . can cut up frogs."

"Cutting up frogs is all he's good for."

"If there's anything I'm not, it's conceited," Betsy declared. But Mr. Gaston continued to think that she was. He thought it all the more after November Rhetoricals.

Rhetoricals were programs which the two literary societies presented in alternate months. In November it was the Zetamathians' turn, and early in the month Miss Clarke asked Julia and Betsy to drop into her room after school. Miss Clarke had long leaned on Julia in preparing the Zetamathian Rhetoricals. Julia loved to oblige with a solo, or to play the piano, or to act in a skit. And Betsy last year had sung the "Cat Duet" with Tacy . . . and had read an original paper.

"My two Rays!" Miss Clarke said happily when Julia and Betsy came in. She was a pretty woman with soft dark hair, soft white skin, and soft eyes behind round glasses which emphasized her gentle guilelessness. Her manner in class was timid and appealing, but out of class she had an innocent girlish gaiety which beamed in her eyes now.

"I've been thinking," she said, "how sad it is that Julia is going to graduate! Of course, I have Betsy coming along, but this is the last year I'll have you both. I've been wondering what you could do for Rhetoricals *together*."

"A duet?" asked Julia hopefully.

Miss Clarke shook her head.

"Betsy's going to repeat that 'Cat Duet' with Tacy on one of the programs this year. No, I have a better idea. A really marvelous one. I want Betsy to write a song which you can sing."

"Not the music!" cried Betsy, alarmed.

"Oh, no, dear! We'll take the music of some popular song. I'd thought of that 'Same Old Story' everybody's singing."

"Just new words? That's a cinch!"

"Listen to her!" Miss Clarke turned to Julia. "I suppose she could do it overnight?"

"Why, yes," said Betsy. She was surprised at such a to-do about something so easy. Julia was delighted with the plan, so Betsy went home and wrote new words for "Same Old Story."

When November Rhetoricals came, Miss Clarke introduced the number with a little speech about the Rays. She told about Betsy's writing the words and the school began to clap. Mr. Gaston, sitting on the platform, folded his arms and looked sardonic. Then Carney sat down at the piano, Julia came to the platform, and everyone clapped again.

Julia had dressed her hair with a long curl over her shoulder. And since this song definitely wasn't grand opera, she dropped all her grand opera airs. She sang like a musical comedy soubrette, sauntering along the platform, with a special smile or toss of her head to end each verse.

There were verses about the Freshman Girl, the Sophomore Girl, the Junior Girl and the Senior Girl, and after each verse the same refrain:

> "*Same old story,*
> *Same old High,*
> *Same old bunch of gigglers*
> *As the years pass by.*

> *She's a hummer,*
> *A shining light,*
> *For she's Deep Valley's High School Girl*
> *And she's all right."*

At the end of the last chorus there was such a clamor of applause that Carney began to repeat. Julia, with true instinct, opened her arms.

"Everybody sing!" she cried, and everybody sang, even Miss Bangeter. Everybody, that is, except Mr. Gaston. He kept his arms folded and looked unpleasant while the assembly room rang.

> *"Same old story,*
> *Same old High,*
> *Same old bunch of gigglers*
> *As the years pass by . . ."*

It was sung over and over. After school it was hummed in the cloak rooms, in the halls, and along High Street. Miss Clarke was triumphant, and Julia and Betsy were decidedly pleased with themselves.

But Betsy stopped being pleased next morning in rhetoric class.

When she came into the room, Mr. Gaston looked up with a smile dangerously bland. It followed her while she went to her desk and sat down.

"We feel fortunate to have a poetess in our midst," Mr. Gaston said, and Betsy blushed. Everyone laughed, but almost no one laughed at his next joke.

"When we come to the study of poetry, perhaps I'd better step down and let Betsy take the chair."

He stacked the attendance cards and grinned maliciously.

"It was reassuring to hear that the Deep Valley High School girl is such a fine specimen," he said.

Betsy was furious, but not so furious as Tacy who fixed him with indignant bright blue eyes. Cab and Tony scowled, Dennie, the new boy in the Crowd, pulled at his curly hair and looked uneasy. Joe Willard, Betsy saw, was gazing out of the window.

Betsy did not enliven the supper table with this encounter. She had decided, wisely, to keep her troubles to herself. But she argued mentally with Mr. Gaston all through the evening, and after she had gone to bed.

"I never claimed it was great poetry." "It was meant to be *funny*." "I'd like to hear what kind of verses *you'd* write!" And so on, into the night.

The next day, however, Mr. Gaston was unusually affable. "Ashamed of himself, probably," Tacy whispered. Betsy struggled faithfully to keep her rhetoric papers as dull as possible and things went smoothly for a while. But then Mr. Gaston assigned another short story. That was her downfall.

He assigned it, of course, only because the schedule required it.

"Any subject . . . any subject you like," he said, waving his hands to express contempt. "Try not to be too flowery."

This, Betsy realized, was probably aimed at her, but she was too pleased to worry. She planned out her story walking home.

It was a sunless afternoon. The look of the world spelled the word November.

"I'm going to put my story in the spring," she thought. "That's what's so nice about writing. You can go into any season you want to."

Her story was about a band of gypsies who stole a child, and before she began Betsy closed her eyes a minute and thought about spring. She thought about the apple orchard behind the Hill Street house, and saw blossoms swaying against a vivid sky. Then she wrote her opening sentence.

"Under a tree hung with rosy apple blossoms, an infant boy was sleeping."

The stories were collected next day. The following day, before returning them, Mr. Gaston faced the class.

"I asked you," he said, "as a special favor, not to be too flowery. But our poetess . . ." Betsy squirmed and blushed . . . "is not only flowery. Her flowers are the wrong color. I haven't read your story, Betsy, and

I don't intend to. The opening sentence is enough for me." He read aloud scornfully:

"Under a tree hung with rosy apple blossoms . . ."

He laid down the paper.

"Rosy apple blossoms! Rosy apple blossoms! Whoever heard of rosy apple blossoms? Apple blossoms, my dear young lady, aren't pink. They are white."

Betsy's blushes receded. She turned, in fact, a little pale.

"I think they are pink, Mr. Gaston."

"You *think* they are pink?" Mr. Gaston glared at her through his thick glasses. "But I *know* they are white."

"It's the under part of the petals," Betsy said falteringly. "They're pinkish, sort of."

"Pinkish, sort of!" Mr. Gaston mocked.

Betsy looked around, a little wildly. Joe Willard was staring out of the window. She brought her gaze back to Mr. Gaston stubbornly.

"We had lots of apple trees when we lived up on Hill Street. I always liked to look at them in May."

"You should have examined them accurately. You would have found that they are white."

"But they weren't white." Betsy was near to tears, but it was from anger.

"They must have been peach trees," Mr. Gaston said.

"They were apples. I've eaten the apples."

"Betsy," said Mr. Gaston, with a maddening, condescending smile. "If you were a little younger, I'd ask you to write a hundred times, 'Apple blossoms are white.' As it is I merely ask you to rewrite your story, and eliminate any inaccuracies."

He picked up another paper.

But the subject was not quite done with. Joe Willard turned from his study of the trees beyond the window and raised his hand.

"Yes, Joe?" Mr. Gaston said, changing his tone.

"It is my opinion sir, that apple blossoms are pink."

Mr. Gaston was silent, stunned.

"Pinkish, rather," Joe continued. "I think Betsy's word 'rosy' is excellent. They're colored just enough to make the effect rosy."

The silence in the room had width, height, depth, mass and substance.

Then Mr. Gaston found his voice, a particularly acid voice.

"Very interesting. But we can't let this turn into a botany class. Tacy, your story is mediocre, but it is at least short, blessedly short."

After class Betsy brushed past marching pupils to go up to Joe. He was wearing the odd coat and trousers and a distant triumphant smile.

"Joe," said Betsy. It was the first time she had addressed him since he told her that her Crowd bored him. "Joe, that was nice of you to speak up about the apple blossoms. I . . . I appreciate it."

The smile left his face.

"It was just simple justice. Nothing personal in it. I'd have done it for anyone," he replied coldly, looking her coldly in the eye.

9
Washington, Lincoln, and Jefferson

THE FIRST SNOW CAME, dramatic as always. One day, unexpectedly, it appeared in the air. Children all over Deep Valley held up their hands to catch the flakes on their mittens, and shouted and raced with delight.

Presently the gray-brown world was covered with feathery white. Boys and girls, walking home from high school, pelted one another with snowballs. Margaret came out with her sled.

She slid with dignity, small skirts spread tidily, her back straight as a ramrod, down to the watering trough. Hugh joined her, and pulled her up the slope so that she could slide down again. He was morose. He had dropped in on Julia, who had said she was busy, giving a lesson to Tacy. Hugh thought it was just another excuse for getting rid of him. But as a matter of fact Julia actually was giving Tacy singing lessons.

Tacy's voice was true and sweet. It was like an Irish harp with plaintive questioning and joy and sadness in it. And Tacy loved to sing. She was so shy that she could not imagine singing in front of the whole school, alone, as Julia did. But standing beside the Ray piano, with Julia whom she had known all her life, she poured out her heart in song.

Julia passed on to Tacy readily all Mrs. Poppy had taught her. "I use Mrs. Poppy's method," Julia liked to say importantly. She was all seriousness during the lesson, and even Betsy was barred from the room.

Julia was busy with the many and lofty activities of seniors, with the choir, and her singing lessons. But presently she grew busier still, for the Episcopalian ladies, wanting to raise money for new hymnals, decided to put on a home talent play. *Wonderland* was its name. It was to be given in the Opera House, and Julia was asked to play the leading part, the princess.

Betsy's crowd of girls was in the chorus. They were to dance a Scarf Dance. Through November the entries in Betsy's journal were all about *Wonderland*: "Rehearsal for *Wonderland*." "Homework and *Wonderland*." "Practised the Scarf Dance for hours. My feet are killing me." Then they began to read, "*Wonderland* and Harry." The references to Harry which followed almost every night thereafter indicated, however, only Betsy's interest in her sister's affairs. It was Julia's life into which Harry had entered.

Harry was playing the part of the prince, and he was not a high school boy. He had been graduated from the High School some years since, had attended the state university for a year, and had now returned to work in his father's bank. He was old. He was so old that he wore a mustache. He was a large self-assured young man, a trifle condescending to the town girls.

He was graciously condescending to Julia at the first rehearsal, where it was discovered that they shared a duet and several love scenes. But they walked home from the second rehearsal, and after that he wasn't condescending any more.

"*Same old story,*" Betsy hummed mischievously when, after the third rehearsal Harry and Julia broke away from the group saying that they were going downtown for a snack. Harry had taken Julia's arm possessively, and in his eyes was a look her sister knew well.

He started coming to the Rays' regularly. He brought Julia flowers and candy. He brought her the score of *The Red Mill*, and he and Julia sang a duet from it:

> *"Not that you are fair, dear*
> *Not that you are true . . ."*

He lifted his eyebrows and puffed out his chest. He quite eclipsed poor Hugh.

But Hugh did not give up easily. In the show window of a hardware store on Front Street some Spitz puppies were being exhibited. Julia took Margaret down to see them and Hugh, making one of his forlorn unwanted calls, heard their enthusiastic descriptions. Late the next afternoon he appeared with one of the puppies under his coat, and presented it to Margaret . . . a delightful little fellow with soft white fur hanging almost to the floor, and a shiny black nose like patent leather.

This gift seemed at first a masterstroke. Julia went into ecstasies more extravagant even than Margaret's. Although the puppy was as white as snow, she gave him a bath and dried him in towels before the dining room fire. She rummaged through her ribbon box for blue and cherry-colored ribbons which she tied into his collar.

"I'll name him Lincoln. It goes so well with Washington. Don't you think so?" Margaret asked.

"Lincoln's sort of hard to say. We could call him Abie, though," Betsy volunteered.

"You're our sweet precious little Abie," Julia cooed, and Hugh looked sheepishly triumphant.

Harry dropped in that night and he wasn't too pleased with Abie. He said that Spitz dogs shed their long white hairs in a most annoying way.

"You won't like it, Mrs. Ray. They have bad dispositions, too, I understand."

After Harry was gone, Mr. Ray looked down at Washington which Julia's last year's beau had given to Margaret, and at Hugh's gift of Abraham Lincoln. They were sleeping peacefully, one on Margaret's lap and one on Julia's. Mr. Ray shook his head and chuckled.

"When will Jefferson appear, and what will he be? White mice? A canary? We'll have a menagerie, Julia, if this keeps up."

Julia's soft white fingers rubbed Abie between the ears. She merely smiled.

Hugh soon discovered that although Julia was so fond of Abie she was no fonder of him than she ever had been. And Harry had an enormous advantage.

Because of the *Wonderland* rehearsals he was with Julia almost daily, and they joked about their love scenes, but they worked hard on the duets. Julia saw to that.

There was a dress rehearsal in which everything that could possibly go wrong went wrong, but by the next evening all had miraculously straightened itself out. The house was packed even to the boxes. The boys in Betsy's Crowd sat in the topmost gallery . . . the peanut gallery it was called . . . and they cheered and whooped when the Scarf Dance was executed flawlessly.

Julia's solo was a glorious success, and at its conclusion the usher presented her with two bouquets: pink roses from Hugh and red ones from Harry. Julia cradled them impartially, one in each arm, while she smiled and bowed. But when she appeared in the next scene she had a red rose in her hair.

Soon after this the evening paper announced that an actress named Rose Stahl would come to Deep Valley in a Broadway success called *The Chorus Lady*. Immediately after supper the telephone rang. It was Anna's night out and Julia, Betsy, and Margaret were doing the dishes, Julia washing, Betsy wiping, Margaret putting the dishes away.

Margaret answered the telephone.

"It's for you, Julia," she said. "It's Hugh."

Julia dried her hands and sat down at the phone in a niche beside the cellar door. In a big checked coverall apron of Anna's, she looked absurdly small. But the poise of her dark head on her slender smooth white neck was alert and resolute.

Listening with interest, Betsy and Margaret heard her say:

"Umm . . . I can't hear you, Hugh." She touched the receiver hook gently and pushed it up and down. "I hear such a queer sound. What *can* be the matter?"

In a moment she said, "The phone must be out of order. You'd better call me back." And she put the receiver into the hook and began to laugh.

"Hugh said there was nothing wrong with this phone except that I was wiggling the hook."

"Well," replied Betsy, "you were."

"Of course I was." Julia was busy cranking to make a call of her own. "He was asking me to go to *The Chorus Lady*. I don't want to accept if Harry is planning to ask me."

"What under the sun are you doing?" Betsy cried. "You can't *ask* Harry whether he's going to ask you."

"No," agreed Julia. "But I can give him a chance."

And in a moment Betsy and Margaret, watching with fascinated eyes, heard her say sweetly, "Harry, what was that song you wanted me to learn? Was it 'Rose in the Garden'? I'm ordering some music and

I just wasn't sure . . ."

There was a silence followed by some unrevealing murmurs. Then Julia cried with a rising inflection, "Really? Why, I'd love to!" There were more unrevealing murmurs, and she said good-by.

But before she could rise from her chair the phone rang again, angrily. Betsy and Margaret stood transfixed. Julia's voice was sweet as honey.

"Yes, Hugh, I hear you perfectly now. What *could* have been the matter? Rose Stahl in *The Chorus Lady?* I'm so sorry. I've accepted another invitation."

She put the receiver on the hook once more and came briskly back to the dishpan.

"Julia," said Betsy. "I don't see how you can be so mean to poor Hugh."

"When he gave us Abie, too!" cried Margaret. She straightened into what Julia and Betsy called her Persian princess air. "I wish I was older. *I'd* go with Hugh to see the show," she said and walked haughtily out of the kitchen.

Betsy too saw *The Chorus Lady*. She went with Winona, Irma, Carney, Alice, and Tacy. Winona could not get passes for so many so they sat in the peanut gallery taking plenty of peanuts and Miss Clarke as chaperone. The boys in the Crowd appeared in a body and after the play they all went to Heinz's, and Miss Clarke had more chaperoning to do than she had bargained for. She took off her glasses and polished them until she almost wore them out.

Harry didn't bring Julia to Heinz's. He scorned this resort of the high school crowd. He took her instead to the Moorish Café, for an oyster stew, an expedition which had two unfortunate results.

In the first place Mr. Ray was displeased.

"She's only a school girl," he protested to Mrs. Ray.

"But it's such a lovely place. And he is such a fine young man," Mrs. Ray replied. "And he asked Mrs. Poppy to join them, so Julia would have a chaperone."

Mr. Ray grumbled, unconvinced. "No judgment! Just what you'd expect from a Democrat!" Mr. Ray was a Republican.

Julia, however, was so dazzled by oyster stew at the Moorish Café, that she broke off with Hugh completely. When he dropped in the next day she remarked that she thought Rose Stahl was as great as Sarah Bernhardt. Hugh protested mildly, and Julia retorted with such provocative fire that before Hugh knew exactly what had happened he was out on the steps going home. He and Julia had quarreled, irrevocably.

"And I don't give two cents for Sarah Bernhardt! I never saw the woman!" he wailed to Betsy, who was full of pity as she always was for Julia's discarded beaus. Margaret was cross with Julia. She wore her Persian princess manner steadily for a week.

Harry was aware that Margaret did not like him. He started bringing her gum drops and picture books.

"How would you like some gold fish?" he asked her one night, and Mr. Ray choked over his cigar so violently that he had to go out to the porch and cough. He returned with dewy, twinkling eyes.

"Harry," he remarked soberly, "I know that you're a rising young Democrat. I wonder whether you've given any thought to Thomas Jefferson."

"Why, sir," said Harry, flattered, "I can't say I ever did."

"I advise you to," said Mr. Ray. "I advise you to consider him seriously."

"Papa," said Julia next morning at breakfast, "that was really too bad of you. He might have caught on."

"I wish he had, the store window dummy!" Mr. Ray said. "Moorish Café, indeed!"

The days slipped along to Thanksgiving. Tom came home, and that meant parties. Carney, Irma, and Winona all gave parties, and Tony took Betsy to Winona's, while both he and Cab accompanied her to Irma's. But Betsy wasn't satisfied. With Julia's great conquest so fresh in her mind, she was very dissatisfied indeed.

"Tony's just... Tony," she said to Tacy. "And Cab...

well, Cab couldn't very well take Irma to her own party. I wish I were more popular with boys."

"Why, Betsy!" cried Tacy. "Your house is always full of boys."

"We feed them," said Betsy glumly.

"It isn't that. They like you."

"Exactly." Betsy was bitter. "They like me so well they slap me on the back. I wish I could be different, suddenly. I wish I could change overnight. Walk into the high school tomorrow just utterly different, so that the boys would be struck dumb . . . even Phil Brandish."

"*Drea-ee-eaming,*" trilled Tacy, and she and Betsy began to laugh. But Betsy grew gloomy again.

"Just wait," she said, "I'll go away some day, and come back all changed like that girl in *The Conquest of Canaan*, languid sort of, and wearing a slinky Paris gown."

"You won't be half so nice as you are right now," said Tacy, who didn't like to hear Betsy criticized even by Betsy herself.

The Rays had Thanksgiving dinner with the Slades this year. The families entertained each other at Thanksgiving, turn and turn about. The dinner was magnificent, as usual, and after it was finished, the grown people napped, Margaret went roller skating, Harry took Julia to the Majestic, and Tom and Betsy went for a walk. Betsy was pleased to go walking with Tom who looked distinguished in his Cox School uniform. They set off across the slough.

They had reached a street which curved up toward the rambling Brandish mansion when a deep horn boomed, and a bright red automobile slowed to a stop beside them.

"Hello," Phil Brandish said.

Betsy was so excited that she almost choked.

"Ah," said Tom. "Greetings and salutations!" This was an expression he had brought home from Cox.

"Want a lift?" Phil Brandish asked.

"No, thanks," said Tom to Betsy's disappointment. She hoped frantically that her hat was on straight, that her nose was not red from the wind. But Phil Brandish was not looking at her. He was looking at Tom's uniform.

"Still in jail, I see," he said.

It seemed to Betsy that he was trying in a heavy inept way to make a joke. But Tom did not take it so.

"Jail, heck!" said Tom. "It's the finest school in the country. And it isn't mourning your departure either."

He scowled and took Betsy's arm.

Phil Brandish looked at her then, but absently. His eyes were yellowish brown. He was big, bigger than Tom, and notably well dressed. His felt hat had a crease down the middle; his overcoat was of rich dark wool, well cut; a checked muffler was folded with care.

"What's biting you?" he said to Tom. "I didn't mean anything."

"Neither did I. So long," said Tom. He and Betsy moved away, and the red auto whizzed away too like an angry hornet.

"He gets my goat," confided Tom. "He means all right, I guess, but he didn't fit in at Cox."

"He doesn't here either, exactly," Betsy said.

"I don't believe he knows how." Tom sounded puzzled. "He's always had too much money. He's traveled with his folks all around the world, gone to one school after another, had things handed to him on a platter."

"Cab says all he cares about is that auto."

"He was nuts about machinery at Cox," Tom replied.

They walked all the way to Page Park, and when they returned it was growing dark. Young and old gathered cozily around the Slade fire, where apples and cider were set out, and Tom's grandmother told stories. She was a very old lady, wizened and small, with thin white hair and sunken lips. She could remember Indians going on the warpath in the valley.

Betsy loved to listen to Grandma Slade's stories, but when the Rays were walking home her thoughts returned to Phil. She was irritated that he had paid so little attention to her. He would have paid attention to Julia.

"I wish I could go away," thought Betsy, harking back to her talk with Tacy. "It isn't practical just to wake up in the morning different. But if I could go away I'd come back so fascinating, so mysterious, Phil Brandish would *have* to look at me."

She planned all the way home and while she wound her hair on Magic Wavers, and after she went to bed, about going away and coming back different, a sirenlike woman of the world.

10

A Letter from Mrs. Muller

BETSY DREAMED ABOUT going away from Deep Valley, but she didn't for a moment suspect that around a bend in her Winding Hall of Fate a journey was actually waiting.

The day she reached that noteworthy bend everything began just as usual. She brought Tacy in after school, which was entirely usual. As usual she dropped her books on the music room table while she shouted for her mother . . . not that she wanted her for anything in particular . . . and when Mrs. Ray answered from upstairs, Betsy and Tacy went out to the kitchen to see what there was to eat.

"Fresh molasses cookies, lovey," Anna said. They heard Mrs. Ray's high heels on the stairs and just as they dipped their hands in the cookie jar Mrs. Ray came into the kitchen.

"Betsy," she said, "you have a letter from Mrs. Muller. I hope it doesn't mean that Tib is sick."

Betsy took the letter quickly, and while she tore it open Mrs. Ray and Tacy waited without speaking. Both of them were very fond of Tib, who for so many years had made the team of Betsy and Tacy a threesome. Betsy unfolded the sheet of creamy white stationery and her face was swept by a smile so amazed and delighted that Mrs. Ray and Tacy were as mystified as they were relieved.

"Mamma!" Betsy cried, "Mrs. Muller wants me to come to Milwaukee for Christmas!"

"Why . . . why . . . what an idea!"

"Do you think I can go?"

"You'll have to ask Papa. What does she say?"

Betsy handed the letter to her mother and threw her arms around Tacy. They danced and squealed.

"Don't get too excited," Mrs. Ray advised, "until you know whether you can go. It's a long trip for you to make all alone. Expensive, too."

Betsy and Tacy took their cookies into the front parlor, where they studied Mrs. Muller's letter. It was brief and concise but it produced an hour or more of uninterrupted conversation.

"Imagine," cried Tacy, "seeing Tib again!"

"And Tacy, I'll see Aunt Dolly!" Tib's Aunt Dolly had visited the Mullers in Deep Valley. She was a doll-like blonde, and Betsy and Tacy had always thought her the most beautiful creature in the world.

"I wonder whether she's as pretty as she used to be."

"Prettier, probably. She's engaged, you know."

"Do you remember her lovely clothes?"

"Do I!"

Julia came in and Betsy and Tacy fell upon her with the magnificent news. Margaret came in and was staggered by it. At last Tacy had to go home, but Betsy promised to telephone her the first thing after supper. She accompanied her out to the porch, and paused there in the twilight, shivering.

"Tacy," she said, "do you realize what this is? It's the chance I've been waiting for."

"Piffle!" said Tacy, and shook her.

"I'll come back completely changed."

"You won't be half as nice."

"Won't you have some tea, Lady Glexter-Glexton?" Betsy drawled in a languid voice. "Celeste, my smelling salts, please!"

Tacy tried to throw her off the porch into the waiting drifts. Betsy struggled, shrieking. She freed herself and ran into the house. There she embraced her mother.

"Oh, I hope . . . I hope . . . I hope I can go!"

"Don't get your heart too set on it, Betsy," Mrs. Ray warned. "You know what big expenses Papa has. Three girls, and this big house. You'd need some new clothes, too."

"I know. If I can't go, it's all right," Betsy said.

She went upstairs and tried to do homework, but her head was whirling. She turned out the gas and went to the window, looked out over the purpling snow. She imagined the lighted train, like a glittering serpent, winding its way to far-off Milwaukee.

"I'd have to eat on the diner!" she thought.

It was a family custom not to broach any new important matter to Mr. Ray until he had had his supper.

"No man, not even an angel like your father, likes to decide things on an empty stomach," Mrs. Ray often said.

But by the time Anna had brought in warm apple sauce and the fresh molasses cookies, Mr. Ray noticed the excitement in Betsy's face.

"What have you got up your sleeve, Betsy?" he asked. "I can see there's something."

"It's not up my sleeve," said Betsy, reaching into

the "V" of her dress and drawing out Mrs. Muller's letter. Smiling broadly she handed it to him.

Mr. Ray read it very slowly. In fact he read it over twice. But that, Betsy felt sure, was only to give him time to turn the matter over in his mind.

"Do you want to go?" he asked then, looking up.

Betsy tried to restrain her smile. She tried to draw it in, to look sober.

"I'd love to go," she said, "if you think we can afford it. But if we can't, it's perfectly all right."

"I wasn't thinking about that," Mr. Ray answered. "I was thinking about your being away from home on Christmas. We have a pretty good time right here."

"I know," said Betsy. But she locked out of her mind the picture of her family on Christmas Eve, trimming the tree, filling the stockings, singing carols and reading from *The Night Before Christmas* and Dickens' *Christmas Carol* and the Gospel according to St. Luke. If she let herself think about this she might not go . . . she might miss the ecstatic experience of visiting Tib in Milwaukee. "I don't think I'd be homesick though," she went on, hastily.

"It would seem pretty funny . . ." Mr. Ray began, and then he stopped and thought awhile. "It would be quite an experience, Betsy," he went on, "to have Christmas in a city like Milwaukee. I've been in Milwaukee. It's so German that it's like a foreign city, and the Germans make a lot of Christmas." He looked across the table at Mrs. Ray and his brow furrowed slightly. "Really, Jule," he said, "for a girl who wants to be a writer, it might be educational to spend Christmas in Milwaukee."

"But can we afford it, Bob?" Mrs. Ray asked. "I think Betsy is quite old enough and responsible enough to make the trip alone. But she'd need some new clothes, and we all know how many expenses you have."

"Never mind about that," said Mr. Ray. "I think she ought to go. Julia went with you to California to visit your mother. It's Betsy's turn to have a trip. Next, we'll send Margaret to Timbucktoo."

The worried look left his face and he began to act happy.

"I want you to get a lot out of this trip, Betsy," he said. "I think it would be a good idea to learn a little about Milwaukee before you go. It was built by Germans, mostly . . . Germans and Austrians and Bohemians and Poles . . . who didn't like old country ways. They had the good sense to come to America.

"The Germans brought a lot of Germany with them, but it was mostly the good part. Singing societies, and coffee cake, and Christmas trees." He got up and went around the table to squeeze Betsy's shoulders.

"Well, well, just imagine!" he said, "Betsy's going off to leave us! She's going to spend Christmas in Milwaukee."

Anna came into the doorway to say that the McCloskeys often went to Milwaukee. It was a tony city, she said.

Mrs. Ray said she would try to get Miss Mix, the dressmaker; they would start sewing at once.

Betsy ran to telephone Tacy, and the Ray family sat in the parlor and talked excitedly about Milwaukee for a long time.

Betsy was exultantly, rapturously happy, and when Betsy was happy, Mrs. Ray often said, she was happier than anyone else in the world. But after she went upstairs to study she began to feel a little queer inside. She remembered how homesick she had been when she visited the Taggarts.

"Tib's different from the Taggarts though, and I'm more than a year older."

Christmas thoughts tried to push their way into her mind. Every year since they were small children she and Tacy had gone Christmas shopping together. They always visited every store in town and each of them always bought just one thing, the same thing every year, a Christmas tree ornament.

"We can go shopping this year, of course. I won't be here though to see the new ornament on the tree."

But Betsy forced back these thoughts with that stubbornness she had in her nature.

"I'm going to go! This is my chance. Maybe I can't change much in two weeks, but I can change a little. Anyway I won't miss a wonderful thing like this, having Christmas with Tib in Milwaukee."

She put on her night gown, and wound her hair on Wavers and rubbed into her face a wonderful new cream she had seen advertised in the magazines. It was supposed to make one's skin as radiant as rose petals.

"I hope it will work by the time I go to Milwaukee," she thought, looking into the mirror wistfully.

Betsy used more creams, lotions, and curlers than most of her friends. Carney and Tacy never used them at all and were very scornful of them. Betsy joked about her beauty aids, but in private she didn't think them funny.

She longed with her whole heart to be pretty, and if . . . as Julia and Tacy insisted . . . she was pretty already, she longed to be prettier still. The heroines in her stories were always beautiful. Some author's heroines were plain but attractive; they had tip-tilted noses, or freckles, or other flaws. Betsy's heroines were perfect, golden-haired and rosy or raven-haired with white magnolia skin. Betsy always made them look just as she wished to look herself.

The rest of December went by on wings. Word of Betsy Ray's holiday visit to Milwaukee spread through the school, and Betsy found herself flatteringly marked out for attention.

Her father bought the tickets. She would leave at eight o'clock in the morning and arrive in Milwaukee at nine twenty-five that night. She would ride in a parlor car, and have two meals in the diner. She would leave on the twenty-first of December.

"I know," said Cab, "you're trying to get away from mistletoe, but you can't do it, Miss Ray."

"Not much," said Tony, looking wicked. "Just when does that train leave?"

"Heaven preserve us!!!" Betsy wrote in her journal. "The boys are coming down to see me off and bring mistletoe to kiss me good-by. Horror of horrors!!!"

The days grew busier and busier. Miss Mix was in the house making a new party dress for Betsy. It was a pink silk with white daisies in it, and with it Betsy would wear a wreath of daisies in her hair. And Miss Mix was making a red and green sailor suit for traveling. Betsy and her mother went downtown and bought a red hat. It was big with a stiff wired bow across the back.

"It will match your red velveteen dress, as well as this one," Mrs. Ray planned.

Mrs. Ray acted like the general of an army. She

shopped, mended, pressed. And Anna, a loyal lieutenant, washed and ironed until all Betsy's clothes were the pink of perfection.

"If only I could put Julia in my trunk and take her along to do my hair," Betsy said.

The trunk stood open in Betsy's room, and slowly it was being filled . . . not only with clothes. The Crowd brought tissue-wrapped bundles to put in it. And Betsy had to buy or make Christmas presents to take along, as well as to leave behind.

It was strange to see home preparations for Christmas going forward. Anna was making fruit cake, plum pudding and mince meat. Betsy would not be there to eat them. Her mother was dressing a doll for Margaret. It was a yellow-haired doll with a red silk dress trimmed with black lace and insertion. Betsy would not be there to see Margaret's delight.

Holly wreaths went up in the windows. Washington and Abie received red and green bows. The house was ready for holiday parties. Betsy would not be there to share in the fun.

Closets and drawers were full of packages at which other people were warned not to look. These would be stuffed in the stockings on Christmas Eve. But Betsy's stocking would be hung in Milwaukee, if it were hung at all.

"I don't believe the Mullers hang stockings. They

just have a Christmas tree," Betsy remembered.

The choir was busy rehearsing Christmas music. Betsy would not be there on Christmas morning to sing in a joyful, pine-scented church.

But she took part in the school Christmas program. It was given on Friday, the day before she left. She and Julia and Tacy sang a trio, a musical setting of Tennyson's poem:

> *"Ring out, wild bells, to the wild sky,*
> *The flying clouds, the frosty light:*
> *The year is dying in the night;*
> *Ring out wild bells, and let him die.*
>
> *Ring out the old, ring in the new . . ."*

Betsy was proud of Tacy that afternoon. Standing between the two Rays she was not frightened, and her voice rang out so sweetly that people spoke of it afterwards.

"You must sing a solo at Rhetoricals, sometime," Miss Clarke said.

"Oh, no," Tacy began, but Julia cut in,

"Certainly she will. In the Spring, Miss Clarke. I'll help her get it ready."

That afternoon Betsy and Tacy delivered Betsy's Christmas presents. It was a pleasant day with sunshine sparkling on the snow and afterward they went on their annual Christmas-shopping expedition.

"We're not going to be cheated out of that," Tacy had said, and Betsy had laughingly agreed.

But now she didn't have the proper feeling. Not the decorated windows, nor the tinkling sleighbells, nor Tacy's arm hooked happily into hers bred the giddy mood in which one could shop gaily for everything from diamonds to bon bons and finally buy only a Christmas tree ornament.

The nearer she came to the moment of departure for Milwaukee the nearer Betsy came to homesickness. She still wanted to go more than she wanted not to go, but she wanted to go less and less.

Tacy sensed that Betsy's spirits were low and tried to cheer her up by acting nonsensical. She drew her to a stop before a toyshop window. It was such a window as they used to gaze at entranced, with jacks-in-the-box, teddy bears, and dolls of every description.

"Now let's choose," Tacy said, speaking in a childish sing-song. "Which one do you want Santa Claus to bring you? I want that big one in the pink dress."

Footsteps behind them stopped and Betsy knew that someone had paused. But she followed Tacy's lead.

"Let me see," she said in baby talk, pointing. "I think I'd like *that* one, and a buggy to take her riding in."

"Oh, no!" cried Tacy. "*I* want that one."

"You can't have it. I saw it first."

"You did not."

"I did so."

As they wrangled Betsy turned her head, and saw a tall boy directly behind them. She looked into the puzzled yellow brown eyes of Phil Brandish.

Aghast, Betsy squeezed Tacy's hand, but Tacy thought it came only from affection and kept on talking. Betsy extended her foot in its sturdy overshoe and brought it down on Tacy's foot, hard.

"Ouch! What the dickens . . ." Tacy exclaimed. She usually caught on quickly but now she had to be nudged in the ribs before she, too, looked around. Phil Brandish, averting his eyes, walked on.

"Tacy!" Betsy wailed. "How perfectly awful!"

"And I got you into it!"

"I'll never get a ride in that red auto now."

They were between laughing and crying. So they went to Heinz's for the consolation of hot chocolate. There laughter triumphed. They laughed so hard thinking what idiots they must have seemed to Phil . . . Philip the Great, Tacy called him . . . that Betsy forgot all her lonesome feelings.

Numbers of boys and girls dropped in at the Ray house that night. Almost the whole Crowd came. Someone wanted to sing Christmas carols but Julia tactfully refrained. She knew what sort of thing made people homesick. Instead she played the newest popular songs.

> *"Baby dear, listen here,*
> *I'm afraid to go home in the dark . . ."*

Tony and Winona clowned through that one. And Carney and Irma, the newly weds, sang in harmony:

> *"I would, if I could, but I can't,*
> *Because I'm ma-a-a-r-r-ied now."*

Again Betsy's laughter kept away tears.

There was something eerie and unnatural about the next morning. The Rays were up and about while it was still dark. Even Julia was up. Mr. Ray went down early to open the drafts in the furnace. Anna followed, and the rich fragrance of coffee floated though the house. They ate breakfast by gaslight, and everyone talked very fast.

Then Julia dressed Betsy's hair, and Margaret polished her shoes, and Anna pressed the tie of the new sailor suit, although it didn't really need pressing. Mr. Ray went out to hitch up Old Mag. He brought her around, sleighbells chiming, while the east was still stained with red. Betsy embraced Anna, and the family went out to the surrey, Julia and Margaret carrying Betsy's grip. Her trunk had been sent on the day before.

The whole Crowd was at the station. Tony looked sleepy, but he was there. Dennie came tardily at a run. Some brought train letters which Betsy stuffed into her purse.

The waiting room was crowded and gay, and brilliant jokes were bandied. The boys had, indeed, brought mistletoe, and Tony held some over Betsy's head.

"All Gaul is divided in three parts, and you have two of them," said Betsy, ducking.

There was a scuffle but she wasn't kissed.

The train whistled far down the track, and everyone poured out into the frosty morning. It was daylight now, but still cold. There was more laughing and joking.

"Don't flirt with the Milwaukee boys," Cab called, as the great black giant of an engine rushed into the station, sending out clouds of steam which froze in the air. Its bell was swinging madly back and forth.

"*Ring out, wild bells,*" Betsy whispered to Tacy, "*Ring out the old, ring in the new* . . . Betsy."

"Piffle!" Tacy said.

Betsy kissed her. She kissed Margaret whose small arms clung tightly, and Julia who smelled sweetly of cologne, and her mother who smelled of violets, and her father who smelled of cigars. His face was ruddy with cold, and wore a determined smile.

"Have a good time, Betsy." "Remember us to the Mullers." "Don't drink too much of the beer that made Milwaukee famous."

Followed by these mingled cries and witticisms, Betsy ascended to the parlor car. Her father gave her grip to the porter, and all four Rays went inside for a minute. When they were gone, Betsy rushed to the window. She rapped on the glass and threw kisses and screamed, "What did you say?" at the frantically moving mouths outside. The boys were yelling through cupped hands.

Then the big bell started to ring again. The whistle blew, aloof and melancholy. The train moved, and slowly the group dropped out of sight . . . the bright tams of the girls, the caps of the boys pulled down against the cold, Margaret's excited, almost anxious face, Julia's smile, her mother's stern look, her father's benevolent one.

They all passed out of sight, and Betsy turned around to the warmth and luxury of the parlor car. She settled herself in the green plush seat. She was on her way to Milwaukee.

11

Tib

THE GRINDING WHEELS of a train are apt to sing a song. The song they sang for Betsy ran like this:

> *"There's a place named Milwaukee, Milwaukee,*
> *Milwaukee, Milwauk, MilwaukEE,*
> *There's a place named Milwaukee, Milwaukee,*
> *A beautiful place to be . . ."*

There was a story behind that song.

One summer afternoon when Betsy and Tacy were five years old, they dressed up in their mothers' clothes, took Mrs. Ray's card case and went to call at a strange, chocolate-colored house which was their particular admiration. No one answered their ring and a neighbor shouted out that the people who lived there were visiting in Milwaukee. Betsy and Tacy were charmed by the word. Walking home, after leaving two of Mrs. Ray's cards in the mail box, they made up a song about Milwaukee.

Later, Mrs. Muller found the cards. Thinking that Mrs. Ray had called she returned the courtesy, and that had begun the friendship of Betsy and Tacy and Tib. They had taught Tib the song and had all sung it together, and now from that distant roseate past, it came back to Betsy as she rolled along toward the city of those dreams.

"There's a place named Milwaukee, Milwaukee, Milwaukee, Milwauk, MilwaukEE . . ."

There was a second verse. It had something to do with Tacy, Betsy remembered. Something about going to Milwaukee with Tacy "ahold of her hand." She wished Tacy were with her now. Not that Betsy, at the moment, felt the need of anyone's hand. She felt poised and confident, and at least thirty years old. But she wished that Tacy were going, just for the fun of the thing.

She rummaged in her pocket book, and found Tacy's train letter, and read it. It was full of love and joy in Betsy's good fortune. Tacy didn't say in the letter . . . she had never once said . . . "I wish I were going." She was never envious, no matter how many nice things happened to Betsy.

This struck Betsy suddenly. She wondered for the first time how she would feel if Tacy were going to visit Tib and she were staying at home. It could just as well have happened that way if the Rays instead of the Kellys had had ten children. Frosting has to be spread thinly over a large cake.

"Tacy," Betsy thought, "is a wonderful person." It was the first time she had ever consciously estimated her friend.

The porter, a colored man in a white jacket, took her hat and put it in a paper bag, which he tucked into the rack over her head. She folded her coat neatly, and put that there too, and looked around the parlor car, which was impressive with wide windows. There were only two or three other passengers, not especially interesting. So she just sank deeply into the soft chair and looked out the window.

The countryside was spread thickly with snow,

against which bare trees showed purplish brown. They were in planted groves mostly, except for scattered oaks in the fields and yellow willows along the frozen streams. The farm houses were small, the red barns big with advertisements for Peruna painted on them. Fences and telegraph poles, horses, sheep and cattle and black and white pigs rushed past.

It was prairie country at first. But near the Mississippi the bluffs began. After leaving Winona, named for the same Indian maiden from whom Winona Root took her name, Betsy gazed with her own eyes on the fabled Mississippi. Her train crossed the river. She was in Wisconsin.

"I've left my native state," she remarked in a jubilant half whisper.

She could hardly wait for noon, having heard about dining cars from Julia after the California trip. When the bluffs flattened out into rolling prairie again, a waiter came through the train calling, "Dinner served in the dining car! First call for dinner!" Betsy was the second person in. She was second only because she waited for someone else to lead the way, and she followed close on the heels of this experienced traveler.

The diner surpassed all expectations. It was pure romance to sit at a table spread with glossy linen and eat a delicious meal while looking out at a flying white landscape. She began to think about her great project of changing herself.

"Two weeks is an awfully short time," she thought. "But two weeks away from home is longer than two ordinary weeks. How shall I change? Shall I change my hair-do? I'm not good at that. Shall I change the way I talk? Make my voice low and musical, and my laugh sort of mocking? That would be good!"

She tried it out softly, but the waiter heard her.

"Is anything wrong, miss?" he asked, looking startled.

"Nothing, thanks," murmured Betsy, blushing. She went on planning.

"Maybe I can copy Aunt Dolly. But she's a different type. I think I'll just try to act worldly and a little bored. The trouble is I never get bored."

She paid for her dinner and left a tip, as her father had done at the Moorish Café.

She had been cautioned in the most urgent terms against talking with strangers . . . indiscriminately, that is. "Probably a woman with small children would be all right," her mother had said. She was delighted on returning to the parlor car to find a woman with a baby. Betsy offered to hold the baby, and soon was in conversation.

Mrs. Gulbertson had been visiting her sister in Baraboo and she told Betsy all about her sister's troubles with her husband. Betsy reciprocated by telling all about Tib, and after Mrs. Gulbertson had left the train, Betsy kept on thinking about Tib.

"I wonder what she'll be like now. She's fifteen, the same as I am. Freddy must be about thirteen and Hobbie is Margaret's age." Frederick and Hobson were Tib's brothers.

Twilight descended and night came on with a rush. The porter pulled down the shades and turned on the lights. Betsy began to feel strange, speeding away through darkness to a big and unknown city. She started to wonder what the family was doing at home, then decided she had better not think about that. She read the last of her train letters, and was glad when the waiter came again calling, "Supper served in the dining car!"

This time Betsy was first into the diner.

She began to think about Milwaukee. She had tried to learn a little about it, and she knew that it had been founded almost a hundred years before by a French Canadian named Solomon Juneau. Before his arrival there was only an Indian village and a fur trading post on the bay where the Milwaukee River emptied into Lake Michigan. Juneau married the half-Indian daughter of the trader, and their seventeen children gave the new town a flying start.

In Europe, through those years, a great hope had

swelled that the people could rid themselves of despotic rulers. Starting in France in 1848, a series of revolutions had gone off like a string of firecrackers. But in Germany and Austria the revolts had been quickly crushed, and many of the brave men who had started them had fled to the new world, to Milwaukee in Wisconsin. Forty-eighters, they were called.

More men followed from Germany, and Austria (including Bohemia, an unwilling part of Austria), and other European countries. They were very industrious, skilled in many trades; and they made Milwaukee a prosperous, well-governed city. But more than most immigrants they had clung to homeland ways. Milwaukee was truly like a foreign city, Betsy's father had said. She could hardly wait now for her first sight of it.

After supper the time dragged. Although not due at Milwaukee until almost half past nine, Betsy went into the washroom at eight o'clock. She washed and shook pink powder into a chamois skin and rubbed it over her nose. She combed her hair and redid her pompadour, very high and stiff.

Back in the parlor car she made friends with a spinsterish lady and told her all about Tib. A married couple from Waukesha made overtures and she talked about Tib to them, too. At last the man pulled up the shade and said, "I believe we are coming into

Milwaukee." And the porter came in and started brushing people.

Betsy watched closely and when her turn came she didn't make any mistakes. He took her new red hat out of the bag and brushed it and she put it on. She stood up while he brushed the red and green sailor suit and wiped off her shoes. When he had helped her into her coat and furpiece, she gave him fifty cents and he said, "Thank you, miss. I hope you have a good time in Milwaukee with your friend Tib."

With her grip close beside her feet, she sat down and waited tensely. The train was running through lighted streets now, and it seemed to Betsy she could not endure the few remaining moments. Then the passengers rose and formed a line and the train entered the station.

"Milwaukee!" shouted the porter, and suddenly she felt very young, nervous, and inadequate. She found herself out on the platform with her grip at her feet.

"Red cap? Want a red cap?" Her father had told her a red cap was a boy who would carry her grip. One was standing beside her now, smiling. She nodded.

"Where to, Miss?" Where to, indeed! Other passengers were scurrying away. If the Mullers did not meet her . . .

"Betsy, darling!" Betsy heard a familiar, high sweet

voice. She turned to see a slight figure running toward her, a girl in a purple coat with yellow hair shining beneath a flowered hat. Betsy threw her arms around Tib.

She had forgotten how tiny Tib was. They hugged and kissed, and Mr. Muller, looking just as he had always looked, large, blond, stoutish, watched them smilingly.

"The little Betsy!" he said, shaking hands. "But she is a young lady now, *nicht wahr*, Tib?"

"*Ja*, Papa," said Tib, "*und sie ist sehr schön.*"

"Tib!" cried Betsy, "You're talking German."

"*Natürlich,*" Mr. Muller said.

Laughing they swept down the platform.

Betsy felt self-possessed again. She heard herself talking like Julia, very grown-up.

"Yes, I had a pleasant trip. The meals on the diner were delicious."

"Before we start home," Tib said, "we thought we'd take you up Grand Avenue to see the Christmas crowds."

"What fun!" Betsy cried.

She had never seen a big city at night, or at any other time for that matter . . . and she found it breathlessly exhilarating. The streets were as bright as day, but the brightness had a different quality. There were trolley cars with glittering windows and a press of horses and carriages, and autos with clamoring horns. The store windows were full of beautiful things to buy.

She and Tib and Mr. Muller pushed merrily through the crowds. Soon, however, they reached a hackstand and Mr. Muller helped them into a horse-drawn hack.

"We must get home," he said. "Mamma and the children, too, are anxious to see Betsy."

They rode for a long time, leaving the business district behind. They didn't talk very much, and whenever they passed an arc light Betsy stole a look at Tib. Usually Tib was looking at her. She seemed younger than Betsy and not only because she was small. She was still wearing a hair ribbon.

"You have your hairs up, haven't you?" she asked suddenly. She said "hairs," Betsy noticed, and not "hair."

"Yes," said Betsy. "I started last year."

"I put mine up for parties."

"Have I changed much?" Betsy asked.

"Have you changed!" Tib gave her little fluttery laugh. "I should say you have changed."

"*Jawohl, Jawohl,*" said Mr. Muller.

They paused at last before a square redbrick house which had lights in every window and a wide entrance door.

"This is our house. It's a duplex," Tib said. "I

guess I told you about it in my letters." She had, but Betsy had not been able to visualize a duplex. There were no duplexes in Deep Valley. "The first floor is our house. The second belongs to someone else," Tib explained.

Betsy was fascinated. "Why, it's like living in a sandwich."

Mr. Muller laughed. "A sandwich, *ja*? Well, we're going to live in this sandwich only until we decide a few things." Betsy wondered what he meant by that.

Inside she seemed to be back in the Muller home in Deep Valley. For Mrs. Muller, who kissed her affectionately, looked just the same. She was still short and square with yellow hair like Tib's and she wore diamond ear rings. The boys were taller, but Fred was still slender and artistic, while Hobbie's face was dimpled and full of mischief. Matilda still wore her hair in braids around her head, and spectacles, and a stiffly starched apron. The lines in her forehead made her look cross, but she smiled when she greeted Betsy.

"This is good!" she said in broken English. "This remembers me of Deep Valley."

The duplex was very spacious. In the big front parlor were a sofa and chairs covered with blue velvet, which Betsy remembered. The dining room had the remembered display of heavy silver and cut glass. Matilda's kitchen, as always, shone like a polished pan.

Betsy was still looking furtively at Tib. Although she was so small she had a rounded bust above a very slender waist. She was feathery-light in her movements as Tib always had been. She was still Tiblike.

She wore a shirt waist and skirt, but it didn't look tailored like other peoples' shirt waists and skirts. There was a fluffy collar on the waist and the skirt was draped up with a velvet bow. She had a new foreign accent. Betsy thought it was cute.

They sat down in the back parlor and Matilda brought Mr. and Mrs. Muller steins of foamy beer, milk and cookies for the children. They were Christmas cookies, kuchen, they were called, some with colored sugar on them.

"I remember these from Deep Valley, Mrs. Muller," Betsy said in Julia's tones, nibbling.

At last Betsy and Tib went down the hall to Tib's room which was fancifully gay.

"I'll bet we'll talk all night," Betsy said as Tib turned back a white organdy spread lined with blue silk.

But they didn't. They weren't well enough acquainted yet. Betsy was still using her company manners and Tib was a little formal herself bringing out towels and wash cloth for Betsy with a perfect hostess air.

Tib put on a thin night gown trimmed with pink

rosettes. She tied up her hair with a pink ribbon. Betsy wound hers on Magic Wavers. She hated to, but she wanted curls next day. She was glad that although her night gown was of flannel it was new and pretty with sprigs of blue flowers in it.

They knelt down to say their prayers on opposite sides of the bed.

"I wrote you, didn't I," said Betsy, rising, "that I'm an Episcopalian now?"

"Yes. Would you like to go to church tomorrow?" Tib asked politely.

"I'd love to," Betsy said. And she added as they climbed into bed, "Now we mustn't talk too late!" But they didn't talk at all. They kissed each other good night and Betsy lay in the dark thinking how strange, how almost fantastic it was that she was here in Milwaukee of which she had heard so much for so many years.

> "There's a place named Milwaukee, Milwaukee,
>   A beautiful place to be . . ."

The words sang in her ears just as though the wheels of the train were still turning. They sang themselves over and over until she fell asleep.

12

Sunday in Milwaukee

THE FOLLOWING MORNING, as agreed, Betsy and Tib
went to church. Prayer books in their kid-gloved
hands, they started off decorously beneath a dull sky.

They went by trolley, an exciting experience for
Betsy, although she tried not to show it. Tib, however,
did not act superior because she was a city girl.

Betsy was still talking like Julia, and Tib's elegant

manner was, Betsy suspected, not quite her own. Even so, they drew closer and closer to the old loving intimacy as they talked about Tib's school. The Sem, she called it.

"It's closed for the holidays. But I'm going to take you to see it. Grosspapa Muller sends me there. All his daughters and granddaughters have gone to Browner."

"Do you like it?"

"Very much. I like to play basketball and act in the plays. And the girls are nice. They're rich," said Tib, "but you'd never know it. We all have to dress conservatively."

Tib, Betsy thought, looked far from conservative. True she wore her fair hair in a braid, turned up with a ribbon, and only a very little, girlish jewelry. But Tib could not look conservative any more than a goldfinch could. Her hair ribbon was lilac color, and she wore a lilac silk dress beneath the purple coat. Mrs. Muller made Tib's clothes, and they were charming, but unusual. People called them "Frenchy." The style was really Viennese. Mrs. Muller's parents were Bohemians and came from the city of Vienna.

"Do many girls board at the school?" Betsy asked, as the trolley hummed along through streets full of large, comfortable homes set in spacious lawns.

"Yes. There are lots of us day girls, though."

"I should think it would be fun to board there."

"It is. I stay overnight with my friends sometimes. The lights blink at nine forty-five and they are called 'first winks.' They go off at ten and that's 'second winks.' At 'first winks' a tray of crackers and milk is put out on the landing in the dorm for anyone who is hungry, but when I stay we have spreads in the gym, very secret and scary."

"I can't imagine your being scared."

"That's part of the fun." Tib laughed. "The boarding pupils, if they are caught, are 'campused' for a while . . . no walks, or trips to town. I'm glad I'm a day girl because I have more freedom. And I certainly need freedom because of Grossmama Hornik."

"Grossmama Hornik?"

"She has her own ideas about my education. The Horniks and the Mullers," Tib continued, "are very different. Grosspapa Muller manufactures beer kegs. He is rich and everyone is a little afraid of him. Grossmama Hornik is strict, too, but no one is afraid of her, except Grosspapa Hornik, perhaps. He is a tailor, and they live up over the shop. I don't know whether it's because they're Viennese or what, but they're gayer. They like dancing and singing and beautiful clothes."

"I remember Aunt Dolly's beautiful clothes."

"Grossmama Hornik wants me to have dancing lessons," Tib continued, "so I have them from the best teacher in Milwaukee. And Uncle Rudy . . . he's Mamma's brother and Aunt Dolly's . . . takes me to concerts and plays. That reminds me, we have tickets for the theatre tonight, you and I."

"How perfectly thrilling!" cried Betsy. "What are we going to see?"

"*Reiterattacke*. That's German. Something about the cavalry. It's very funny."

"Will it all be in German?"

"Yes. There's a German stock company at the Pabst. Uncle Rudy didn't remember that you don't understand German, I guess. But I'll tell you what's going on."

"I love the theatre so much," said Betsy, "that I wouldn't care if the play was in Chinese. But Tib!" She grasped Tib's arm suddenly. "It can't be tonight we are going."

"Why not?"

Betsy laughed merrily at Tib's mistake. "It's Sunday!"

"Yes," answered Tib, "that's the night Uncle Rudy got the tickets for, Sunday, the twenty-second."

Betsy was silent, astonished. She could hardly believe her ears. They were going to the theatre on Sunday. It was certainly Sunday, for they were on their way to church.

Nobody Betsy knew ever went to the theatre on Sunday. The Rays were not straight-laced, but they wouldn't have dreamed of doing such a thing . . . any more than they would have danced on that night, or played a game of cards.

For a moment Betsy wondered wildly whether she should refuse to go. Elsie Dinsmore, she remembered, had refused to play the piano on Sunday; she had fallen off the piano stool instead. But Betsy had never thought much of Elsie Dinsmore.

"I'm almost sure," Betsy thought, "that Papa would say, 'When in Rome, do as the Romans do!'"

Tib lifted a gloved finger and rang a bell.

"Here's where we get off," she said.

The church with its tall spires was impressive, and they walked up the broad stairs in silence. Inside it was lighted by candles and drenched with color from the stained glass windows. It seemed to be full of prayers, and as Betsy and Tib knelt to add two more, an organ started playing.

Betsy was carried away by the beauty of the service. The voices of the boy sopranos were like angel voices . . . so high, sweet, and unearthly.

"I wish Julia could hear them," she thought.

As though in a dream she went through the familiar service, kneeling and rising and making the proper responses. Her heart seemed to open up into one great wish . . . to be good.

Outdoors again, they found that it had been snowing. Fresh soft snow covered the steps, walks and lawns. It lay in mounds on the lacy branches of the evergreens. Still uplifted by the service, Betsy looked around.

"It seems like a miracle!" she cried.

"We should have worn overshoes." Tib took off her kid gloves and put them into her pocket. "You'd better do the same," she advised. "Dampness isn't good for kid."

"When the choir sang, I felt as though the heavens were opening," said Betsy.

"Did you?" asked Tib, looking puzzled but impressed.

She hadn't really changed, Betsy thought.

Back at home Tib put on a ruffled apron trimmed with pink bows which made her look like a valentine. But she helped Matilda with brisk efficiency. This, too, seemed natural. Tib had known how to cook, sew and bake before either Betsy or Tacy could boil water.

Betsy offered to help, but Tib pushed her out of the kitchen, just as she used to do.

"You . . . you . . . *Dummkopf*," she said affectionately. "Go away until you are called."

Feeling agreeably incompetent, Betsy withdrew to their bedroom. She was glad to have a few minutes in which to bring her journal up to date. She wrote a letter home, too, and one to Tacy. Then she was called to the table, and it was a table worth drawing a chair to.

Dinner began with noodle soup and ended with *Schaumtorte*, piled high with whipped cream. In between were *Sauerbraten*, with red cabbage and potato dumplings, hot raised biscuits and several kinds of jam.

Mr. Muller had beer. He gave sips to Fred and Hobbie and offered one to Betsy.

"It's bitter," Tib warned.

"No thanks," said Betsy, smiling. Going to the theatre on Sunday was, she thought, concession enough to the Romans.

Mrs. Muller said that since they were going to the theatre that night they had better rest. So after dinner they went to their room and while Mr. and Mrs. Muller napped, and Fred and Hobbie looked at the funny papers, Betsy and Tib stretched out on the bed and talked.

Now, for the first time, the bars of strangeness came completely down. Betsy was not acting like anyone else any more, and neither was Tib. They were Betsy and Tib again, mutually adoring. As of old Betsy talked and Tib listened, her blue eyes flatteringly round.

Betsy talked about the Crowd. She showed Tib snapshots of the various boys and girls. Tib knew Tacy, Winona and Tom but almost none of the others.

Tib had not yet started going out with boys.

"That's odd," said Betsy, feeling very worldly. "You're so pretty and cute."

"Oh, they like me," said Tib . . . not boasting, just telling the truth. "But I don't know many boys. I take my cousin Heinrich to school dances."

She was enthralled by Betsy's picture of Deep Valley gaieties, and Betsy painted with a lavish brush.

She told about Tony with his bushy black hair, his bold eyes and laughing mouth. She told about being in love with him last year, and how strange it was that she had stopped. She described Cab, Dennie, Pin.

"Betsy, you sound terribly popular."

"Oh, no," said Betsy with elaborate carelessness. "They just like to come to our house."

"Oh, that's it!" Tib replied matter-of-factly, which was not at all the thing to say. But Betsy understood Tib.

She described Joe Willard and told about their feud. She even went up to Olympian heights and described Phil Brandish.

"Brandish?" Tib repeated. "A Phyllis Brandish goes to the Sem."

"Why, she's Phil's twin sister. I knew she went to a boarding school. Do you like her?"

"I don't know her very well. She's a junior and she's . . . well . . . different."

"I know what you mean. So is Phil," said Betsy.

She kicked her heels reflectively in air. "I think Phil Brandish is the most thrilling person in school. I'm not in love with him, but I'd die with joy if he ever paid any attention to me."

"If you wanted him to, you could make him," said Tib with utter confidence.

"I wonder," said Betsy. "I wonder whether I could."

Mrs. Muller, who had waked from her nap, called in just then to remind the girls to rest. So they stopped talking, and Betsy closed her eyes but her thoughts continued in the path where Tib had set them.

It led, of course, directly into her plan for changing herself.

"I haven't changed a bit so far," she admitted. "In fact I'm getting more like myself all the time."

Yet here in Milwaukee with the aura of Tib's adulation about her, the idea seemed more practicable than ever. She dreamed about going back to Deep Valley completely, stunningly different, until Mrs. Muller called them to coffee.

The Mullers, like most Milwaukee families, had coffee every afternoon. On Sunday, because of the big dinner, coffee came later and combined itself with supper. The table was spread with cold meats and *Kartoffel salat*, sweet rolls and cakes and, of course, kuchen.

Before they had finished Uncle Rudy came in. He was tall and slim in impeccably tailored clothes. He had a yellow pompadour, and yellow mustaches, waxed and twisted upward.

Betsy promptly fell in love with Uncle Rudy. She was madly in love, for at least a week.

He was accustomed to it; many women were in love with him. He was a jaunty, carefree young man. He could play the piano, Tib told Betsy, better than Paderewski. He joked with Betsy about not liking the beer that made Milwaukee famous. He sold it on the road. He was the uncle who had sent Tib Schlitz beer calendars, long ago, in Deep Valley.

He drove them to the Pabst in a dashing cutter behind a high stepping horse whose harness was strewn with bells. His auto, he said, was put up for the winter. It was a Steamer, and it took him thirty minutes to get up a head of steam.

"But then it goes like blazes. If you were here in the spring, I'd give you a spin," he declared, giving Betsy a smile which turned her head completely.

He left them at the Pabst. Betsy was so excited by the festive crowd that she felt almost helpless, but Tib with her usual calm got them safely to their seats. The audience was very well dressed. The women rustled in silk or satin dresses and sparkled with jewels. Everyone seemed to know everyone else.

The orchestra played Christmas airs.

"*Reiterattacke,*" Tib explained, was a military farce. It was full of handsome officers (but not so handsome as Uncle Rudy), clanking swords and sabers, and pink-cheeked girls. The audience laughed uproariously and Betsy laughed, too, even before Tib had a chance to explain the jokes. Tib understood almost all the German, and when her knowledge failed, their neighbors helped them out. During intermission the talk was all in German.

"It doesn't seem as though we were in America," Betsy said, looking around.

"Papa," observed Tib, "thinks Milwaukee isn't American enough. He and Mamma like it better in Deep Valley. He argues with Grosspapa Muller about it. That is," Tib added, laughing, "as much as one *can* argue with Grosspapa Muller."

"Why can't one argue with Grosspapa Muller?"

"You'll see on Christmas Eve."

13
The Seven Dwarfs

BETSY AND TIB, FRED and Hobbie were busy on Monday stringing cranberries for the tree. Mr. Muller was away at his office. He was an architect, and Fred wanted to be an architect, too. He was always sketching town halls and cathedrals on a drawing board like his father's. Mrs. Muller was doing last minute shopping, and Matilda was busy in the kitchen. The heavenly aroma emanating therefrom was in contrast to her temper.

"She'd better be careful," Hobbie murmured resentfully, after he had been refused a sixteenth cookie. "The *Christkindel* comes tonight."

"The *Christkindel*?" repeated Betsy, puzzled.

"The fairy Christ child," Tib explained. "He comes on the twenty-third of December to see whether children have been good. See that you behave today, Betsy *Liebchen*."

"He comes again on Christmas Eve to Grosspapa Muller's," Hobbie said, fitting a cranberry on his needle with stubby fingers.

"He brings the presents," Tib explained again.

"But what about Santa Claus?" Betsy demanded.

"He's called the Christmas Man," said Tib. "He's not so important in Milwaukee as he used to be in Deep Valley."

That night Mr. Muller brought home a Christmas tree. Even though the Mullers were to spend Christmas Eve at Grosspapa Muller's and Christmas Day at Grosspapa Hornik's there had to be a tree in their own home. Unlike Santa Claus, Christmas trees seemed to be very important in Milwaukee. The older people were as excited as the children when Mr. Muller carried in his huge fragrant bundle.

The next afternoon, which was Christmas Eve day,

all of them trimmed it. They put on candles, and carved wooden toys, and cookies hung on ribbons, and little socks with candies in them, as well as the usual bright balls. They draped the strings of cranberries around the spiraling branches and placed a star angel on the top.

Tib and Fred were very artistic and it was a beautiful tree. They had fun trimming it, too; but it seemed strange to Betsy to be hanging the Mullers' balls and angels and to think that at home a tree was being trimmed with the dear familiar ornaments . . . some that she and Tacy had bought on their Christmas shopping trips.

As early twilight gathered outside the windows she thought of the Christmas Eve ritual at home going on without her. She remembered the doll her mother was dressing for Margaret and was swept by homesickness almost as acute as she had suffered at the Taggarts.

But no one suspected it, and it didn't last. Hobbie made her laugh by shouting, "We must get gedressed for Grosspapa Muller's."

"Yes," said Mrs. Muller. "We are expected there at half past five. Dress, and make quick."

So Betsy brought out her new party dress, the pink silk with daisies in it, and the daisy wreath.

"I'll fix your hairs for you," Tib offered.

"Hair, hair, beautiful Dutchman!" Betsy teased,

but she was glad to have Tib dress her pompadour and pin on the wreath. Tib was almost as clever as Julia was with Betsy's silky, hard-to-manage hair.

Tib put her own hair up because this was a party. Her pompadour made a pale golden cloud. She wore a wreath too, and her filmy white dress was trimmed with loops of rosebuds.

"You look just like a fairy tale princess, and you always did," said Betsy.

Tib lifted her skirts and waltzed about.

Mr. Muller wore his best waistcoat. Mrs. Muller wore a rich, dark silk. The boys were dressed in their Sunday suits, with white shirts and carefully knotted ties. They had scrubbed their faces until they were pink, and brushed their blond heads until they shone. Mr. Muller's face looked like Hobbie's tonight, full of fun and mischief, all care gone.

Matilda had left to spend the evening with relatives. The hack was waiting in front. Mr. Muller shooed them all out and they drove off to Grosspapa Muller's. It was a long ride through the spectral winter evening, a ride Betsy was never to forget.

It was memorable just to be outdoors, instead of indoors, on Christmas Eve. And the city was so given over to Christmas that it seemed as though the *Christkindel* really was abroad. Lighted trees shone through many windows and there were roving groups of singers in the streets. *"Stille Nacht, heilige Nacht."* Their voices came plaintively over the snow.

They passed a small band, four shabby men with trumpets, horn and drums, who were playing raucously, *"Du bist wie eine Blume."* Mr. Muller sang with them. He asked the hack driver to stop, and put out his head and cried, *"Fröhliche Weihnachten!"* which meant "Merry Christmas." The leader came running, pulling off his cap, and Mr. Muller tossed a coin.

They crossed the frozen river, and went on toward Lake Michigan. The houses grew bigger. Betsy felt as though she were in a dream.

Grosspapa Muller's house sat on a corner. It was a large gray stone house with wrought iron balconies. There was a carriage house in back. Old Johann lived over that and took care of the horses, Tib explained. All the windows were full of light.

There was a wide lawn, now buried deep in snow.

"In the summer Grosspapa Muller has a row of seven dwarfs on his lawn," Tib said.

"Each one," Hobbie added, "has a different colored hat."

"They are in the basement now. Johann repaints them every winter. I'll take you down to see them," Tib promised squeezing Betsy's hand.

Betsy felt more dream-bound than ever, listening to this talk of seven dwarfs.

The hack drove up to the porte-cochere. It was the first time Betsy had ever alighted at a porte-cochere. A massive carved door hung with a holly wreath was flung open by a smiling servant and the Mullers trooped into a crowded hall.

The house seemed bursting with Mullers, old and young. Betsy and Tib laid off their wraps in the Yellow Room upstairs and when they descended the wide, deeply carpeted stairs, they found themselves surrounded by uncles, aunts and cousins. The great hall, the front and back parlors, richly furnished and hung with mistletoe and holly, were swarming with them.

All the uncles were large and stout, and so were the aunts whom Tib called *Tante*. They wore diamond ear rings, such as Mrs. Muller wore. Grosspapa Muller had given all his daughters-in-law diamond ear rings, Tib said. Their dresses were rich and elaborate, but none of them looked stylish, somehow. Tib's mother, Betsy thought, was the only stylish looking woman there. She seemed more American, too, than the others, and so did Mr. Muller.

The children ranged from pig-tailed twin girls Hobbie's age to the tall cousin Heinrich whom Tib took to the Seminary dances. He was nice looking, with curly brown hair, but not half so fascinating, Betsy thought, as Uncle Rudy. Men and boys alike, when introduced to Betsy, bowed stiffly from the waist. Some said "How do you do?" but others said, *"Guten Abend, Fräulein."*

"Come," said Tib. "I want you to meet Grosspapa."

"And Grossmama?" asked Betsy mischievously. It was funny the way all the Mullers referred only to Grosspapa Muller.

"Grossmama, too, of course," said Tib, not knowing that she was being teased.

Grosspapa was larger and stouter than any of his sons. He had a gleaming bald head which seemed to begin at his black overhanging eyebrows. His black beard, speckled with white, almost concealed his snowy waist-coat. He addressed Betsy in German, and she found herself answering, *"Guten Abend, Herr Grosspapa,"* and curtseying, as Tib did.

Grossmama Muller was small and timid. Her graying hair, which had once been fair was drawn back into a tight bun. She too wore diamond ear rings.

The double doors leading to the library were closed. The children kept trying to look through the cracks and were pulled away by their elders. At last a bell was heard.

"There's the *Christkindel*'s bell," Tib whispered to Betsy. But the company was not yet ready to answer the summons.

One of the young lady cousins went to the piano,

and it developed that the pig-tailed twins had pre-
pared a surprise for their Grosspapa. Why not for
Grossmama, too, Betsy wondered? They played a
Mozart duet, somewhat shakily, with violin and flute
and Grosspapa was pleased.

After that everybody sang Christmas songs. From
Grosspapa to Hobbie they sang with a will, and Betsy
joined in, although she was the only one singing in
English.

But in the library the bell became imperative. The
great doors slid back, and Betsy saw a Christmas tree
so tall and majestic that it seemed to fill the large,
high-ceilinged room. It was twinkling with lighted
candles, sparkling with ornaments, and it threw off
a delicious woodsy fragrance. After a long-drawn
breath the company joined hands and marched
around the tree singing . . . but in German . . .

"*O, Christmas tree, O, Christmas tree,*
How lovely are thy branches . . ."

Betsy wanted to pinch herself, to make sure she
was awake, but she couldn't manage it very well with
Tib holding one hand and a pig-tailed twin swinging
from the other.

All around the room were tables covered with sheets.
The smiling servant girl hurried about taking off the
sheets, and there were tables for everyone . . . the

servant girl, the cook who came in from the kitchen, and old Johann, wrinkled and nut-like. There was even a table for Betsy laden with boxes of candy and cakes, hair ribbons, pin cushions, pen wipers, and sachet bags.

The children were mad with excitement. They were throwing paper to the floor, and the aunts were picking it up and folding it neatly. Everyone was kissing and thanking everyone else.

Then Betsy was swept on the tide of Mullers into the dining room for a delicious cold supper . . . roast fowl and ham, potato salad, pickled herring, pickles of many kinds and little curly anchovies; cream filled horns, cakes glazed with sugar and others decked out with peaches and cherries. There was hot chocolate for the children, and the men and women had wine. They toasted Grosspapa and Grossmama, and the President of the United States and Kaiser Wilhelm.

"Grosspapa Hornik," Tib whispered, "won't toast Kaiser Wilhelm nor Kaiser Franz Josef either. He doesn't like Kaisers. He and Grosspapa Muller don't get on very well."

The children went back to the tree to play with their dolls and toys. Soon the younger ones began to grow sleepy. At last with mingled cries of *"Fröhliche Weihnachten"* and "Merry Christmas," oldsters began to put on coats and furs.

"Tib!" said Betsy. "I haven't seen the dwarfs!"

"Come quick!" cried Tib, catching her hand.

She pulled Betsy toward the dining room and Fred and Hobbie and Cousin Heinrich followed. They ran through the pantry and kitchen, down spotless stairs, into the largest cleanest basement Betsy had ever beheld.

There, indeed, were the seven dwarfs standing in a row. The biggest one didn't come to Betsy's shoulder. The smallest was about a foot high. They were made of cast iron and wore short Alpine jackets and little Alpine hats with feathers in them. Each hat was a different color . . . red, green, purple, yellow, pink, blue and brown.

"Every winter," said Tib, "Grosspapa has them repainted. And every spring, as soon as the snow melts, he puts them out on the lawn. Since he has retired from business he takes more interest in his dwarfs than in anything else, Papa says. Every year he puts them out differently. Some years they head north, and some south, and some east, and some west. But always the big dwarf leads."

"Grossmama Muller," said Fred, "wishes that some year the little dwarf could lead. Every spring she asks Grosspapa . . . 'Just this once, Gerhard, just this one year let the little dwarf lead.' But he won't. He always has them go in a straight line with the big dwarf at the head."

"He had them made to order," Tib remarked. "The molds were destroyed after they were made."

Hobbie looked reflective.

"Do you know," he said, "I've always thought that the big dwarf looks a little like Grosspapa."

Everyone looked at the big dwarf but nobody replied.

14
The Brave Little Tailor

"You always did look like a fairy tale princess," Betsy told Tib, "So I'm not surprised to find that you live in a fairy book."

"I live in a duplex," said Tib.

"In a fairy book," repeated Betsy firmly. "One grandfather has seven dwarfs, and the other one is a tailor. Fairy books are full of tailors. You remember

The Brave Little Tailor? 'Seven at one blow'?"

"That's right," said Tib, and laughed.

They were walking to Grosspapa Hornik's ahead of the rest of the family so that Tib could help Aunt Dolly and Grossmama with dinner. It was midway of Christmas morning. At breakfast Betsy had given the Mullers the presents she had brought for them . . . except Tib. Tib had had hers earlier.

Returning from Grosspapa Muller's, the night before, Betsy had insisted upon hanging her stockings.

"But we don't hang stockings," Tib had protested.

"You're you, and I'm me," Betsy had returned. "I'm hanging my stockings. And if you have a spark of feeling, Fräulein Muller, you'll fill them with those packages I brought from Deep Valley. By the way," she added, "if you should happen to hang your own you might find something at the bottom of it in the morning."

So Tib had hung her stocking, too, over the foot of the bed, and there had been a mysterious scurrying about after the gas was turned out. In the morning they had taken the stockings into their bed and unpacked them jubilantly.

Betsy's gifts had included photographs from Tony and Irma at which Tib had gazed long and earnestly. The Deep Valley Crowd seemed as story bookish to Tib as the Milwaukee grandfathers seemed to Betsy.

"The Brave Little Tailor," Betsy repeated musingly now, pleased with her fancy.

To reach the tailor shop they walked toward the central part of the city. Arms hooked, they swung along happily through a white world full of chiming sleighbells.

"Grosspapa Hornik," said Tib, "is a very good tailor. You noticed what handsome clothes he makes for Uncle Rudy. He makes clothes for the very best people."

"The brave little tailor! But why, oh why, is he afraid of Grossmama?"

"Oh," said Tib. "She has the head for money. And besides, they wrangle about Emperor Franz Josef. Grosspapa's father . . . he was Alois Hornik, too . . . was a Forty-Eighter, if you know what that is."

"I should say I do!" cried Betsy, stopping still.

"Grosspapa was only a little boy when he came to Milwaukee, but he hates the emperor and everything about the court."

"He was a Bohemian?" prompted Betsy.

"His father was a Bohemian. His mother was a Viennese, and she's famous in the family because she was so beautiful, with golden hairs. She was a revolutionist, too. Grosspapa looks like her pictures, and so does Aunt Dolly. So do I, a little."

"How romantic!" Betsy exclaimed. "What was her name?"

"Catherine Wilhelmina."

They proceeded in silence, Betsy thinking of the revolutionist, Alois Hornik and his beautiful, golden-haired wife, fleeing from Vienna after 1848. How strange that Tib, her friend, now walking calmly along a Milwaukee street, should look like that distant, lovely Catherine Wilhelmina.

"And Grossmama Hornik?" she asked, after a while.

"Her parents were Bohemian, too," said Tib. "But they lived in Vienna until Grossmama was twenty-five. As a girl she did embroidery for the Court; and she was given the right to use a five-pointed crown on her linens, calling cards and stationery. She is very proud of it. Grosspapa doesn't like it at all, and she doesn't like his ideas either. When he talks against the Emperor, Grossmama says, '*Ach, der pa!*' But they're very fond of each other." She broke off. "Here we are at the tailor shop already."

"Already yet so soon," Betsy teased.

The tailor shop was in a two-story brick building. A sign in gold letters read Alois Hornik, Schneider. It added in English in very small letters, "Tailor." At the right of the door which led into the shop was another door on which two calling cards were tacked. One of them said *Herr* Alois Hornik, and the other said *Frau* Alois Hornik and that bore a tiny five-pointed crown.

"Even a crown you have in your fairy tale, already yet," Betsy said.

Opening the door they walked down a long, dark, carpeted hall. At the end were two doors.

"Dining room and kitchen," Tib said. "The rest of the rooms are upstairs."

She opened the left-hand door and they went into the dining room which was small and dark but papered in a handsome, red, floral design. A table was set for dinner with polished glass and silver on a gleaming damask cloth.

Tib lifted a corner of this cloth and showed Betsy the five-pointed crown again, in embroidery so fine that Betsy wished Carney could see it. No needlewoman herself, she knew she could not appreciate it but she clicked her tongue admiringly.

Turning right through a small hall from which a carpeted stairway ascended they entered the kitchen. It was large and bright and full of savory odors. Shiny copper pans hung on the walls and you could see your face, although a trifle askew, in the polished nickel trim of the cook stove. The stove was covered with sauce pans in which things were bubbling briskly. Three open-faced apple pies sat ready on the table.

"Everybody must be upstairs," Tib was saying, when an exquisite apparition floated in. Yellow curls were piled on top of a small proud head. A pink messaline tea gown clung to a delicately molded figure. Long sleeves, like angels' wings, hung almost to the floor. Betsy saw a pink and white doll's face, blue eyes. It was Aunt Dolly, and she hadn't changed a bit!

"Why, Betsy!" she cried. She tripped across the room and lifted her cheek for Betsy to kiss. She was so tiny and dainty that she made Betsy feel like a giant . . . all the more so, when she said, "How tall you are, child!"

"Wasn't it nice," cried Tib, "that Betsy could come for Christmas?"

"Very nice. It's too bad, though, that you had to find me looking such a fright."

"Why, Aunt Dolly! You look lovely!"

"A perfect fright!" she repeated happily. "Aren't you ashamed, Tib, to bring your guest in before I'm dressed?" Then she began to trip about the kitchen, lifting sauce pan lids and changing dampers . . . capably, too, in spite of the swinging sleeves.

She ought to be wearing an apron, Betsy thought frenziedly, but Aunt Dolly did not soil a single ribbon. She stirred with a practised hand, tasted critically, added salt and pepper, pinches of sugar, dashes of vinegar. Betsy watched fascinated, until she found herself between Tib and Aunt Dolly, going upstairs.

At the top they came out into a room so large and

gracious that you would not have expected to find it above a tailor shop. The carpet was of soft green, strewn with flowers. There were gold chairs, as fragile as Aunt Dolly. There were long lace curtains, and vases of red and white glass . . . Bohemian glass, Tib said. A grand piano stood in one corner, and in another a Christmas tree.

From a door at the back leading toward the bedrooms, Grosspapa and Grossmama Hornik emerged. Tib embraced them both, and introduced Betsy.

Grossmama spoke only German but she did not, Betsy found, present the problem which Grosspapa Hornik did. With Grossmama nothing was expected except curtseys and smiles. But Grosspapa prided himself on his almost unintelligible English.

"How does it happen," Betsy asked Tib later, "that he doesn't speak English better? He was born here."

"Plenty of people in Milwaukee speak only German," Tib replied. "You get on better here with only German than with only English, I can tell you that. Grosspapa likes to speak English but he can't do it with Grossmama, or with most of his customers, so he doesn't get much practise."

Grosspapa Hornik was small but erect, in a glossy cutaway coat. He was as blond as his famed mother had been, but his hair was thin and his graying mustaches turned down. He had a dimple in his chin, a small mouth, and a sweet spontaneous smile which showed even white teeth. There were two deep lines between his brows . . . a result of concentration over the tailor's bench . . . but the look of severity vanished when he smiled.

Grossmama Hornik was large and stately with dark hair parted in the middle and drawn smoothly back. A fresh apron partly covered her black satin dress which buttoned tightly over an imposing bosom. Presently she and Tib started down stairs.

"You wait here," Tib said to Betsy. Aunt Dolly departed to dress, and Betsy was left alone with Grosspapa Hornik.

"Vat tink you of diese Milvaukee?" he asked Betsy. *"Es ist gemütlich, nicht wahr?"*

"I like it very much," said Betsy politely.

"I am here sixty years already," he said. "*Und es ist gut* here. *Ja, sehr gut.* Here is no Kaiser, no *Soldaten* marching, marching all de time. Kaisers are *nicht gut.* Der Kaiser Franz Josef und der Kaiser Wilhelm are de same, *beide nicht gut. Verstehen Sie?"*

"I verstehe," said Betsy.

"Die Grossmama versteht nicht. Weil der Kaiser likes her *Stickerei,* her embroidery, de Grossmama *versteht nicht."* He frowned. "Here in Milvaukee ve have fun, *nicht wahr?* De people has joy mit his wife und *Kinder* und his Christmas tree und his music und his beer."

"Und his kuchen," Betsy added.

"*Ja, ja!*" Grosspapa Hornik's sweet smile broke over his face. He patted her shoulder. "De Grossmama," he said "has made so many kuchens you can't count dat many yet."

"Grosspapa Hornik," Betsy said, "do you have a picture of your mother?"

"*Was? Was sagen Sie?*" Grosspapa Hornik was so startled that he lapsed into German.

"Your mother," Betsy repeated. "I want to see a picture of your mother, the beautiful Catherine Wilhelmina."

Then indeed, Grosspapa Hornik smiled. His face shining, he led Betsy to one of the slender-legged tables and picked up a miniature, framed in chased gold. Betsy took it in both hands and stared. Catherine Wilhelmina did indeed look like Tib. It was the fearless expression in her eyes.

"Oh, thank you, thank you!" Betsy cried, and to be sure he understood she added, "*Danke, danke schön.*"

Grosspapa Hornik struck his chest. "Mit me, *mein Kind*," he said, "you may speak alvays de English. Only mit de Grossmama *müssen Sie Deutsch sprechen.*"

Fred and Hobbie came pounding up the stairs followed by their parents, and Grossmama Hornik and Tib. Uncle Rudy strode in also, and Aunt Dolly's fiancé arrived, a dapper pleasant-faced young man, called Ferdy.

Wearing a trailing blue lace dress now, Aunt Dolly tripped across the room to slip her arm possessively into Ferdy's. There were mingled shouts of *"Fröhliche Weihnachten!"* and "Merry Christmas!" Packages were opened with cries of *"Wunderbar!"* and *"Sehr schön!"* and *"Danke, danke sehr!"* Again, as at Grosspapa Muller's, there were presents for Betsy, too.

They all went down stairs to goose with onion dressing, and potatoes, and gravy, and apple sauce, and various vegetables with piquant flavors. The apple pie was heaped with whipped cream. There was beer for everyone, and coffee.

Most of the conversation was in German, but Betsy didn't feel left out. Everyone kept smiling at her, and when they began raising beer mugs and proposing toasts, Uncle Rudy toasted her. Betsy blushed, but she was very pleased.

They toasted Grosspapa and Grossmama Hornik, and Christmas time, and the President of the United States. But they didn't toast a single kaiser . . . not Wilhelm nor Franz Josef.

Grossmama Hornik said something in German and Tib whispered to Betsy, "She says that if Grosspapa were not such a stubborn *Esel* we should drink to the dear Kaiser Franz Josef who appreciates her beautiful embroidery."

"Those who likes kaisers should go back to the *alt* country," Grosspapa Hornik muttered fiercely.

"The brave little tailor," Betsy thought.

She said it to Tib after dinner and Tib answered, "Grosspapa is a very good American, even though he can't speak English. And Grossmama is proud that he was a Forty-eighter, although she would never admit it."

The older people went to take naps, and Uncle Rudy asked Betsy and Tib whether they would like to go skating.

"I'm giving all my girls the go-by on account of you," he said, winking at Betsy.

Fred and Hobbie wanted to go, too, and they all piled into the cutter and drove to the Mullers' house for skates and on to the river. Betsy, a very poor skater, was silently thankful that she hadn't brought skates to Milwaukee. She refused firmly, although politely to borrow any.

"I'll just adore watching," she said. And she did.

For the sun glittered on the ice, a band was playing, and the skaters moved merrily in time to the music. Many glances followed Tib and Fred waltzing together. They made a charming pair for they looked much alike and moved like one person. They stayed until the sun, a round red eye without a single lash, dropped suddenly below the river bank.

Back at Grossmama Hornik's they were all soon eating again. Coffee was made, sandwiches were set out, along with the inevitable kuchen. Uncle Rudy and Aunt Dolly didn't eat with the others. They were going to a Christmas ball.

"Let's watch Aunt Dolly dress," Tib proposed. "She won't mind. I often do." So they went upstairs and knocked on her door, and she called them in.

Her room was all in white and pale yellow. The curtains were white over yellow, the bedspread was white over yellow. There were dozens of small yellow cushions tossed about and a snowy white fur rug.

There were mirrors everywhere. Wherever Aunt Dolly looked she was sure to see her own exquisite reflection. There was a tall, three-sided, pier glass, and an adjustable mirror on her dressing table.

Before this Aunt Dolly now was putting the finishing touches to her toilet: She was wearing a low-cut, green satin ball gown. She had fastened jewels into her ears, and around her neck and wrists. She looked charming, but she gazed into the mirror with a dissatisfied expression.

"This green," she said, petulantly, "makes me look as yellow as cheese." Casually she opened a drawer of the dressing table and took out a round cake of something pink. She took out a soft object, a rabbit's foot, and rubbed it across the pink cake. Then slowly, with complete concentration, she tinted her round cheeks, and the tips of her ears and her chin, which was dimpled like her father's.

For the second time since coming to Milwaukee Betsy was completely astonished. First, the theatre on Sunday, and now this! A hot tide swept up her body coloring her face more vividly than Aunt Dolly was being colored with the rabbit's foot. The blush came partly from embarrassment. It must be, she thought, that Aunt Dolly had forgotten her presence. If she were going to . . . paint her face like an actress . . . she would certainly do it only when she was alone. Betsy didn't know which way to look, and by chance she looked at Tib. Tib was watching Aunt Dolly, and her expression was one of mild interest.

"I'll be glad when I can use that stuff," she said.

"*Ach*, you're too young!" Aunt Dolly put down the rabbit's foot. She picked up a hand mirror for intensive study, took up the rabbit's foot again and gave her dimpled chin another dab.

Betsy's horror was tempered now with a thrill of self-importance. She had seen rouge used, and not by an actress! She could tell her mother and Julia about it.

Aunt Dolly sprayed herself with perfume, and rose. She turned, inch by inch, before the pier glass. She took up a fan, a lace handkerchief, and a small silken bag . . . it was called a vanity bag . . . which she slipped by its cord over her wrist. She handed Tib her white opera cloak and floated out of the room.

Ferdy and Uncle Rudy were waiting in the drawing room. Ferdy's face flushed when he saw Aunt Dolly. Both he and Uncle Rudy had changed into evening clothes, and Uncle Rudy, Betsy thought, looked dazzlingly handsome.

He sat down at the grand piano, throwing the tails of his black coat clear and ran his fingers along the keys.

"I've a new waltz I want Mamma to hear. She talks so often of the great Strauss. Here is a piece as good as any of his and it is also by a Viennese."

He began to play.

The opening phrases were short and artless. They sounded like a rocking horse. But the swing began to grow longer, the rhythm stronger. The waltz began to ask questions, wistful, poignant. It took on a dreamier sweep.

Then a gayer theme sent Uncle Rudy's fingers rippling over the keys. The melody wove in and out. It circled, swayed, as though it were music and dancer in one. It was irresistible.

Aunt Dolly threw her train over her arm. She smiled that sweet sudden smile like her father's, and asked Ferdy to dance. Tib motioned to Betsy but she shook her head and they both sat silent, watching. Fred, too, was motionless but he smiled as though in his mind he followed every undulating curve.

Grossmama Hornik turned her stately head slowly in time to the music. Grosspapa Hornik and Mr. Muller slowly waved their steins.

"What is the name of it?" Betsy asked Tib breathlessly, after it was over.

Uncle Rudy spoke over his shoulder. "It's 'The Merry Widow Waltz,'" he said.

That night, in bed, before she fell asleep, Betsy chuckled.

"What are you laughing at?" Tib asked.

"I'm thinking of the presents I'm going to take home. I'm certainly going to surprise people."

"What are you going to take?" Tib asked drowsily.

Betsy chuckled again.

"A fairy book to Margaret. And it must have *The Brave Little Tailor* in it, and *Snow White and the Seven Dwarfs*. And 'The Merry Widow' to Julia. And a stein for Papa. And for Mamma . . ." her mirth shook the bed . . . "a rabbit's foot."

"I don't see what's so funny. I think they sound very nice," said Tib as she dropped off to sleep.

15
A Week of Christmases

CHRISTMAS DAY WAS OVER, four days of her visit were gone, and Betsy had not yet begun to change.

"I *must* get started," she thought, lying in bed, waiting for Tib to wake up. "I want to be so completely different by the time I go back to Deep Valley. Of course, I've been busy with Christmas. But that's over now . . ."

Little she knew!

"Everyone's coming here for the Second Christmas Day," Mrs. Muller said at breakfast.

"Where are we going for the Third Christmas Day?"

"What is planned for the Fourth Christmas Day?"

Betsy listened in bewilderment. "How many Christmas Days do you have, for goodness' sake?" she demanded, and everyone laughed.

"New Year's puts a stop to them," Mr. Muller said.

The reason for this week of Christmases was clear. It would have been impossible in any lesser period to exhaust the holiday spirit which foamed in the city by the lake. Everyone must see everyone else's tree, and these visits of tree-inspection were virtual parties, with coffee and a great display of kuchen. Betsy learned to recognize a few different kinds . . . *Pfeffernüsse*, *Sterne*, *Kipfel* . . . but some of the most delicious had names she never mastered. She and Tib were not able to attend all these gatherings . . . too much must be crammed into two short weeks . . . but Fred and Hobbie reported on the kuchen every night.

Betsy reflected sometimes on how different Tib's life was from her own. Here the telephone did not ring all day. There wasn't perpetually a crowd of boys and girls around. But that did not mean Tib's life was empty. It was crowded with uncles, aunts, cousins and grandparents . . . and with other interests which the rapidly passing days revealed.

One afternoon they took the trolley to Tib's school. Tib was pleased to be showing her Sem to Betsy. When they crossed the Milwaukee River she said eagerly, "We have a regatta every June. I wish you could see it." When the turreted buildings loomed in sight among bare elms, she remarked with a sidelong glance, "It's prettier, of course, when the trees have leaves."

"I like it now," said Betsy, gazing about. The red-brick walls were clothed warmly with ivy. There were towers and friendly bow windows, and roguish gargoyles peering down.

Tib pointed out the athletic fields, the tennis courts, and when she had received permission from the resident teacher to show Betsy around, she took her first to the gymnasium.

"At basketball games," she said, "the girls who aren't playing sit in that balcony, and when a basket is made they yell out the spelling of the name of the one who made it."

"Like T-I-B?" said Betsy.

"That's right," Tib answered, smiling.

"They'd never call B-E-T-S-Y," Betsy said.

They looked in at the chapel, the library, the dining room. They peeked into the Dorm.

"I'm getting boarding school fever," Betsy said. Of course she knew in her heart that no school could ever be more than second best to the Deep Valley High School.

Tib chattered happily of beach parties on nearby Lake Michigan, of plays for which the girls themselves made scenery and costumes. She showed Betsy the large hall with a stage at one end where plays were produced.

"We have our dances here, too," she said.

"Do the girls ever go out with boys?" Betsy asked when they were walking toward the lake.

"Oh, yes, but you take a chaperone and you have to be in by 'second winks.' And Browner girls are allowed to go to only certain places. I remember when . . . one of the girls . . . was 'campused' for sneaking out to a restaurant not on the approved list." Betsy wondered over Tib's momentary hesitation. Could the girl have been Phil Brandish's sister?

"If I were a boarding pupil," Tib continued matter-of-factly, "I wouldn't do a thing like that. Browner is a school with high standards. And schools are like people. They have to have standards and live up to them, or they don't amount to much."

The lake was in sight now. Betsy and Tib clasped hands and ran. It was Betsy's first glimpse of the big inland sea, so different from the gentle, willow-fringed lakes of home. She felt very small standing on the sand, with the gulls swooping overhead and that vast expanse of water before them. The water was gray today, with whitecaps in a neverending race.

Betsy liked Lake Michigan, but best of all she liked downtown Milwaukee . . . the shops and the trolleys and especially the crowds which, like the whitecaps, were never ending. She liked the shipping in the bay, and the Milwaukee River nosing its way so determinedly through the city streets. Tib took her to see the statue of that Solomon Juneau who had started the whole thing.

They went downtown several times, once to a matinee at the Davidson Theatre called *Father and the Boys*. As they waited for the curtain to go up, eating caramels busily, Tib said she saw almost everything good that came to Milwaukee.

"If Uncle Rudy doesn't buy me tickets I buy them out of my allowance. I go alone. I like to, and Papa doesn't mind. I've seen Otis Skinner, and Sothern and Marlowe, and Minnie Maddern Fiske. Betsy, I even saw Sarah Bernhardt!"

"You did?" cried Betsy, and began to laugh. She told Tib about Julia's quarrel with Hugh as to who was greater, Sarah Bernhardt or Rose Stahl.

"Why, I saw Rose Stahl, too!" Tib exclaimed.

"Didn't you love *The Chorus Lady*?"

"Adored it! Betsy, do you remember when I played Meenie in *Rip Van Winkle*?"

"I'll never forget it. You were perfect! Tib, do you think you might like to be an actress when you grow up?"

Tib did not answer immediately. She swallowed a caramel, licked her fingers and looked thoughtful. The orchestra was tuning up now. Fiddles were twanging on the G string, flutes were making rippling excursions into the stuffy, scented air.

"Maybe," she said. "I like to dance, too. But it all goes together."

"I only thought . . . if you're going to be an actress, when I'm a famous writer, I'll write a play for you."

"I'd love that!" cried Tib, and then the theatre darkened, and the curtain went up.

On another afternoon they went shopping for Betsy's presents, the fairy book for Margaret, the stein for Mr. Ray, the score of *The Merry Widow* for Julia. They bought Anna a sewing basket, lined with purple silk, and Tacy fancy hat pins.

Betsy did not have courage enough to buy the rabbit's foot. But Tib, as usual, had courage for two. With Betsy trying to act as though they were perfect strangers, Tib danced up to the drug counter and made the shocking purchase.

"I'd better get Mamma something else," said Betsy,

"and pretend that this is just a joke, in case she doesn't like it." So they bought her a vanity bag like Aunt Dolly's.

Betsy bought dozens of postal cards for the Crowd . . . views of Lake Michigan, of Juneau Park, of Browner and the famous Schlitz Palm Garten. On some of them she wrote, "I want you to meet my friend, Miss Muller, otherwise known as Tib." And Tib scribbled in, "Pleased to meet you," and sometimes, *"Prosit!"*

All these expeditions unfailingly led to a coffee shop called Webers. Every afternoon at four, as Betsy soon learned, that part of Milwaukee which was not at home to put the coffee pot on, gathered at places like this one. There was a bake shop in front at which, on your way back to the tables, you selected a cake from tantalizing displays. Almost everything was covered with drifts of whipped cream.

"Whenever I see whipped cream, all my life, I'll think of Milwaukee," Betsy said.

Choosing a cake required the weightiest concentration. But when they had finally made their selections they proceeded to the tables where one could have either coffee or chocolate from silver pots, with, of course, a bowl of whipped cream handy.

"What a nice custom this is!" Betsy sighed blissfully. "Coffee in the afternoon!"

"But the women in Milwaukee are mostly very fat."

"This is worth getting fat for!" cried willow-thin Betsy. "Let's go back and choose another cake!"

Many of Tib's relatives strove to make Betsy's visit pleasant. One of the stout aunts took the girls to the Turnverein to hear Handel's *Messiah*. A stout uncle sent them to *The Rat Catcher of Hamlin*. Grosspapa Muller took the family and Betsy to dinner at the fashionable Deutscher Club . . . Johann in livery on the box of the carriage. Grosspapa Hornik, not to be outdone, took them to the Schlitz Palm Garten.

On New Year's Eve Tib invited all the cousins to a party for Betsy. While dressing Betsy had an inspired idea.

"Tib, do you know what I think we ought to do?"

"What?" asked Tib.

"Stay up all night tonight, and talk."

"You mean, all night, until morning?"

"Yes. I never did it; did you? And New Year's Eve is a perfect time for it, such a mystic kind of evening. Besides I'm going home day after tomorrow, and goodness knows when we'll see each other again!"

A curious expression crossed Tib's face. Then she replied, "All right. I'll make coffee to help keep us awake. After Papa and Mamma are asleep of course. We'd better not mention it to them."

"Oh, of course not! *Natürlich*."

The evening was passed pleasantly with cousins large and small. Even the twins and Hobbie stayed up for the New Year. They sang and played games, and there were ice cream and two kinds of cake for refreshments.

When the cuckoo clock started to sing for twelve o'clock, everyone made a fearful racket. They yelled at the tops of their voices, "Happy New Year!" and *"Prosit Neujahr!"* They shook hands, and laughed, and Heinrich threw up the window in order that the gaiety of the surrounding houses might come in.

Betsy put out her head. Whistles were blowing, bells were ringing.

"Ring out the old, ring in the new . . ."

But the new Betsy had not yet been rung in. She didn't even seem to be on the way.

"She is, though," Betsy resolved, staring firmly at a star. "I'll start with the new year."

"If you want to get married, Betsy," Heinrich called, "this is the year for you. Nineteen hundred and eight is Leap Year, you know."

"There'll be another in four years."

"But you may not have me around then."

"I'll have to make a special trip to Milwaukee."

This banter made her feel almost as though she were back in Deep Valley.

With the New Year, the party broke up. Singing out good wishes, the cousins departed. Fred took a sleepy Hobbie off to bed. Mr. and Mrs. Muller, too, retired. Tib and Betsy undressed, put on bathrobes and sat down to wait. When the house was quiet, Tib whispered, "Now I'll make the coffee." And they tip-toed toward the kitchen.

While the coffee boiled, they loaded a tray with cream and sugar, kuchen, and what Tib called *Butter-brot*, slices of buttered bread; also some cold beef, two or three kinds of cheese, what was left of the cakes, and dill pickles. The coffee reached a fragrant boil . . . all too fragrant.

"Heavens! Mamma will be sure to smell it!" Tib opened a window and Betsy waved her hands franti-cally, trying to push the smell out into the night.

Tib took the tray, and Betsy took the coffee pot, and they tiptoed back to their room. The cuckoo clock sang one.

They closed the door and pushed a rug against it and arranged their dishes on a little table. Tib had even brought a lace-edged cloth and two napkins. Neither one was very fond of coffee but they diluted it liberally with cream and spooned in sugar. They made themselves sandwiches from the *Butterbrot*, beef and cheese. Betsy realized suddenly how much fun it was.

"Tib," she said, putting down her cup. "I've had the most glorious time visiting you."

"I've loved it, too," Tib answered soberly. "I wanted you to come. I like the girls at the Sem very much, and I like my cousins, but there's never been anyone like you and Tacy."

"We've never gotten over missing you."

"I was so afraid you wouldn't come," said Tib. "I know how much you think of Christmas in your family. And besides, you have so much fun in Deep Valley during vacation."

"Oh, I was wild to come," Betsy answered. "I was wild to see you. And there was another reason. Tib," she said earnestly, "I want to change myself. I want to get a different personality. And I thought that going away, especially to a romantic place like Milwaukee, would give me a good chance to do it."

Tib stared. "But you're only here for two weeks."

"I know. But two weeks seems like a long time when you're away from home. Do you think I've changed any?"

"Not a bit."

"I was afraid not," said Betsy. "I think I've changed inside though. You couldn't see and do all the things I have, and not be a little different. And when I go back to Deep Valley, I'm going to be changed on the outside, too, so that people will notice it."

"How? What are you going to be like?"

Betsy put her hands behind her head.

"I can't decide," she said dreamily, "whether to be Dramatic and Mysterious, or Ethereal and Intellectual . . . sort of unhealthy in an attractive way, like Elizabeth Barrett Browning. Being tall like I am is good for the first thing, and being so thin is marvelous for the other. Which one do you like best?"

"The first one," said Tib. "Dramatic and Mysterious." She looked at Betsy keenly. "I know a wonderful way to do your hair."

"How?"

"Come here and I'll show you."

They went to the dressing table, and Tib asked for Betsy's biggest rat. She pinned it on firmly, and erected a magnificent pompadour, topped off with a high, pointed knot.

"Marvelous!" cried Betsy. "I ought to stick a jeweled dagger through it. Oh dear, I wish I had one!"

"I haven't got a dagger," said Tib, "but I'll give you this." Rummaging through her jewel box, she brought out a rhinestone pin which they poked into the knot.

"Stunning!" cried Betsy. She stalked about the room acting Dramatic and Mysterious. "A darned shame," she remarked, stopping before a mirror, "that I'm too young to wear ear rings. But I'm going to drench myself with perfume. And I'm always going to use the same kind, so that whenever anybody smells that odor they will know it's me . . . like Mama with violet perfume, only I want something more exotic."

"I have some Jockey Club," said Tib. "Would that be exotic enough? Somebody gave it to Aunt Dolly, but she said it didn't smell a bit like her, so she gave it to me. It doesn't smell like me either, and I'll give it to you if you want it."

"Jockey Club is perfect!" Betsy doused her flannel night gown rapturously. "And Tib, I've read that women of the kind I'm going to be always match their eyes in clothes and jewels. So I'm going to start wearing green."

"Your eyes are hazel," Tib objected. "And blue is your best color, Betsy. Always has been."

"Blue!" scoffed Betsy. "It's namby pamby. And there's lots of green in my eyes. Green for jealousy," she cried in a thrilling voice, resuming her stroll around the room.

"Whom are you jealous of?"

"Oh, nobody! I just like the sound of it. Pour me another cup of coffee; will you?"

Tib poured. "But, Betsy," she said, "you can't throw all your clothes away and get new ones. Can you?"

Betsy shrugged. "I suppose not. Fortunately, though,

my new sailor suit is green. And I can start wearing green hair ribbons and neck bows. I'm going to, too. Gee, I wish I'd bought some green ribbon to wear home!"

"Mamma has a whole bolt of green ribbon. She'll give us some."

"My jewels, from now on, are going to be emeralds."

"Well, that's one thing I don't have," said Tib. And the cuckoo clock sang two.

Betsy sipped her coffee meditatively.

"I'm going to try not to laugh so much," she said. "I'm laughing all the time. And when I'm not laughing, I'm smiling, which is worse. Oh, *why* did my teeth have to be parted in the middle!"

Tib looked at her critically. "You might paste white court plaster over them," she said.

Betsy, forgetting her recent resolve, burst out laughing. She laughed so hard that Tib said, "Hush! Be quiet, *Dummkopf*! you'll wake Mamma."

But Betsy rocked with mirth. "Let's try it. Do you have some court plaster?"

Tib obligingly found some. She measured Betsy's two front teeth, cut the court plaster meticulously, and pasted it on. But by that time she was laughing, too, and they heard a door open down the hall. They grabbed for handkerchiefs, stuffed them into their mouths, and waited tensely. The door closed again, and they removed the stuffing, but alas, the court plaster was gone!

"It's getting cold in here," said Tib. "I wish I dared heat up the coffee. But we'll have to wait until Mamma goes back to sleep."

"Let's move our chairs over to the radiator. There's a little heat left, and we can wrap up in blankets. Let's raise the shade, too. I'd like to see the dawn."

They tucked themselves in cozily on either side of the radiator.

"Betsy," said Tib, "I believe I'll change myself, too. What shall I be like?"

Betsy gazed at her through half closed lids.

"You," she declared, "are the silly type."

"What do you mean?" cried Tib. "I'm not a bit silly."

"That's just the trouble. You ought to be. You disappoint boys, probably, all the time. You look so little and cute and foolish, and they don't like to find out how sensible and practical you are."

"Don't they?" asked Tib.

"No, they don't. You ought to laugh lots . . . just the opposite of me . . . a silly little tinkling laugh. You ought to act too helpless to pick up your own handkerchief. And don't let on that you were ever inside of a kitchen."

"Oh, dear!" said Tib. "I thought boys would like it

that I'm such a good cook."

"Tib," said Betsy. "For a boy who was in love with you to see you making *Hasenpfeffer* with potato dumplings would be an absolutely disillusioning experience."

They started to laugh again and grabbed their handkerchiefs. The cuckoo clock sang three.

"I'm simply frozen," said Betsy then. "We have to warm up the coffee; that's all there is to it." So they took the rug away from the door and tiptoed down the hall again. To their great relief they could hear Mr. Muller snoring.

The rooms of the house were silent, cold and empty, and beyond the windows they could see the ghostly snow. The flame on the gas stove was comforting somehow, and so was the warm pot. They carried it back to their bedroom.

And now waiting for morning began to be hard. They were both very sleepy. They turned down the gas and stared out the window, but they saw only snow and a cold starry sky. There wasn't a trace of dawn. The cuckoo sang four times.

They turned the gas up again and talked some more about their new personalities, but even this fascinating subject could not keep them awake.

"Let's say the alphabet," Betsy proposed. And they did.

"Let's say the multiplication tables," Tib suggested.

"Heavens!" said Betsy. "I don't remember them." But she tried, and it took time. The cuckoo clock sang five.

"Perhaps we might get into bed," Betsy conceded. "It's so darned cold. We'll leave the gas high though, so we won't fall asleep." They jumped into bed gratefully. Then Betsy bounced up. "If we don't turn out the gas," she said, "we can't see the dawn, and I particularly want to see the dawn."

"I'll turn it out," said Tib hopping out of bed. Tib was always quick to do disagreeable things.

They lay in bed staring at the gray square of window. And suddenly Tib spoke. Her voice didn't sound sleepy any more. It was serious, grave.

"Betsy," she whispered. "Can you keep a secret?"

"Yes. Very well."

"I'll tell you one then. Mamma told me. Papa doesn't even know I know it. He came back to Milwaukee because Grosspapa Muller likes his sons around him. But Papa and Mamma like better to be independent, and to raise their children in a more American way. That's why we haven't bought a home, or horses here in Milwaukee. We still own our house . . . the one you always loved so much . . . back in Deep Valley. Maybe, just maybe, we're going back!"

"Tib!" cried Betsy. She sat up in bed again in spite

of the cold. "Why, that would be glorious! Divine! Wait 'til I tell Tacy! Oh, dear, I can't tell her."

"Yes, you may," said Tib. "You and I and Tacy have kept secrets before. But not anyone else."

"Oh, Tib, Tib! Won't we have fun? The Crowd will be crazy about you. Who do you think you'd like to go around with, especially? Dennie is cute. And Tony, of course."

Tib grasped Betsy's arm. "Look out the window! It's beginning to get light."

It was. The stars had faded. The sky was the color of smoke, just a little darker than the gray city snow. And behind the rooftops to the east a fire seemed to be burning.

"We've done it!" Betsy cried softly. "We've stayed awake all night. Happy New Year!"

"*Prosit Neujahr!*" answered Tib sleepily. "And now, for goodness' sake, let's get some sleep!"

Betsy snuggled down. "When I get my new personality," she said, "I'm going to throw in foreign phrases all the time. Things like '*nicht wahr*' and '*wie geht's*' and '*Prosit Neujahr!*'"

"*Prosit Neujahr!*" murmured Tib, plainly too far gone in sleep to understand.

After a few minutes Betsy said, "And I'm going to add an 'e' to my name. B-e-t-s-y-e. Would you like that?"

"Um! What did you say? I was asleep. Good night, dear." Tib turned over.

Betsy laughed. "When you come to Deep Valley," she said, "we'll make a wonderful team. Me, so tall, dark and mysterious, and you so blond and silly." But this time Tib did not answer at all. So Betsy, too, closed her eyes.

The cuckoo clock sang six.

16

Betsy into Betsye

ON NEW YEAR'S AFTERNOON they called on Grosspapa and Grossmama Muller and the dwarfs, and on Grosspapa and Grossmama Hornik above the tailor shop. Uncle Rudy said that it was Leap Year now, and wasn't Betsy going to ask him for a kiss? Aunt Dolly invited her back to Milwaukee for her wedding.

"I hope I'm coming back sometime," Betsy said,

and meant it heartily. The following morning she started home.

She and Tib went to the depot alone on the trolley. In spite of the consoling secret they shared, they felt sober about parting. Tib wheedled the conductor into letting her go through the gate and aboard the parlor car.

"See what I can do when I act silly like you told me?" she asked with an airy trill of laughter.

"That reminds me! Dramatic and Mysterious," said Betsy, drawing herself up.

They laughed as they embraced, but both of them had wet eyes.

"See you in Deep Valley," said Tib and went quickly down the aisle. Outside the window she smiled and blew kisses, a gay little figure in her purple coat.

The trip to Deep Valley was different from the trip to Milwaukee. The flavor was different. Anticipation was there, of course, but now it was for home. For the first time Betsy dared think wholeheartedly of home.

Her company in the parlor car was different too. There was no sociable Mrs. Gulbertson today. There were five bridal couples, and bridal couples, Betsy discovered are not sociable at all. She looked out the window. It had rained the night before and then turned colder. Every twig on every bush and tree was sheathed in ice. They looked like clouds of silver in the sunshine as Wisconsin hurried past.

Betsy took out a tablet and pencil, but instead of writing a story or a poem as she usually did to amuse herself, she made a list.

"*List*," she wrote, "*of Things I Must Do to be Different.*"

She smiled as she began for the list reminded her of the glorious time she and Tib had had staying awake all night. But she grew serious before she had finished.

1. *Start signing your name Betsye.*
2. *Don't laugh so much.*
3. *Seldom smile.*
4. *Keep your voice low.*
5. *Wear green.*
6. *Wear emeralds . . . when you can get them. (Jade would do.)*
7. *Use only Jockey Club perfume . . . be lavish with it.*
8. *Use foreign phrases . . . be lavish with them, too.*
9. *See that your waists don't pull out at the waist-band.*
10. *Keep your clothes in press, your shoes polished, and your fingernails manicured.*
11. *Take at least one bath a day; two would be better. Lavish with bath salts also.*

She memorized this list grimly; then she tore it up.

She had dinner in the diner, passing through Madison. Supper came at Winona, back in her own state. Expectancy now became joyful suspense. She sat with her hands tightly clasped.

It was dark outside, and the shades had been drawn. She wondered whether the family would meet her. "Just Papa, probably. But the rest will be waiting up, even Margaret." And that proved to be the case. When the porter had finally brushed her as before, and the train, its bell ringing, had slowed down for Deep Valley, she found her father waiting. The sight of him, so tall, ruddy and dependable-looking, with a happy smile on his face, brought a lump to her throat.

"Well, well! Home again!" he said, as Betsy hugged and kissed him.

She tried to talk about her trip, but he kept stopping her. "No! I promised the family I wouldn't let you tell a thing. They're half crazy, waiting."

Betsy felt half crazy herself as they neared High Street. Welcome lights streamed out across the snow. Margaret's small erect figure with the hair bow and the English bob was outlined in the big front window. The door opened and everyone rushed out, Abie barking and leaping.

Inside everything looked beautiful.

"Mamma has even scoured the coal scuttle," Mr.

Ray said. He always made that joke when one of them came home after being away. There was a fire in the dining room grate, and a lunch on the table beneath the hanging lamp.

"Did you get anything fit to eat in Milwaukee, lovey?" Anna asked.

"Nothing half so good as this," Betsy replied. But she hardly knew what she was eating. There was so much to tell and to be told.

Margaret brought out the new doll in its red silk dress. Julia told about all the parties.

"That Phyllis Brandish was visiting here."

"Is she nice?"

"She took quite a liking to Harry," Julia said. "But I kept him safely by my side."

"Harry," said Mr. Ray, "spends altogether too much time by your side." He seemed a little disgruntled.

Betsy asked for her grip and, smiling broadly, brought out her presents.

"I want you to know, Margaret," she said presenting the book, "that I've seen those seven dwarfs with my own eyes, and I've met *The Brave Little Tailor*."

Julia seized her *Merry Widow* score and dashed to the piano. Anna exclaimed that the sewing basket was tony. Mrs. Ray loved her vanity bag and Mr. Ray, with a chuckle, put his stein on the plate-rail. Slowly, last of all, Betsy brought out the rabbit's foot.

She held it behind her back while she told of Aunt Dolly getting ready for the Christmas ball.

"And if she can use rouge, you can," she ended, extending the package to her mother.

"Here! Here! Give that to me!" Mr. Ray made a grab. Betsy ran, her father following. Margaret screamed joyfully, Abie barked, and Washington yowled. Eluding her father by a breath, Betsy put the gift into her mother's hands.

"This begins a new life for me," said Mrs. Ray. "From now on I'm going to be different." That brought sharply to Betsy's mind the changes she had intended to make in herself. She had been laughing not less, but more than usual. Her waist had pulled out, and the high peaked knot Tib had made on top of her head had fallen down. But her mother noticed the Jockey Club.

"What is that new perfume, dear? Isn't it a little heavy?"

The new personality had hard going that night, and the next day, too. Tony appeared right after breakfast. Cab and Dennie followed. Tacy came to dinner, was given her hat pins and told the joyful secret of Tib's possible return. The Crowd had gathered by evening for a Welcome Home celebration which did not lend itself at all to Dramatic and Mysterious poses.

Betsy told them all about Milwaukee, especially all about Tib. Tib would never have recognized herself in Betsy's extravagant descriptions.

"Gosh, isn't she coming to visit you sometime?" Tony demanded.

"I must say she's changed since we were in school together," Winona remarked skeptically. "She was just a little white-haired kid."

"I should say she has changed," Betsy replied. And reminded of her own plans, added hastily, *"Aber ja! Unglaublich!"* But nobody seemed impressed.

As the days ran on, she made discouragingly little progress. She had no luck with the hair-do, and her mother objected to too much Jockey Club. Now and then she had a trifling triumph. She heard her father say to her mother, "Don't you think Betsy seems a little serious since she got home?" He complained, too, that he could never get into the bathroom. That, of course, was on account of the two baths a day.

"Do you think I seem any different?" Betsy asked Julia. And Julia's reply was satisfactory but surprising. "Of course. Travel is so broadening. But do *I* seem any different?"

"Why . . . why . . ." said Betsy. She realized that she had been so wrapped up in herself that she hadn't paid much attention to Julia. "I don't know," she added.

"Maybe it doesn't show on the outside," said Julia. "But I've been going through a good deal. Harry is . . . quite serious. I think he's in love with me."

"There's nothing new about that."

"Yes there is. Harry isn't just a kid. He's a grown man; and Bettina . . . I like him, too."

"Julia!" exclaimed Betsy.

Julia looked solemn. "I almost think I'm in love with him. And Bettina . . . what do you suppose?"

"What?"

"Papa doesn't like it," Julia said.

Betsy was inclined to take this lightly, but Julia looked grave and uplifted as she looked when she sang.

"It just breaks my heart to upset Papa," she said. "But I can't help it that I have this wonderful feeling. What do you think I ought to do?"

Betsy warmed as always when Julia turned to her for counsel.

"Have you talked to Mamma about it?"

"Yes. She tells Papa not to take it too seriously. It may be," added Julia darkly, "that it's more serious than she thinks."

"Julia, has he . . . he hasn't . . . proposed?"

"Not yet. I don't think he will until I graduate."

"Then don't worry! Because if you do, you may not even graduate." Both of them began to laugh, and remembered that school started next day with examinations imminent.

Examinations, as usual, quite changed the character of life. After school and in the evening, alone and in crowds, everyone was studying. Julia was memorizing a speech from *Hamlet* for Miss Bangeter's Shakespeare class. It was Polonius' speech to Laertes, his son.

Betsy heard it so often that she inadvertently learned it and would chant along with Julia through the various admonitions to the end.

> *"This above all: to thine own self be true,*
> *And it must follow, as the night the day,*
> *Thou canst not then be false to any man."*

Betsy needed such soothing exercise. She was really worried.

"Usually I can rely on a good grade in English. But with Gaston . . . I don't know what to expect. History and Caesar aren't so bad. I think I can manage if I study *diligentia*."

"*Cum diligentia,*" Julia corrected.

"*Cum diligentia*. But oh this geometry!"

Julia explained the proposition in hand. "Do you understand it now?"

"If I don't I can memorize it."

"But Bettina, it would be so much better to *understand* it. Geometry is so *interesting*. It's so much fun."

"About as much fun as the dentist," Betsy growled.

She was in her own room, wearing an ancient bathrobe and decrepit slippers. Examination week was definitely not the time to be Dramatic or Mysterious.

When it was over, with Julia and Betsy passing in all subjects, the Winding Hall of Fate took a momentous twist.

Betsy had an attack of la grippe. And her convalescence was not happy. Usually Betsy, who loved to read and loved even better to write, rather enjoyed being kept in bed. But this time, although she had a new dressing sacque and a pile of notebooks and sharp pencils, she did not have a good time at all. She had been running away from some thoughts from which she could now run no further.

The humiliating truth was that she had not succeeded in changing herself.

She had had fun telling Tacy that she was going to change, and even more fun plotting out with the admiring Tib a thrilling glamorous transformation. But facing the facts in her lonely bed Betsy realized that it was much easier for her to plot out something than it was for her to do it. Just as, when they were younger, she and Tacy had loved to dream up wild deeds but it had usually been Tib who carried them out.

This particular plan was unusually difficult to translate into action. It really amounted to play-acting, and Betsy had never been any good at that. Julia could play-act any time, any place, before any audience. She could be haughty or coquettish or melancholy as the occasion required. But Betsy, in the family circle at least, was always the same. She was always plain Betsy.

Right now, the day before the doctor had said she might get up, she was heartily sick and tired of being Betsy.

"I'm so disgustingly young!" she thought, digging into a pillow. "Not in my age but in the way I *am*."

Harry was practically on the point of proposing to Julia. Carney had gone with Larry for four years and now had Al Larson, the football hero, paying devoted attention. Irma enthralled everyone just by widening her big eyes. Winona was not an absolute siren, but plenty of boys followed gaily along her madcap path. Tacy and Alice, of course, weren't interested in boys.

"But I *am*," thought Betsy, tears squeezing beneath her lashes. She was ashamed and dashed them away. "It isn't that I have a crush on anyone. I haven't. But I'd like to be dazzling, popular, a belle. I always thought I would be."

She sat up in bed violently and blew her nose.

"And I *will* be," she said, aloud this time. She went

on silently. "There's no reason why I can't be. I'm not so pretty as I wish I were, but I'm plenty pretty enough. The trouble is that Tony and Cab and Dennie all know me too well. They see me doing homework and washing dishes and things. I can't put on in front of anyone I know. But I can with people I don't know, sometimes. I could with Phil Brandish."

She remembered her thoughts after talking with Tib the first afternoon in Milwaukee. Tib had said that Betsy could probably get Phil Brandish if she tried. All at once everything seemed to fit into place like the pieces of a puzzle. Betsy felt alert and confident.

"I'm going to get Phil Brandish crazy about me," she said, and began to put her bed in order, flapping the comforter so energetically that notebooks and pencils flew in all directions. Julia just back from a lesson at Mrs. Poppy's, looked around the door.

"What do you think, Bettina? The Metropolitan Opera is coming to St. Paul this spring. Caruso's coming, and Farrar."

"Um . . . is that so?" said Betsy. "Julia, what do you do when you want to get some boy interested in you?"

"I tell him I had a dream about him," said Julia, and laughed, and went on to her own room.

So! That was the way! Betsy plumped her pillow and sat up, very bright eyed. She couldn't very well tell Phil Brandish that she had had a dream about him, for she never saw him. You can't buttonhole a virtual stranger in the middle of the street and tell him that you had a dream about him.

"But you can spread the news," thought Betsy, bouncing with determination. She was, she knew, in an excellent position to spread news. The Ray house was headquarters for the Crowd. At any moment now boys and girls would begin trooping in. In fact, the advance guard had already arrived.

"Yoo hoo! Betsy!" Tacy, Winona, and Carney clattered up to Betsy's room.

"What are you looking so excited about?" Tacy asked at once.

"Girls!" cried Betsy. "I had the craziest dream about Phil Brandish."

"You what?" "Phil Brandish?" "For heaven's sake!"

"Yes, I had a dream about Phil Brandish. But don't ask me to tell you what it is, because I won't." And Betsy began to laugh merrily.

Winona started to tease her into telling, but a voice from down stairs interrupted. "Hello! It's Cab and Irma. May we come up?"

"Irma can, but not Cab until I get beautified," cried Betsy, taking pins out of her hair. Irma ran upstairs, and Cab, joined shortly by Dennie, sat down at the piano to play "Chopsticks."

"Irma," Winona said, "Betsy has had a dream about Phil Brandish."

"What was it?"

"She won't tell!"

"I certainly won't! Will you call Julia, and ask her to come like a lamb and fix my hair?"

"Do *you* know what it is?" Winona demanded of Julia.

"Know what what is?"

"Betsy's dream about Phil Brandish."

"Betsy's . . . dream?" Julia looked at Betsy. "Did you have a dream about Phil Brandish, Bettina?" Julia asked easily taking up the comb.

Cab and Dennie, joined now by Tony, shouted up the stairs. "If we can't come up, some of you women come down."

"Go keep the poor things company," Betsy said. And Carney and Irma rose.

Tacy stayed curled on the foot of the bed, and Winona was too curious to leave. She stared with speculative eyes while Julia deftly twisted and pinned and gave Betsy a hand mirror in which to see the effect.

The boys downstairs were calling for Julia to come play the piano.

"Play 'Dreaming' for me, will you, Julia?" Betsy asked.

"'Dreaming'? That old thing?"

"It's so appropriate," said Betsy, and she and Tacy went off into gales of laughter.

"See here," said Winona. "You *have* to tell me what you're laughing about."

"Nothing," said Tacy.

"Oh, Tacy and I made up words for that song . . . ages ago," Betsy said.

"What are they?"

"Shall we tell her, Tacy?"

Julia had started to play, and Betsy and Tacy began to sing, in parts, with sobs of mock feeling.

> *"Dreaming, dreaming,*
> *Of your red auto I'm dreaming,*
> *Dreaming of days when I got a ride,*
> *Dreaming of hours spent by your side."*

"Betsy!" interrupted Winona. "Do you have a crush on Phil Brandish?"

"I never said I didn't."

"But *have* you?"

"I never said I did."

Winona pounced on her, and the scuffle grew so pronounced that Mrs. Ray came out from her bedroom where she had been sewing.

"Is this the way to behave with la grippe? I'm certainly thankful that you get up tomorrow."

"So am I," said Betsy. "And I can go back to school on Monday. Can't I, Mamma?"

"I expect so."

"I hope so because the class officers are meeting. We're making plans for the sophomore party."

Tony, Cab and Dennie roared up the stairs.

"Is Betsy beautiful yet?" "What's this about your dream?" "Why don't you ever dream about me?"

Betsy shouted appropriate replies, and Winona ran down stairs.

Betsy was up and dressed next day, looking pale and interesting, she hoped. The rest of the week passed quickly, more than a little enlivened by talk of her dream.

"Do you know," asked Winona, again dropping in after school, "it wouldn't surprise me if Tony had told Phil Brandish that you had a dream about him."

"What makes you think so?" Betsy simulated horror.

"I saw them talking in school."

"He wouldn't be so mean!"

"Maybe," suggested Winona looking wicked, "he did it on a dare."

"If he did, I know who dared him. Winona Root, you . . . you . . ." Betsy made a dash.

"Be careful," warned Mrs. Ray, "if you want to go to school on Monday!"

"I have to go to school. I wouldn't miss that officers' meeting for a farm."

"Why? What's so important about it?" Winona asked.

"I told you. We're planning the sophomore party. And I have some ideas," Betsy said. "At least," she added, "I have one wonderful idea."

She went to school on Monday wearing her prettiest waist . . . its lofty collar was encircled by white ruching . . . green bows in her hair and a green belt around her slender waist. Just before leaving she sprayed herself with Jockey Club and hurried out before her mother could protest.

It was good to be back. She was even glad to see the teachers, she announced as supreme proof of her joy. Joe Willard smiled at her. Notes flew briskly up and down the aisles. A Welcome Back present from Tony, in the shape of a piece of licorice, passed hand over hand to her seat and was much appreciated, in spite of the fact that it left a black rim around her mouth.

A short time later . . . she had removed the rim . . . she passed Phil Brandish in the hall. He looked at her keenly. For some reason Betsy did not think at that moment about her much discussed dream. Meeting his yellow-brown eyes brought back the terrible moment when she had discovered him listening to her and Tacy in front of the toyshop. She blushed down to her snowy ruching and Phil Brandish turned away.

The sophomore class officers met after school in the Social Room. The president was named Stan Moore. Cab was vice-president, and a nice freckle-faced girl named Hazel Smith was treasurer. Stan at once introduced the subject of the party.

"This is a pretty important affair," he said. "We need to raise money. Next year we'll be juniors and we'll have to entertain the seniors and do a lot of expensive things. And our treasury is as empty as a drum." He looked around the group. "Any ideas?"

Betsy was almost bursting with her important idea but she thought it better strategy not to speak first. Hazel Smith proposed a bazaar with a candy booth. The response was unenthusiastic. After a suitable interval Betsy looked up brightly.

"I have a brainstorm."

"Good! What is it?"

"Let's hire Schiller Hall and give a dance."

"That wouldn't make money," Stan objected. "It would probably lose it for us."

"Not if we open it to all the classes," Betsy answered. "The juniors and seniors give dances at Schiller Hall all the time."

"But, Betsy," put in Hazel, "we sophomores haven't

started dancing much. I'd adore a dance, and I think most of the girls would, but I don't believe . . . to tell the truth . . . that we'd be invited. A few sophomore girls, like Irma would probably get to go and maybe you would, Betsy," she added politely. "But I don't think most of the sophomore boys would ask girls. Would you now?" she appealed to Cab and Stan.

Before they had a chance to answer Betsy spoke. "Oh, but you haven't heard all my brainstorm. This is Leap Year, and I want to give a Leap Year dance. Let the girls do the asking."

"Hooray!" cried Cab. "And the paying?"

"Certainly the paying. Of course, if you are gentlemen you'll return the party soon."

"That would make two parties! Fine for the treasury," grinned Stan.

It was unanimously decided to announce a Leap Year dance for the coming Friday, the last one in February.

Betsy went straight home and up to her room. Since the trip to Milwaukee she had kept a pad of Jockey Club sachet in her stationery which was, of course, pale green. On one of these heavily scented sheets, she wrote a note . . . but not until she had written several trial versions on tablet paper.

The note, which she immediately sealed, stamped and mailed, was signed . . . Betsye Ray.

17

The Leap Year Dance

NEXT DAY AT SCHOOL news of the Leap Year dance blew like a mischievous wind through the cloak rooms, the Social Room, even the assembly room. Not for four years, not for a high school generation, had girls had a chance to invite boys to a party.

"That was a good idea, Betsy," said Stan, stopping her in the hall. "I didn't realize that girls were so crazy about dances. There's such a rush for tickets that it keeps Hazel busy taking in the money."

Betsy smiled, one of the new smiles she was practising. "I'm awfully glad it's working out," she said. "I hear that Hazel's taking you?"

"That's right. Who are you going to take?"

"I don't know yet," Betsy replied. And that was what she said to everyone. It wasn't, she argued, an untruth, although it certainly gave a false impression.

"Who are you taking, Betsy?" Irma inquired. "I'd like to ask Cab, but not if . . ."

"Ask him. He'll be delirious with joy."

Carney approached her. "I'm taking Al. Who are you taking, Betsy?"

"I don't know. Wish I did."

"While you're thinking," Carney warned, "everyone will be snatched up."

"I'll risk it."

Winona complained good-humoredly that Joe Willard had turned her down.

"You ought to take Pin anyway," said Betsy.

"I will. You're taking Tony, I suppose?"

"I believe Tacy's taking him," Betsy answered evasively, and hurried away.

Tacy knew the secret of the pale green, scented note. She was much more interested in that than in whom she would take. "I wish I didn't have to go, but Alice and I are on the program committee. Alice is taking Dennie."

"Why don't you ask Tony?" Betsy suggested, remembering the talk with Winona.

"I'd like to. I know him so well. But you might want to take him yourself, in case you . . . he . . ."

"No," said Betsy, firmly. "If I get turned down I'll have another attack of la grippe."

Phil Brandish did not seek her out that day. But then she didn't give him a chance. She hurried through the halls like a fugitive, not meeting his eyes, and, of course, during the morning she was not certain that he had received the note.

"He must have received it by now," she thought at the afternoon session. But he didn't speak.

The next day there began to be real curiosity about her plans. Winona cornered her.

"Betsy," she said sternly. "Are you asking Joe Willard?"

"I wouldn't dare to ask him after he turned you down."

"Well then, what do you have up your sleeve?" Winona demanded. But even after all the talk about Betsy's dream, not Winona nor anyone else suggested that Betsy might have asked Phil Brandish.

"Any mail?" Betsy asked, bursting in after school.

"No, dear." Her mother looked up in surprise.

"Were you expecting something? Betsy, I've just been saying to Julia, you ought to make up your mind about that party. Decide on some boy, and invite him."

"Um . . . er . . . that's so," murmured Betsy, and asked Julia, hastily, "You're taking Harry, I suppose?"

"Unnecessary question!" Julia replied. She looked straight at Betsy and her eyes held a knowing twinkle.

But Betsy was beginning to think that this was not a laughing matter. Today was Thursday. The dance came tomorrow night.

"I may have to have la grippe awfully quick," she thought. At supper that night she refused dessert, paving the way for disaster.

Shortly after supper the telephone rang.

"You might as well answer it, Betsy," Mrs. Ray said, "It's sure to be for you." The members of the Crowd were wireless telephone conversationalists. Betsy answered with a cautious hello, but her heart dropped and rose several times like a runaway elevator when she heard a deep and unfamiliar voice on the other end of the wire.

"Hello . . . er . . . Betsy, do you know who I am?"

"N . . . no," murmured Betsy, "I don't believe I do." Mentally she groped for her new personality, for the list she had written on the train. She laughed the low laugh she had practised in the diner. She tried to make her silence full of mystery.

"I'm Phil Brandish. I . . . I'd like very much to go to

that dance, but . . ." At the "but" her heart sank to the ground floor. "But," he went on, "you haven't sampled my dancing."

"You haven't sampled mine!" In glad relief she gave the laugh again. "I can tell you will be a good dancer . . . from the way you walk, I mean."

"I was just going to say that about you," he answered. This was almost more than she had hoped for. "I'm sorry that my auto is put up, but I'll try to get the local hack."

"Oh, no!" cried Betsy. She could never live down going to a dance in Mr. Thumbler's hack. "Everybody walks to Schiller Hall to parties. It's just at the foot of our hill."

"All right," he said. "I'll be around about . . . eight?"

"Eight," said Betsy.

She walked back to the parlor with a thistledown tread.

"Surprise! Surprise!" she announced to the assembled family. "I'm taking Phil Brandish to the Leap Year dance."

"Betsy!" cried her mother, "Why, you hardly know him . . ."

"I suppose," said Julia slyly, smiling, "he wants to find out about that dream."

"The Brandish boy? How did you happen to ask him?" her father inquired, sounding annoyed.

"Oh, I just wanted to," said Betsy, pacing excitedly

about the room. "You don't mind, do you?"

"I guess not, I don't know anything against the boy."

"I should think you'd take Tony," said Margaret, looking up from *Little Women*. Tony was a great favorite with Margaret.

Betsy patted her head and ran to telephone Tacy. When she returned she and Julia went upstairs.

"It's such fun, Bettina," Julia said, "that you're starting to go to dances. Now we'll be going to them together all the time."

"Isn't it wonderful!" cried Betsy.

"What are you going to do now?"

"Wash my hair!"

"Come into my room to dry it, and we'll talk."

Betsy washed her hair, adding plenty of Jockey Club to the last rinse water. She dried it over the register in Julia's room, rubbed it and brushed it, and put it up on Wavers. Then she and Julia manicured their nails, buffing them to diamondlike brilliance, and Betsy told Julia all about the pale green note and Julia told Betsy about dances at Schiller Hall.

"You go up three flights of stairs," she said, "and there's a ladies dressing room just outside the hall. You leave your cloak there, and beautify yourself at the mirrors. They're always crowded with girls. When you come out into the hall you're given your program, and the boys rush up to ask for dances . . ."

"Rush up?" asked Betsy. "You mean they rush up

to *you*. What do I do if nobody asks me for a single dance and my program is a perfect blank?"

"It won't be," Julia said. "But if, by any chance, there's one dance you're not asked for, you go to the dressing room and spend the time doing your hair. You don't sit out on the side lines and let everybody notice you're not dancing as some dumb girls do."

Betsy made a mental note. "There are going to be fifteen dances," she said. "Tacy and Alice are making the programs. They're terribly cute, with a bar from 'The Merry Widow Waltz' painted on the cover. But fifteen dances, Julia! Cab will ask me for one, of course, and Tony, and Dennie, and Pin, and Al, probably, and Squirrelly, and Harry, but that's only seven. I've fifteen to fill."

"Your escort," said Julia, "always writes his name down for the first dance and the last one, and usually one in the middle. If he really likes you, he asks for four." She laughed. "Harry," she said, "wants me to give him every other dance. But I won't. People would talk and Papa wouldn't like it."

"I can just see my program," said Betsy, "with yawning vacant spots." She did have cold chills of fear that she would not be asked to dance, but right along with them was a warm conviction that she would be. This was her first dance. It just had to be wonderful.

"And, Bettina," said Julia, "I think it's swell that

you asked Phil Brandish. It's time you stepped out and did something for yourself. But he isn't one of the boys that comes to the house. We don't know much about him, and if he shouldn't be our kind, if he should be . . . spoony going home, let him know right off that we don't do that sort of thing."

Betsy nodded wisely. She remembered something Tib had said.

"Don't worry. I have standards. If people don't have standards and live up to them, they don't amount to much."

She went out with the thistledown tread again.

She was still walking like thistledown when she went to school next morning. The girls in the Crowd came up as soon as she entered the Social Room.

"Betsy," said Winona, "have you asked anyone yet? That party is tonight, you know."

"Why, yes, of course," said Betsy. "Haven't I told you?"

"Of course you haven't told us!"

"Really? I thought I had. Let's see. Who *am* I taking!" Betsy rubbed her forehead.

"You tell us!" Winona shook a warning fist.

"All right! Philip J. Brandish."

For a full moment everyone thought she was joking. Irma said, "Betsy! Tell us, please."

"I did tell you," answered Betsy and laughed but she was really flustered. She began to blush and blushed all the harder when necks craned toward Phil. Betsy did not look his way nor meet his eyes. It would be easier to establish that new personality when they were alone than in front of the Social Room. She was thankful that the last bell rang just then. Everyone had to hurry off.

The boys, at the Ray house after school, were equally bewildered.

"What are you going to take that big stiff for?" Cab demanded. But Betsy only smiled, a cool superior smile she had acquired. Cab didn't find it attractive and he didn't like the green bows either, nor the clouds of perfume nor the *"nicht wahrs"* scattered through her speech. He had told her so several times. "What's got into you, Betsy?" he asked with irritation.

Tony's black eyes were laughing. Perhaps, Betsy thought, he considered himself responsible because of having told Phil about her dream.

"I always thought," he said, "that when you started going to dances, you'd go with me. I'd know enough to take a curling iron along in case it started to rain."

"Dummkopf!" said Betsy.

"Never mind! I can mention to Brandish that he'd better put a curling iron in his pocket."

"Tony! You wouldn't!"

"I won't take you to the party if you do," Tacy threatened. "Come on, Betsy. We have to hurry if we're going downtown."

They were going downtown because Tib, off in Milwaukee, always wore lace stockings to parties. Betsy ran up to her mother's room and searched through the rag bag for a scrap of her pink silk dress. With this in her pocket she and Tacy went down to the Lion Department Store and bought lace stockings of the same shade of pink. Tacy, too, had purchases to make. Reassured because she was going with Tony, with whom she had long since ceased to be shy, Tacy was beginning to feel that she might like a dance.

At supper Betsy refused dessert again.

"It's delicate pudding, lovey."

"Put mine in the icebox for me. Will you, Anna? Maybe I'll eat it after I get home."

Betsy was upstairs ready to start dressing at half past six. By the time she was out of the bathroom, smelling sweetly of talc, her mother, Julia, and Margaret, with the cat in her arms, had gathered in her room. Margaret's eyes were as big and watchful as Washington's while Betsy pinned starched ruffles across her chest, donned her prettiest corset cover, strung with pink ribbons, three starched petticoats, the outer one also strung with pink, the pink lace stockings, her high shoes. Dancing slippers, of course, would be carried in a slipper bag.

Julia, who was never in a hurry to start dressing, and Mrs. Ray who by now knew the entire plot, perched on the bed and made lively suggestions.

"Tell him you dreamed he was patching a tire."

"Tell him you saw him staggering under a big bouquet of roses."

"Tell him you saw P H I L written in letters of fire."

Betsy laughed but for once she did not talk. Her eyes were bright, determined. Slipping on a kimono, she ran down to the kitchen to refresh her curls. As she wound her locks on the iron she thought of Tony and giggled.

"That *Dummkopf*!" she said aloud. It would be fun to be going to the dance with someone she knew well like Tony but not so exciting, not so demanding, not . . . she felt . . . so good for her as this.

She ran back upstairs.

"Want me to do your hair?"

"Will you, like an angel?"

Julia did her incomparable best.

Betsy slipped on the pink silk dress. Julia pinned on the daisy wreath. Betsy sprayed Jockey Club perfume and her mother did not say a protesting word.

Ready, down to a filmy handkerchief. Betsy stared into the mirror. Her pompadour made a dark cloud; her neck was white like Julia's. Her figure in the rosy, flower-sprinkled silk looked slender, insubstantial.

"I love the way I look," she thought. "Thank you! Thank you!" She smiled resolutely into her own eyes.

When the doorbell rang she felt like a racehorse, just ready to start. Anna answered and Betsy went swiftly down the stairs. Her mother did not follow immediately and her father did not look up from the paper he was reading in the parlor. Again Betsy was unutterably thankful. She could not have taken the first difficult steps with her family looking on.

Nobody looked on and the expression in Phil Brandish's yellow-brown eyes made it easy to act her part. She put out her hand; he took it in a large strong grip. Both of them smiled.

Betsy heard herself chatting about the party, the sophomores' need for funds.

"That's so we can entertain you juniors next year. I thought I'd start now and get in practise."

"An excellent idea!"

Smiling down at her, his hat in his hand, a white muffler folded with care inside his overcoat, he was very impressive. He was tall, and a lock of his thick light-brown hair hung over his forehead. His skin was a clear olive tint. His eyes were heavily lashed.

He had very good manners . . . pounded into him, Tom had said, by schools all over the country. But he had none of the easy, foolish give-and-take of the other boys she knew.

"I want you to meet my father," Betsy said, and led him into the parlor. Her mother came downstairs shortly, acting gracious . . . not at all as though she had recently been perched on Betsy's bed and thought up ridiculous dreams.

The great Phil Brandish held Betsy's coat, took her slipper bag. She kissed her father and mother. Then they were out in the icy night, walking along sidewalks walled by snow, his hand protectively beneath her arm, going to the dance.

Talking was easier than Betsy had thought it would be. He told her how sorry he was that his auto was put up. He explained what happened to autos in cold weather. Betsy, looking up, mentioned Uncle Rudy's Steamer.

"Steamer!" He gave a disparaging snort. His car was a Buick, he said, and he wouldn't have anything else. He talked on, comparing Steamers and Buicks in technical detail. No one could have comprehended less of this than Betsy but at least she knew well that when a man talks it is a woman's part to listen. She listened, starry-eyed.

"The Buick must be ever so much better!"

He tightened his grasp on her arm.

"In the spring, maybe we'll go for a whirl."

That brought them to Schiller Hall and the three flights of stairs. At the top Betsy left him and went into the dressing room. It was warm, crowded, smelling of mingled scents. Junior girls like Carney had been to dances before, and so had Winona since Pin was a senior, but most of the sophomore girls shared Betsy's palpitating excitement.

Betsy changed into her dancing slippers; she rubbed a chamois skin over her nose. The mirror was a blur of faces in which she recognized her own shining eyes. Out in the ballroom a violin was being tuned. She went to the door to peek out over the glistening empty floor. There were knots of boys talking here and there.

At all high school dances music was provided by a violin and Mamie Dodd's piano. Mamie was a senior but she never danced at high school parties. She earned money playing the piano for them. No one, not even Julia, could play dance music as Mamie Dodd could. She was up on the platform now, twirling the piano stool to conform to her square shortness, smiling and winking at her friends.

On either side of the ballroom door Tacy and Alice were handing out programs. Tacy hurried over.

"You look lovely."

"So do you."

"Are you scared?"

"Petrified."

"If nobody dances with us, we'll hide in the dressing room together."

"Play 'buzz,'" Betsy said.

Alice called Tacy back to her duties and Betsy took a deep breath. She strolled through the door.

Phil came to her immediately. Taking her program he said, "How many may I have?"

"I believe," said Betsy, "three is the usual thing."

"I want four."

She smiled, and he wrote his name four times.

Other boys pressed in upon them. Pin with senior confidence asked for a schottische . . . they were hard to do. Tony, with typical Tony bravado, asked for nothing but wrote his name down for a two-step and a waltz.

"I brought that curling iron . . ." he whispered.

Cab and Dennie had been watching. They nerved themselves visibly, came up and took her program. The other boys in the Crowd came, and Julia's late lamented Hugh, and Stan. In no time at all her program was full, even the four extras at the end. In fact she had to divide one extra between Al and Julia's Harry who arrived late, of course, because of Julia.

Betsy and Phil went to speak to the chaperones, Miss Clarke and Mr. Gaston. Miss Clarke beamed while Mr. Gaston looked sardonic. Betsy gave him her cool, superior smile.

Then Mamie Dodd brought her hands down on the keys in warning chords. The violinist following, she swung into a waltz. Betsy in Phil's assured arms swung out on the polished floor.

The waltz was one they sang around the piano:

"Waltz me around again, Willy,
Around, around, around."

Phil waltzed her around, and around, and around. He was an easy dancer; not inspired, as Tony was. Dancing was one of Betsy's few accomplishments. She loved it, down to her feather-light toes. She even breathed in time to the music and lifted a radiant face.

All too soon the waltz ended and Cab came up for his two-step. He was annoyed by Betsy's faraway look. But they had fun two-stepping . . . just as they did it in the Ray front parlor.

Pin came up for his schottische.

"First the heel and then the toe . . ."

Away they went, Pin's long legs quick and deft.

Next she danced with Phil again, and the words of the song caused smiling faces to turn in their direction.

"Come away with me, Lucille,
In my merry Oldsmobile . . ."

"Only it isn't an Oldsmobile," he murmured in her ear.

She went from Phil to Dennie, to Tony. Dancing with Tony was cloudless joy as always. She smiled beatifically at Tacy . . . who also seemed to be enjoying herself . . . at Julia, who was dancing with Harry. But Julia looked rapt and uplifted.

"That's the way *I* ought to look," thought Betsy, and remembered her resolution not to smile so much. She quickly assumed a wistful expression. But it didn't last, for next on the program came the circle two-step.

When this dance was under way, the violinist called out to make a circle. The company joined hands and circled gaily around the big room until he called again, "Grand right and left." Then you did the grand right and left until he shouted, "Everybody two-step," and you two-stepped with whomever you found yourself facing, until he cried, "Everybody circle," again.

It was glorious fun. Betsy met Pin; she met Cab; she met Tony.

"Well, look who's here!" "Of all the luck!" "Where did *you* drop from!" Those were the proper things to say.

Blissfully two-stepping, Betsy glanced toward the doorway and saw a familiar blond head. Joe Willard was leaning against the door jamb, hands in pockets. He was smiling, a somewhat superior smile, Betsy thought.

She waved, and he waved back, and she concentrated on her dancing, thinking that if he noticed her admirable performance he would ask for a dance. Of course, her program was full. But it would be a satisfaction to have him know it. And she might, she just might, split another extra. But when she looked toward the doorway again, he was gone.

The ninth waltz was her third dance with Phil. He walked toward her eagerly. He really liked her, Betsy realized, and not just as Cab and Tony did. He looked actually . . . infatuated.

"I've been talking with Mamie Dodd," he said. "I've made some special arrangements . . ."

"What," Betsy wondered, "did he mean by that?"

She soon discovered. Mamie smiled and her fingers, roving up and down the keys, seemed to say, "You're going to like this one." Then piano and violin together began famous and now familiar strains:

> *"Tho I say not,*
> *What I may not,*
> *Let you hear . . ."*

It was "The Merry Widow Waltz."

Betsy looked up at Phil and smiled. He smiled back, but neither of them spoke. The waltz rocked through the artless opening phrases. They whirled in happy harmony.

Then the swing grew longer, the rhythm stronger. The words sang dreamily in Betsy's head.

> *"Every touch of fingers,*
> *Tells me what I know*
> *Says for you,*
> *It's true, it's true,*
> *I love you so . . ."*

Betsy was certainly not in love with Phil Brandish. She was well aware of the fact. Yet the words seemed sweetly appropriate. The melody wove in and out in dulcet sadness and their feet followed in glad obedience.

The melody changed. Mamie's fingers rippled as Uncle Rudy's fingers had.

> *"And to the music's chime,*
> *My heart is beating time . . ."*

"Exactly," thought Betsy, swaying.

A deep voice spoke in her ear. "Wasn't it clever of me to ask her to play it?"

"Oh, yes!"

"She might have played it for the thirteenth waltz, the one you'll be dancing with that Markham guy."

He had noticed that Tony took two dances! He was jealous! This was the glittering mountain peak of the evening.

Talking breathlessly during the next intermission

Betsy began to tell about Uncle Rudy. He interrupted.

"The one who owns the Steamer?"

"Yes."

"That's a bum car!" He scowled. He seemed to be jealous of Uncle Rudy, too. Oh, beautiful! Beautiful!

Another two-step, another schottische, Tony's waltz, another two-step, and then Mamie Dodd, still smiling but looking a little weary, began the significant bars of "Home Sweet Home."

Phil found Betsy, as boys everywhere were seeking the girls who had brought them to the party. Everybody sang now as they waltzed. Then the girls broke away from their partners and rushed for the dressing room.

"Wasn't it fun?" "Wasn't it divine?" "We're going to Heinz's; are you?"

Out of the babble of voices, and down three steps of stairs! Phil was holding Betsy's arm. They waited there for Julia and Harry, and when they had joined forces Phil asked casually: "How about the Moorish Café?"

Betsy's glance toward Julia was rapturous. Of course they could not go. But to have been asked!

"It's really more fun," said Julia, "to go with the Crowd."

It was fun at Heinz's. All their friends were there consuming banana splits and Deep Valley Specials and Merry Widow Sundaes. Merry Widow Sundaes were the rage. To be sure Phil did not mix well with the Crowd. He took a table for two and devoted himself entirely to Betsy. But that was all right. It was flattering. She hoped Irma noticed it.

Going home they walked slowly up the Plum Street hill. The night was icily cold under icy stars. And just as Julia had warned her he might, he tried to act spoony. She put her hand into her coat pocket for warmth, and his hand followed.

Betsy wondered what to say. She wondered with an intense concentration that was almost prayer. She didn't want to sound priggish; she didn't want to make him mad. But she had to put a stop to this . . . quickly!

In the bottom of her pocket she felt something soft and silky and pulled it out, upsetting his hand.

"Here's what you're looking for. Something to remember me by."

"I don't need anything to remember you by." He took her hand again. "I'm not going to forget you, and I'm not going to let you forget me."

She answered quickly and, for the first and only time that evening, she sounded like Betsy and not Betsye.

"You might as well know," she said with desperate honesty. "I don't hold hands. I just don't hold hands."

He laughed, and let go.

"What were you going to give me?"

"This."

They stopped beneath a street lamp and he scrutinized the silken scrap.

"Why, it's a piece of your daisy dress!" He put it to his nose. "It smells like you too." He reached inside his overcoat and drew out his purse, opened it, and put the scrap in.

"But it's not," he said, "to remember you by. My only trouble will be to forget you."

They climbed the hill dreamily and behind them Julia and Harry were climbing it dreamily, too.

18

Philip the Great

JULIA ALWAYS SLEPT LATE after dances and Mrs. Ray thoroughly approved. Mr. Ray, having country ways, had objected at first. But Mrs. Ray had counted out for him the hours of sleep a growing girl requires, she had stressed Julia's delicacy and had otherwise talked him down. Now it was taken for granted that although on other mornings the girls must appear for breakfast, fully dressed, on the mornings after late parties they might sleep.

Betsy, therefore, would have been privileged to sleep late the morning after the Leap Year Dance; but she didn't. She was awake very early. While the sky was still leaden she heard through the open slot in her storm window the liquid whistle of a bird; a spring bird, she felt sure. It was amazing how that clear, cool whistle, although it came across a snowy world, brought the whole feeling of spring into her heart.

She could see the snow melting and rushing down the gutters where Margaret and her friends would sail boats. She could see pasque flowers—wind flowers, the children called them—on the soggy green hills, and marigolds goldening the slough. She could see buds swelling, feel the warmth of the sun. It was wonderful to have spring come on and be crazy about someone and have someone crazy about her.

If he really were! Perhaps he wasn't? Perhaps he treated all his girls the way he had treated her? Unable to stay in bed with that awful thought gnawing Betsy jumped up. She dressed swiftly and was out of the house before anyone was stirring, except Anna.

"I'm going up to Tacy's," she told Anna. "I'll have breakfast up there."

Climbing toward Hill Street she walked rapidly, her hands thrust into the pockets of her coat. There was a soft south wind. Early as it was, with a copper fish left over from sunrise still hanging in the east, the snow was beginning to melt. She heard another spring bird call and walked faster. She had to talk with Tacy.

The Kellys, surprised but delighted, made room for her at their big table. Although she had thought she couldn't possibly eat breakfast and had told Anna she was eating at the Kellys' only to avoid dispute she found herself eating with a hearty appetite. She and Tacy talked a great deal, too, happily describing the dance. Mrs. Kelly excused Tacy from the dishes, and Betsy and Tacy went for a walk.

Now Betsy poured out her heart. She told Tacy everything Phil had said and done, even about the scrap of pink silk. She confided more than was her wont, even to Tacy, because she had to have her tormenting fears assuaged.

"It can't be that he's really crazy about me! Not Phil Brandish!"

"I don't see why not. Certainly he is!"

"I think he is . . . and yet . . . How could he be?"

"How could he help but be?"

"I don't see how I can go to school Monday," said Betsy. "I'm so afraid he'll just look at me casually, as though I were any girl. And yet I can't bear not to go. I'd die if I had a sore throat or something and had to stay at home."

"Don't get your feet wet in this slush then," said Tacy, looking down anxiously. But even in the throes of her love affair Betsy had remembered to wear her overshoes, which made them both laugh.

Even harder than waiting for Monday was doing homework. There was actually homework. No teacher was more sympathetic to young love than was Miss Clarke and yet she had inadvertently assigned for this particular weekend an outline of the French Revolution. The only advantage to this blunder was that it gave Betsy an excuse to refuse to see Tony, Dennie, and Cab. She didn't enjoy their company today; they had no conception of her feelings.

"I still can't see why you asked that big stiff Brandish to the party," Cab said frankly.

"Betsy's going to be a heart-smasher like sister!" Tony teased.

Invoking the French Revolution, Betsy sent them off home. But it would take more than this remote upheaval to keep them away on Sunday night.

"After all, Betsy, we don't come here just to see you," said Tony. "We like your father, too, you know."

"His sandwiches, you mean. I certainly *do* know!" Betsy thought.

On Sunday night there was the usual Crowd around. Betsy kept listening for the telephone. When

Phil didn't call, she was almost sure it meant that she wasn't important to him. And yet in her heart she felt sure that she was.

Torn by these confused and contradictory thoughts she was up early on Monday. She dressed with the greatest care, wearing a crisp openwork waist over a pale green under-waist, and her most becoming ten-gored skirt. Her cheeks were so red that her father asked her at breakfast whether she had a fever. He actually looked down her throat. But there were no white spots. She was allowed to go to school.

As soon as she saw Phil she knew that everything was all right. She sensed again that—incomprehensible, astounding as it was—he felt about her as Julia's beaus felt about Julia. She even felt sure that he, too, had been wracked with doubts and fears over Saturday and Sunday. The first glances from both of them were questioning, urgent. They were answered by smiles; and relief poured over Betsy like honey.

During the fifth period he wrote her a note. "You haven't told me what that dream was." This was his first reference to the dream.

Betsy wrote back, "I didn't have a chance over Sunday."

He smiled and scribbled rapidly, "May I see you tonight?"

Fearfully Betsy answered, "It's a school night."

Again he wrote rapidly. "May I walk home from school with you, then?"

Betsy answered yes.

Acting as intermediary between them was that same nice, freckle-faced Hazel Smith who was treasurer of the class. She sat at a strategic point between Betsy's aisle and Phil's. After passing Phil's last note to Betsy, she wrote one herself.

"That Leap Year Dance was a good idea. Yes? No? Yes?"

Betsy smiled broadly and answered, "Very!!!"

Phil walked home from school with her and just to be contrary she didn't ask him in. They stood on the steps talking until it grew so late that the melted snow began to freeze in the late afternoon chill. Inside the house Julia was singing from *La Boheme*, that song in which Mimi, the little seamstress, whose name was Lucia, tells how the flowers she embroidered transported her out into flowery meadows. Betsy felt transported now into a fragrant flowery world.

Tony arrived, said "hello," and went inside. Cab and Dennie arrived and walked past with jeering remarks, trying to act as though they hadn't been headed for the Ray house. When Betsy went in, absent and dreamy, her mother reproved her gently.

"I really would prefer, Betsy, to have you ask your friends inside. Phil must have felt as though he wasn't welcome, and of course, he is very welcome. All your friends are."

"How do you like him, Mamma?" Betsy asked eagerly.

"He has beautiful manners."

"Hasn't he?" Betsy answered rapturously. She hugged her mother and floated upstairs.

After that he walked home from school with her every day and on Friday night he took her to the Majestic. Saturday night Betsy took him to a party at Irma's. Sunday night he came for lunch and after that it was Phil, Phil, Phil all the time around the Ray house, just as it was Harry, Harry, Harry.

Phil separated her from the Crowd. It was hard to say just why. Everyone was polite to him; he was polite to everyone else. Perhaps it was because Betsy acted differently when he was around. Cab said she put on airs, acted la de da. Certainly she didn't sing so wholeheartedly around the piano and when the rugs were rolled up she danced mostly with Phil.

Phil was flatteringly inclined to be jealous. One afternoon she went for a walk with Tacy on the hills. They picked pasque flowers, found skunk cabbage in the woods, saw a chipmunk pale from its winter hibernation. Betsy talked about Phil all the time but, of course, Phil didn't know that. He was annoyed with her for having gone.

And he didn't like her correspondence with Herbert. Ever since the Humphreys moved away, Herbert and Betsy had corresponded ardently. They still called each other C F, meaning Confidential Friend, and Herbert told Betsy all about his affairs of the heart. Of course Phil didn't know that either, and when he and Betsy, coming in from school, found these thick missives waiting, he was plainly put out.

But more, much more than Tacy or the far-removed Herbert, he resented Cab and Tony. Gradually the boys in the Crowd almost stopped dropping in.

Not but what their presence wasn't often felt! Sometimes when Betsy and Phil sat by the fire there were mock romantic serenades under the window. Once they made fudge and put it out to cool. When they went to bring it in, it was gone, and Betsy saw footsteps in the snow.

Those long fireside conversations and all their conversations everywhere dealt with two subjects: Phil and his car.

Betsy dug out of her memory something Julia had said last year. "That reforming line is one of the oldest in the world, and one of the best." Betsy started reforming Phil. He smoked. He smoked a pipe. He was the only boy in Betsy's circle who smoked, except behind the barn. It was a wonderful evening when Phil gave his pipe to Betsy. She hung it on a ribbon over her dressing table.

The second and even more successful topic was the auto. He was counting the moments until he could get it out of storage. Melting snow meant pasque flowers to Betsy. But to Phil it brought nearer the joyful moment when he could bring out his car. He described it to Betsy in the most technical detail, and she paid devout attention.

The warm weather continued and one never to be forgotten day he took the Buick out of storage. He could hardly wait to bring it, polished so you could see your face in its red sides, brass work gleaming, up to the Rays' front door. It was the proudest moment of the spring when Betsy walked down the steps and was helped by Phil into the high front seat.

He went around in front to crank it. All the neighborhood children looked on. After considerable rushing from the crank to the seat to work the throttle he climbed in beside her. They started off, and the wind created by the rapid motion blew her hat so that she had to cling to it with both excited hands.

"I must buy myself an automobile veil," she said. "That is," she added with a sidelong glance, "if I'm going to have very many of these wonderful rides."

"Don't buy it," Phil said, and her heart stood still in dismay. But it soared again when he continued, "I've been wanting to bring you a present. You won't let me bring candy, now it's Lent. What about an automobile veil?"

"Mamma wouldn't let me accept it," Betsy laughed. "She's strict about things like that. It's sweet of you to think of it, though." ("I'll buy myself one tomorrow, a green one," she thought.)

The ride was very bumpy for the roads were still frozen into great deep ruts, and more than once Phil had to get out and do things with wrenches and hammers. But when they were riding they went at a thrilling twenty miles an hour. She half closed her eyes and a blurred enchanted world rushed past. Now and then Phil squeezed a rubber bulb. The deep horn sounded.

"Get out of the way! We're coming! Phil and Betsy!"

They did not ride again for a while. The unseasonably warm spell ended. Flakes as big as pieces of paper whirled in the wind; and snow dressed the world in white once more.

But March could not be obnoxious enough to trouble Betsy this year.

This was entirely different from being in love with Tony. Tony hadn't been in love with her. That affair had consisted mainly of her own wistful yearnings. Phil Brandish—it was still unbelievable—felt now as she had felt then. The ecstatic feeling was mutual, or almost so. Deep inside, Betsy admitted that there was something lacking in her own emotions.

But Phil was big and handsome; he was rich and he was a junior. He was very exciting.

An almost equally great excitement came from her new prestige. The girls in the Crowd were respectful about this affair. And there was no need now for Betsy to worry about who would take her to anything. Phil asked her the moment any sort of party or entertainment was rumored.

The sophomore boys, returning the Leap Year compliment, gave another dance in Schiller Hall. Betsy was almost the first girl invited. And the second dance was almost as wonderful as the first one. Again Phil asked Mamie Dodd to play "The Merry Widow Waltz."

It was understood now that they would be together on Friday nights and Saturday nights, and that he would come to Sunday night lunch, and although they saw each other so often they exchanged notes every day in school via Hazel Smith at the fifth period.

Betsy slaved over these notes which were all signed significantly, "Betsye." She wrote and rewrote them when she should have been doing geometry, and copied them carefully on pale green stationery, heavy with the Jockey Club scent. Phil's notes were mere untidy scribbles; he didn't like to write. But the sight of his handwriting on a paper torn from a notebook made Betsy's heart palpitate. She kept these notes in her handkerchief box.

Betsy slaved over her notes, her hair, her clothes, her fingernails. Although Phil was so enchanted by her, she had a feeling that it couldn't last. She didn't dare just be herself. The common ordinary Betsy that Cab and Dennie and Tony all liked would not, she felt, be sufficient for Phil Brandish. She couldn't imagine him liking her with her hair uncurled or when she was having a riotously good time.

In high school they had formed a Girls Debating Club. Carney was excited about it and anxious for Betsy to join. But Betsy thought debating sounded intellectual, unfeminine. She thought Phil wouldn't like it. She said no.

Miss Clarke asked her and Tacy to sing the Cat Duet at Rhetoricals, as they had sung it every year since they were in sixth grade. Betsy couldn't imagine singing the Cat Duet in front of Phil. She and Tacy always clowned through the Cat Duet. Each one tried to make her yowls worse than the other one's yowls. She simply couldn't do it. Again she said no.

When in mid-March Miss Clarke asked her to be the sophomore representative in the Essay Contest, Betsy had a feeling of being actually torn. The Essay Contest was like debating. It wouldn't seem important to Phil. Her being chosen would not raise her in his estimation. It might even lower her. And it would take time! For if she went into the Essay Contest this year she was resolved to do a good job. It would mean hours spent in the library, away from Phil, and in those hours some other girl might very well take him away from her. Irma, for example. Betsy had a deep-down fear of Irma.

And yet there was something in her stubborn nature which would not let her turn the Essay Contest down.

"What is the subject this year?" she asked.

"James J. Hill and the Great Northern Railroad," Miss Clarke replied.

"James J. Hill and the Great Northern Railroad!" Could anything be more remote from spring and the red auto?

"Do you happen to know . . . who the Philomathians have chosen? I suppose it's Joe."

"Yes. And they seem very confident about the sophomore points. But I am equally confident, if you will represent the Zetamathians, Betsy."

"Of course I will," Betsy replied quickly.

Everyone was surprised to hear that she was going out for the Essay Contest. At home they were surprised.

"I'd rather you didn't do it, Betsy, unless you can do it justice," her father said.

The Crowd was surprised.

"What will Phil do?" "Who's going to console Phil?" "Look out for Irma!"

Phil was surprised.

"What do you want to do that for?" he grumbled. "It's just getting to be good autoing weather."

"I'll take books on James J. Hill along, read them while you patch the tires," she said. But Phil didn't think that was funny.

"I don't have to patch tires as much as you think," he answered sulkily.

Joe Willard was surprised. He actually stopped to speak to her on the way out of class. She was wearing the usual green bow at her collar, a green pin in her pompadour, and was scented with Jockey Club perfume.

He looked mischievous, his blue eyes were shining.

"I hear," he said, "that we're competing again. I didn't know you knew anything about railroads. I thought you specialized on autos."

Betsy blushed.

Troubled, she sought out Julia, but before she managed to make her worries known Julia began confidences of her own. Surprisingly enough they didn't deal with Harry's love, nor her father's objections, nor the rapidly impending proposal. They didn't deal with Harry at all. It came to Betsy suddenly that Julia hadn't been talking about Harry quite so much lately.

She was obsessed with a longing to go to St. Paul for grand opera.

"It's perfectly fantastic, I know," she said, low-voiced. "There isn't a chance in the world."

"Why not?"

"Too expensive! I couldn't go alone. There'd be railroad fare and hotel bills, besides the opera tickets for both Mamma and me." It was indeed a daring wish. Deep Valley's rich and great went to the Twin Cities for shopping, concerts and plays. But the Rays were neither rich nor great. Mr. Ray's shoe store didn't yield an income of a size to support grand opera. Besides, Betsy had recently had her expensive trip.

"Does Papa know you want to go?" asked Betsy.

"No, and even Mamma doesn't realize that I've thought of it seriously. It would never even enter Papa's head to send me. But, oh, how I'm longing to go!"

She took out the folder Mrs. Poppy had given her. Enrico Caruso was there in a clown suit, Geraldine Farrar in a ruffled dress and a poke bonnet as Mimi in *La Boheme*.

"'*Mi chiamano Mimi*,'" hummed Julia gazing at her.

"Don't feel badly," Betsy said, deciding to postpone her confidences. "They aren't coming until the end of April. Lots of things can happen in a month." This proved to be absolutely true.

19
April Weather

LOTS OF THINGS CAN HAPPEN in a month, especially if the month is April. Never, it seemed to Betsy, had April been so full of moods. She was especially conscious of them because of Phil who followed Nature's mutations as a fish hawk follows the ripples in a blue Minnesota lake. This was because of the auto, of course. He wanted the weather to settle and the roads to dry so that the Buick could come out and stay out.

But it rained and it snowed. The sun emerged and the snow melted, but it promptly rained and snowed again, sometimes with hail for good measure. Each time, however, there was a little progress. The bushes greened over; the buds on the maples burst open; and Margaret came down from the hills with small tight bouquets of blood-roots and Dutchman's breeches and pinkish lavender hepaticas.

Slowly the world was getting dressed for spring, and so were the girls in the Crowd. Talk was all of new suits and hats, especially hats. The Merry Widow hat had made its appearance this spring. It was as devastating as the Waltz.

Merry Widow hats were sailors, very wide, the wider the better.

"In New York," Julia said, "ladies get stuck in the trolley car doors."

Miss Mix was at the Ray house making Easter out-fits and her visit was as confusing as the weather. The house was filled with the hum of the sewing machine. There were fittings and conferences, pins in the mouth, bright scraps and snarls of thread, touchy tempers and company meals. Everyone was heartily glad to see her go although she left lovely things behind.

For Betsy it was a suit, her first suit, blue serge piped with green. Her Merry Widow hat was blue, extravagantly wide, trimmed with green foliage and ribbon. Betsy doted on that outfit. Of course, she was saving it for Easter and this gave her an interest in the weather almost as acute as Phil's. What if Easter should be rainy? A rainy day, always a minor tragedy because it straightened out her curls, would be a major tragedy this year, when she had her first suit and a Merry Widow hat.

She needed to look pretty for Phil's moods were Aprilish, too; and April at its worst, right now. Betsy was starting work on the Essay Contest, and he didn't like it at all. She had bought a new notebook and written on the first page, "James J. Hill and the Great Northern Railroad." Armed with that, and plenty of sharp pencils, she had set off for the library. She would have been exhilarated if it weren't for Phil.

Books dealing with the assigned subject did not circulate. Miss Sparrow had assembled them on a special shelf in back of the stalls, near a table set apart for the contestants. There were eight of these . . . two freshmen, two sophomores, two juniors, and two seniors. One of each pair was a Philomathian, the other a Zetamathian. The essays were graded on the point system, and the society whose team piled up the most points won.

Sometimes the table was almost empty; sometimes all eight were working busily at once. There was a good feeling of respect at that table, and a pleasant mingling of camaraderie and rivalry. Betsy enjoyed her sojourns there in spite of her nagging worry.

Joe Willard came only in the late afternoon or evening. He was friendlier to Betsy now. He looked up and smiled from under his thick light brows when she came in and when she left. But he didn't, this year, ask to walk home with her.

"And just as well," Betsy thought, although she admitted that she would have been pleased. Phil wouldn't have been pleased. He was more and more inclined to be jealous and Betsy ceased to find it flattering.

The approach of Easter, as usual, brought Tom home. He was Betsy's oldest friend among the boys. Not knowing how Phil had changed the atmosphere of the Ray house, Tom came hurrying up the day of his arrival.

"Grandma's making sour cream cake," he said. "The kind with cinnamon in it, and she said I could bring you back to supper."

"Wonderful!" Betsy cried. "Maybe she'll tell us about the Indian massacre again."

"She's sure to," Tom replied.

She did, and Betsy had a very enjoyable evening. But when she told Phil about it next day he began to act stiff and unnatural. At first Betsy could not make out what was wrong. It was too, too ridiculous to be jealous of Tom. Then she remembered that he and Tom did not like one another because of Cox. Something, she realized, would have to be done about that.

"You and Tom will just have to be friends," she said with what she hoped was appealing frankness. "Our families get together, you know. He brings his violin to play with Julia. Why, during his vacations, he almost lives at our house."

"Just don't expect me to come when he's here," Phil relied.

"But Phil, you wouldn't be coming at all."

"All right, I won't be coming at all."

Betsy was appalled. She couldn't possibly tell Tom to stay away. The whole family would protest. And as for having Phil stay away . . . why, Easter was almost here. What would be the fun of a new suit and a Merry Widow hat if she had a quarrel with Phil?

They were coming, however, perilously near to a quarrel. He left, saying coldly that she might let him know whether or not he would have to run into Slade. Betsy didn't telephone him and he didn't telephone her. The next day, the last before Easter vacation, the fifth period came and went without a note. Hazel Smith turned around in her seat. She raised her eyebrows at Betsy and gesticulated wildly. Betsy tried to smile but the result was feeble. Another evening passed and Phil did not 'phone. She cried herself to sleep.

Betsy was stubborn, but she wasn't so stubborn that she wouldn't have patched up the quarrel if she could have seen a way to do it. She really couldn't see one. It was absurd for Phil to expect her to bar Tom from the house.

"Tom's of no romantic interest to me!" she cried in her thoughts. "Never has been! Never will be!" It was all too utterly silly.

But silly or not she came down stairs Saturday morning with red eyes.

The family had noticed, of course, that Phil hadn't 'phoned or come to the house for several days. Everybody tactfully refrained from mentioning him.

Mrs. Ray and Julia went downtown to shop for accessories for the new Easter suits . . . gloves, jabots, and so on. Anna was baking a cake, and Betsy, remembering all the precepts about doing something kind for someone else when you're feeling down in the mouth, offered to help Margaret dye Easter eggs.

They both put on kitchen aprons, and Betsy twisted her hair in a tight knot out of the way. Unhappy as she was, she could not help enjoying the business of dyeing eggs. She had always loved it. The rich glowing colors brought back a procession of happy childhood Easters. She was telling Margaret gaily about how she and Tacy used to save their Easter dyes and dye sand and have sand stores, when the front door bell rang.

Anna was folding in egg whites. Margaret's hands were dripping purple. Betsy pushed back a wisp of hair and rushed through the music room to answer the door herself. On the porch stood Phil looking his handsomest and most immaculate, and he was not alone. Beside him was a slight graceful girl, beautifully and expensively dressed in a gray suit with a big fluffy fur and a Merry Widow hat so wide that it made the one Betsy cherished in a box upstairs look positively narrow.

She was small where Phil was large, but they had the same heavily fringed, yellow-brown eyes, the same olive skin, the same somewhat sullen faces. Betsy almost collapsed in a heap, for she knew that this was Phil's twin sister, Phyllis.

Betsy had heard that when you are drowning one moment may seem like a lifetime. That was the kind of a moment she experienced now. Beyond Philip the Great, and his even greater sister, she saw the red auto and beyond that the greening hill with the German Catholic College on the top. Behind her she heard Margaret happily calling, "Betsy, come and see! It's the most bee-utiful purple!"

There was another aspect of the moment which suggested drowning, too. Betsy's thoughts went so deeply into the gray waters of the past. She was like a diver going down for a pearl and she found it . . . the almost forgotten incident which could help her.

She remembered a distant afternoon back in the Hill Street house when Mrs. Ray was housecleaning and the minister's wife had come to call. Her mother had ignored the fact that she was in the midst of washing windows. She had not mentioned the towel around her head nor the wildly disordered parlor. She had calmly dried her hands and sat down to chat. When her mother referred to the housecleaning, at last, she had merely said that the hard work made her long for a good cup of coffee. She had made coffee and the two of them had drunk it, with a cookie for Betsy. When Betsy dredged up this memory now, she smiled and put out her hand.

"How nice of you, Phil," she said, "to bring your sister to see me!" And she asked them into the parlor.

Betsy perspired but she tried to hew to her mother's line.

"Margaret and I are dyeing Easter eggs. Did you ever do that? Margaret, dear, bring in the eggs. . . . Aren't they beauties?"

Phyllis Brandish did not help her as the minister's wife had helped her mother. Gracious but chilly, Phyllis managed to give the impression that she thought Easter eggs were silly, that she had certainly never dyed them even as a child (if, indeed, she had ever been a child, which Betsy doubted).

While Margaret displayed the eggs Betsy excused herself, went into the kitchen, washed her hands and took off the stained apron. That was the best she could do. The miserable call ended somehow, just as Old Mag drew up before the house and her mother and Julia came in triumphantly laden with small packages. They helped immeasurably in covering the farewells, but when the callers were gone Betsy both laughed and cried.

"If he's worth a fig, he'll like you just as well this way," Julia comforted her.

"You look cute!" her mother said.

Betsy knew better. She went upstairs finally and blew her nose and combed her hair. She wished Cab and Tony had not stopped dropping in. Their presence would have been cheering now. Tom came, but aware of the great concession Phil had made in ending their quarrel by bringing his sister to call, Betsy didn't have the heart to be very nice to Tom. In fact, she wasn't nice at all, which hurt his feelings and didn't help anyone.

Her mother and Julia went into action. Families can be wonderful sometimes.

"Betsy," said her mother, "we're having an extra good lunch tomorrow night because of its being Easter. Don't you want to ask Phil to bring his sister?"

Betsy nerved herself to telephone him, and somewhat to her surprise he accepted the invitation promptly. He even seemed pleased to receive it.

That brought a little of the glory back to the new suit, the Merry Widow hat, and Easter day. In gratitude, next morning, Betsy went to early church. She hadn't gone for a long time, and it was good to be there.

> *"Lift up your hearts."*
> *"We lift them unto the Lord."*

Betsy loved those sentences always, but especially today in a church white and fragrant with lilies.

She went to church again at eleven o'clock, to sing in the choir. Julia sang a solo.

After dinner Phil drove up in the auto and took Betsy for a ride. Neither of them mentioned the quarrel and they were very happy. He said the new suit was spiffy, and the Merry Widow hat a dream. He took pictures of her with his big expensive camera. They drove up to see Tacy, and over to see Irma, and down to see Carney, and around to the rest of the Crowd.

"Time now to go over and pick up Sis," he said, and they turned toward the slough.

The snow was gone except for absurd patches in

shady hollows. The sun was so warm that even the new suit felt heavy. Robins were everywhere, and in the slough, red winged blackbirds swung from the cat tails. Betsy exclaimed over them, and he said absently, "Um . . . pretty; aren't they? Listen to that motor! Did you ever hear anything sweeter?"

The Brandish mansion had a porte-cochere at the side like Grosspapa Muller's house in Milwaukee. Betsy was pleased to be grandly familiar with porte-cocheres.

Phil took her in to meet his grandmother who had bright spots of rouge on her cheeks. Betsy had liked rouge on Aunt Dolly, but she didn't care for it on this small, over-dressed, smilingly tight-lipped old lady. She liked old Mr. Brandish, though. He was a big, warm, alive sort of man with a curly gray beard. He could tell stories, Betsy imagined, to match Grandma Slade's.

"Phil is going to bring you over to dinner soon," his grandmother said, as the young people departed.

Phyllis, Betsy thought, was just like her grandmother. Betsy seldom had trouble making friends with people, especially with other girls, but she could not feel close to Phil's sister. They spoke of Browner, of Tib, of Milwaukee, but they seemed to speak in a vacuum.

"It's not that way with Phil and me," Betsy

thought, puzzled, for they were, she realized, equally uncongenial. Between them, however, paucity of interests did not matter.

Julia got on with Phyllis better than Betsy did. Phyllis seemed taken with Julia. Yet Julia was not very nice to her. In fact, she came as close to snubbing as you could come and not do it.

Phyllis was interested in Julia's music and while Harry watched Mr. Ray make sandwiches and Phil talked with Mrs. Ray, Phyllis and Julia and Betsy looked over opera scores.

"I suppose you'll be going up to the Twin Cities for opera," Phyllis said.

Betsy knew what a sore spot that put a finger on, but Julia gave no sign.

"I'd be glad if I could," she answered casually. "Farrar will be singing in *Boheme*."

"I'm crazy about Farrar."

"Oh, have you heard her?"

"Yes. Many times." Phyllis circled the group with a daring smile. "They say that she and the German Crown Prince have been having quite an affair."

"I don't believe it, and I don't think it's important," Julia answered. That was one of the times when she came near to snubbing. "Just what roles have you heard?" she asked superciliously.

The sandwiches were never better and the cake was

superb. They had a very pleasant time. To be sure, Phil was not at his best in gatherings like this one. He always seemed a little ill at ease with the family as he did with the Crowd.

But he wasn't ill at ease with Betsy. The quarrel was over and things were as nice or nicer between them than they had been before.

20

Julia Sees the Great World

JULIA WAS SINGING, *"Ni-po-tu-la-he."* When she had sung it a number of times with a look of critical attention, she opened her copy of *La Boheme* and began Mimi's song about being called Mimi although her name was Lucia.

"'Mi chiamano Mimi,'" she sang in her own version of Italian. She greatly preferred the Italian text to the English translation.

"How do you think my voice sounds in that aria?" she asked Betsy, breaking off.

"Fine!" said Betsy.

"I wish I could hear Farrar sing it. Then I'd know what I do wrong."

"You don't do anything wrong," Betsy replied.

Julia sighed and closed the book. She sat still on the piano stool, her hands in her lap.

"They're coming next week, and they're going, and not one soul who will hear them needs to hear them so much as I do."

"You mean the grand opera?"

Julia nodded in profound dejection. Before Betsy could find a word of comfort, Anna poked her head in from the kitchen.

"Your pa hasn't come in yet? I don't like to complain about such a nice gentleman, but Mr. McCloskey always came home on time the night I made cheese soufflé."

"I hear him outside now, Anna," Betsy answered.

"Strike the gong for me; will you, lovey? Then he'll hurry up his washing."

Betsy beat a brisk tattoo, and the family gathered expeditiously. It was light at supper time now, and tonight the windows were open, for the day had been unseasonably warm. The soft yet exhilarating air came into the dining room. Julia began to tease her father.

"I don't know about *your* father, but my father brought me up to be on time for meals."

"Especially," chimed in Betsy, "the nights we have cheese soufflé."

"Anna's soufflé," said Mr. Ray, "actually improves by waiting. And I was busy tonight, Anna. Had to pick something up."

"A birthday present for Betsy?"

"When is Betsy's birthday?"

"You know perfectly well. It's next Thursday."

"By George!" said Mr. Ray. "I'd forgotten. That's bad." He looked worried. "Anna, do you know how to make a cake?"

"Do I know how to . . . what?" Anna stared.

"Make cake?"

"Stars in the sky!" she said. "The man's taken leave of his senses."

"I'm only thinking about a birthday cake for Betsy," said Mr. Ray in an injured tone.

"Bob," said Mrs. Ray. "What are you driving at? Anna makes the best cakes in the world, and for that matter there's nothing wrong with mine."

"But you won't be here."

"I won't be here on Betsy's birthday?" Mrs. Ray sounded amazed.

"It's going to hurry you awfully to get back," Mr. Ray answered. He reached into his inside pocket.

Sudden silence fell on the table. A song sparrow perched on a greening shrub outside gave vent to his joy in three notes and a trill which echoed through the dining room.

In a leisurely gesture Mr. Ray brought out a long envelope. He carefully extracted a pack of papers, sorted them thoughtfully on the tablecloth while Anna and the family gazed entranced. There were railroad tickets. And there were two small packs in rubber bands containing four pink tickets each. And there was that folder Mrs. Poppy had given Julia with pictures of Farrar and Caruso and information about the St. Paul grand opera season.

Julia grabbed Betsy's knee under the table.

Mr. Ray looked the folder over slowly. "Maybe, you can make it home by Thursday night. It will hurry you though."

Julia put her napkin down.

"Papa," she said in a choked voice.

"Bob!" said Mrs. Ray. "What have you done?"

Mr. Ray flipped the tickets thoughtfully.

"I'm just sending you and Julia up to St. Paul to grand opera. That is, if Betsy and Margaret can keep house and Anna knows how to bake a birthday cake."

"Papa!" cried Julia again. This time she jumped up and ran around the table to her father's chair. She pressed her cheek against his shiny dark hair.

Mr. Ray said, "Hey! Do you think I need my face washed?" for a tear was trickling down his forehead to his cheek.

Julia ran to kiss her mother. She kissed Betsy and Margaret and Anna.

"I'm going to grand opera! I'm going to grand opera!" Tears were running down her cheeks, and she didn't even seem to know it.

Mrs. Ray jumped up too to kiss Mr. Ray. And Betsy and Margaret jumped up just to jump up and down. Julia ran into the music room. She sat down at the piano and began to play *La Boheme*. She didn't sing. Suddenly the music stopped.

"Julia, you idiot! Come and finish your supper."

No answer.

"Will you come? Or shall we come and get you?"

"I'll come," said Julia, and she came back, blowing her nose and wiping her eyes. She sat down but she didn't eat any more supper. She just sat at the table, smiling, a faraway look in her eyes.

Anna brought in the dessert, but she didn't go back to the kitchen. As usual on exciting occasions she leaned against the door jamb.

"How long will they be away?" she asked.

"Five days, Anna."

"Where will we stay?" Mrs. Ray wanted to know.

"The Frederick Hotel. Reservations are all made."

"That's where Mrs. Poppy is staying," Julia cried.

"Farrar and Caruso are staying there, too."

"What?" cried Julia jumping up again. "I'm going to be under the same roof with Geraldine Farrar?"

She went into the parlor, out of sight, and sat down.

"Bob," said Mrs. Ray. "Whatever made you think of it?"

"I've got a pretty good think tank."

"You've got a wonderful think tank. But what about Betsy's birthday?"

"You leave that to Anna and Margaret and me. I remember now, I remember perfectly, Anna *can* make cake."

"Stars in the sky!" said Anna, shaking her head, and went back to the kitchen.

Mrs. Ray and Julia left on the four forty-five train. Julia was missing almost a week of school but Miss Bangeter had agreed that the trip was educational. Mr. Ray hitched up Old Mag and took the whole family to the train. Harry came, too, of course.

Mrs. Ray and Julia wore their new Easter suits and Merry Widow hats. Mrs. Ray looked excited, and Julia looked as she had looked when she was baptized, and confirmed, and when she sang. She didn't pay much attention to Harry.

Mrs. Poppy was there, large, elegant and radiant,

and Mr. and Mrs. Home Brandish, and others of Deep Valley's rich and great. They all had seats reserved in the parlor car. So had Mrs. Ray and Julia.

"You shouldn't be doing this, Bob," Mrs. Ray said. "We can't afford to be going up to Grand Opera along with all these millionaires."

"I'd like to know who will appreciate that music any more than you and Julia."

"It isn't a question of our appreciating it. It's a question of your being able to afford it."

"You leave that to me," Mr. Ray said.

Julia came up to her father.

"Papa," she said formally, "I want you to know that I'm going to get everything possible out of this trip. I do appreciate all the advantages you're giving me."

"I know you do, my dear," Mr. Ray replied.

Betsy squeezed Julia's hand. "Julia," she said, "you're going to see the Great World."

"At last!" Julia answered.

Betsy felt important in her new position as lady of the house. She sat in her mother's chair and poured the breakfast coffee. She conferred with Anna about meals and told Margaret what dresses and hair ribbons to wear. She asked Phil to dinner, that he might see her in this new dignity, and he was properly admiring.

As her birthday approached Anna suggested that she ask the Crowd to a party but Betsy thought it better not to. Phil still didn't get on any too well with the Crowd, and he was feeling grumpy anyway because Betsy was working so hard on the Essay Contest.

"I'll just have the girls come in for birthday cake in the evening," she decided. "And Tacy for supper, if that's all right."

"Lovey," said Anna. "On your sixteenth birthday, anything's all right!"

Her sixteenth birthday! It was, Betsy realized, a pretty important occasion! Her father and Margaret awakened her by squeezing a wet sponge in her face which wasn't a very dignified beginning. And Betsy chased them all over the house until she stumbled on her long night gown, which made it worse. And at breakfast she was given sixteen spanks, with one to grow on; and sixteen more, when Tacy came in. All very childish! But the day, as it wore on, grew up, quickly, just as Betsy was doing, to adult stature.

Home presents were to wait until her mother's return but when she came in from school at noon she found two packages.

One was from Tib, a pair of stockings with tiny blue flowers embroidered on them. "Very Frenchy!" Betsy thought. "They look just like Tib."

The second package was from Herbert, a Japanese

print showing a big white bird with a long beak and long legs, among some rushes. Betsy liked it . . . not just because it came from Herbert. It reminded her of the quiet bay, smelling of water lilies, and the faintly rocking boat, in which, last summer, she had started her novel.

She hurried up to her room and hung it over Uncle Keith's trunk. If she left it down stairs she would have to show it to Phil. It was more and more inconvenient, having Phil so touchy.

Before the afternoon was over, however, she forgave him everything.

He walked home from school with her but he did not mention her birthday and neither did she. She could not help wondering, though, whether he remembered it. She did not ask him in, and later Tacy came and they went up to Betsy's room where Betsy changed into a white duck skirt and a white silk waist.

"Just think," Betsy said. "I'm older than Juliet."

"Juliet who?"

"Juliet out of *Romeo and Juliet*. She had a big love affair and died before she was sixteen."

"Well, you've had the love affair," said Tacy who always said the right thing.

And with equal rightness at just that moment the doorbell rang.

The girls hurried down. A florist's boy stood on the porch with a long green cardboard box. Boxes like that had often come for Julia but never for Betsy before. Betsy and Tacy began to squeal in unison, and Betsy seized the box and unwrapped it while Tacy, Anna, and Margaret hovered near.

Inside, in a nest of glazed paper, were sixteen pink roses—sixteen perfect pink roses, surely the most beautiful roses that had bloomed since the world began.

Betsy hugged them, ignoring the thorns. She buried her face in their fragrance. She ran swiftly to telephone Phil while Anna put the roses into a tall vase.

Her father teased her about them all through the supper, and the girls when they arrived, laden with packages, exclaimed and teased too.

Irma ran out to the kitchen and got sixteen cubes of sugar and tied them by ribbons from a chandelier.

"Sweet sixteen!" someone cried.

"Sweet sixteen and never been kissed!"

"She gets pink roses, though."

It was glorious.

There was chocolate ice cream, and Anna outdid herself on the cake.

"What do you think, Mr. Ray?" she asked as she brought it in, candles gleaming, "Can I make cake or can't I? Stars in the sky! You should have heard Charley when I told him what you said."

And before Betsy blew the candles out (at one puff, with a secret wish that Phil might keep on being crazy about her forever), her mother and Julia walked in. They had come from the train in Mr. Thumbler's hack. Mr. Ray had not met them, for the ecstatic jumbled postal cards and letters which had flooded the mails ever since they reached St. Paul had not made clear just when they would return.

Both were radiant and even before Julia took off her Merry Widow hat she gave Betsy her present. The box bore the name of a St. Paul jewelry store. The girls crowded around as Betsy opened it.

"Oh, how beautiful! How lovely!" It was a gold linked bracelet, the first really fine piece Betsy ever had owned. She hung it on her wrist, pushed it up her slender arm.

She wore it over the wristband of her night gown when she sat on Julia's bed later hearing the story of the trip. Her hair was wound on Magic Wavers which always made her face look childishly round. Julia was in bed, her dark hair loose around her shining face.

"It was too unutterably wonderful," Julia said. "I was longing for you, Bettina. I could hardly stand it that you weren't there."

"It would have been over my head," Betsy said.

"Nonsense! You're much more musical than you

let on," said Julia, who had a gracious habit of investing Betsy with all the qualities she most admired.

The first opera had been *Die Walküre*.

"That was over *my* head," Julia said. "I came back to the hotel so blue. I thought, 'Can I possibly be mistaken? Can it be that I don't like opera after all?' But I know now it was because *Walküre* is so hard. It's the ultimate, Mrs. Poppy says."

"The next was *La Boheme*! I saw Geraldine Farrar come in with her candle. I heard her sing '*Mi chiamano Mimi*.' Oh, Bettina how I cried! And I knew then. *Cavalleria* and *Pagliacci* only made me surer, and so did *Aïda*, although that's pretty hard, too. Not like Wagner, of course. He's just the ultimate."

"I thought *Die* whatever-it-is was the ultimate?"

"But that's Wagner. Don't you see, darling? I'm going to send for *all* the scores, and then you'll understand."

"Tell me about seeing Farrar and Caruso around the hotel," Betsy said, reaching for some bedclothes. The room was growing cold.

"Well, I saw them. You did Caruso an injustice in your essay on Puget Sound last year. He isn't really short and fat, and he's *very* magnetic. Farrar is adorable. She was wearing a suit, just as simple as could be. And, Bettina, she does look like me!"

"Does she really?"

"Yes. Or I look like her. It might be more respectful to put it that way."

Julia paused a moment, and when the talk stopped the room was very quiet. For it was late now. Betsy's sixteenth birthday was a thing of the past.

"The trip settled one thing for me," Julia said. "I belong in the Great World. There's no doubt about that. I'm definitely going to be an opera star."

"But, Julia?" asked Betsy. "What about Harry?"

"Harry?" asked Julia vaguely. "Harry?" She sounded almost as though she were asking, "Who is Harry?"

"Oh, Harry!" she said, bringing her thoughts back from far spaces. "Harry will get along all right."

21

Dree-eee-eaming Again

HARRY PROPOSED TO JULIA. He didn't wait for her to graduate. Perhaps he thought the coolness which developed so rapidly after her return from St. Paul would be checked by laying his heart and his hand at her feet. So he only waited for a moonlight night, and laid them there.

Julia refused him. Naturally she was gratified by

having received a proposal . . . her first. Coming into the house, after it happened, she went to Betsy's room and told her all about it, and called her mother who slipped on a kimono and came in to hear, too. Julia described the proposal in detail, but she hardly bothered to mention that she had turned him down. That was taken for granted.

"Poor Harry!" mourned Betsy. "Did he feel badly, Julia? I hope you were nice to him."

"Oh, I was lovely," said Julia, and went out of the room singing *"Mi chiamano, Mimi."*

"We all know your name is Lucia!" Betsy called after her. "What we want to know is how poor Harry felt."

But Julia was already taking the pins out of her hair.

"I must say," said Mrs. Ray, going back to bed, "that Papa does a lot of unnecessary worrying."

Harry stopped coming to the house but Julia didn't seem to mind. She was busy just then with Tacy's lessons. Miss Clarke had asked Tacy again to sing at Rhetoricals and Julia had almost hypnotized her into accepting. Now they were working hard on the song Tacy would sing.

> *"There's a bower of roses,*
> *By Bendemeer's stream . . ."*

Tacy sang it over and over. Sometimes Betsy, in the parlor, heard her break off and say;

"Julia! I just can't do it!"

But Julia would answer, "Nonsense!" and start over again. When Tacy wasn't thinking about Rhetoricals, she sang it very sweetly.

On the great afternoon Betsy was as nervous as Tacy. They walked to school together, and Betsy kept tight hold of Tacy's icy hand. Tacy's eyes were full of misery. Her cheeks which were usually flushed were so pale that Betsy could see the freckles on them. She was dressed up, of course, in her Sunday blue silk, but she wore her red hair just as always in Grecian braids. No one had been able to persuade Tacy into a pompadour.

"Cheer up!" said Betsy. "Maybe the school will burn down. I'd touch a match to it if I weren't so sure that you're going to sing like an angel."

Tacy tried to smile.

Rhetoricals got under way, with a chorus number. Betsy among the second sopranos kept looking anxiously at Tacy among the first sopranos and then accusingly at Julia. It was all Julia's fault, but her expression was guiltlessly bright. Katie looked as grim as Betsy. She and Betsy were feeling just the same.

Alice recited a piece. *"Johnny gets a hair cut."* It

was humorous and people laughed. But Betsy could not laugh, looking at Tacy's stony profile; and neither could Katie. Julia laughed and clapped.

Number by number, inexorably, the program went forward. At last Miss Clarke announced a solo by Tacy Kelly. Betsy twisted her fingers and looked into her lap. She could not watch Tacy going down the aisle, like a sleep walker, white and stiff.

Julia, who was to play her accompaniment, went forward with her usual assurance. She swung the piano stool up to a proper height, sat down and opened her music. The piano was placed so that she could look at Tacy, and she looked up now, full in her face, and smiled.

She played the opening bars and her lips formed the words. She was almost singing. Tacy began to sing.

And Betsy began to breathe again, and Katie gulped and color swept into her face. For Tacy was singing beautifully, as she sang by the Ray piano.

> "There's a bower of roses,
>   By Bendemeer's stream . . ."

Her voice was tender and plaintive like an Irish harp.

She was tremulously happy afterward. Miss Clarke

said, "You're not going to get out of singing solos after this, Tacy. You're going to sing often for Rhetoricals."

Betsy and Katie were radiant, and Julia was proud.

"I always knew she could do it. She has temperament. Lesson tomorrow at three forty-five, Tacy dear."

Julia was engrossed with Tacy's lessons, but being Julia she was soon engrossed also with more romantic affairs. May had warmed up gradually. On the hills around Deep Valley the wild white plum was in bloom, and one fine afternoon the faculty and the seniors had a picnic. It was an annual event, which Betsy considered important because it gave a holiday to the rest of the school. She and Phil had a splendid ride, and he had just left her at home when Julia came in.

She ran up the steps and into the house calling, "Bettina! Mamma! Bettina!"

"Yes, yes!" "What is it?" Mrs. Ray and Betsy came running.

Julia's hair had blown loose and her small hands were grubby. She was holding a gigantic bouquet of purple violets.

"Bettina!" she said, looking mischievous. "You can now have your revenge."

"What do you mean? What revenge? I don't want any revenge."

"Any time you want it."

"But who on?" Betsy demanded.

"Who do you think fell for me at that picnic? And I didn't try, Bettina. I give you my word I didn't."

"Who?"

Julia began to laugh, showing her pretty teeth, set close together like Geraldine Farrar's. She looked more mischievous than ever.

"Gaston!" she cried. "Your precious Gaston!"

Betsy was thunderstruck.

"I don't see how you can even be interested in such a horrid person," Mrs. Ray said.

"But don't you see?" asked Julia. "I can help Betsy get her revenge."

"Maybe you can get me an 'E,'" said Betsy. "I'd like that better. But I simply can't believe it. He isn't human. He cares for nothing but cutting up frogs."

"He cares about violets," said Julia and gave the big bunch to Betsy to smell while she went to get a vase.

It was true. Astounding as it seemed, Mr. Gaston now followed Julia with calf's eyes. Betsy did not think she could count on an "E" but she did notice a marked softening in his attitude. He smiled at her sometimes, a little sheepishly. He reminded her that she was excused from her homework because she was studying for the Essay Contest.

She was certainly working hard on that. Oftener and oftener now she braved Phil's displeasure and went to the library. Almost in spite of herself she had become fascinated by the life of James J. Hill. She came to know the tough-fibered young Canadian who arrived in Minnesota at the age of seventeen and was soon directing the boats on its rivers and the course of silvery rails across its land. She came to see the majestic northwest country, its Indians and trappers, its pine-encircled lakes and the rivers with magic names. Red River of the North! She said that over and over to herself. She read more than she needed to read, everything she could find, and her essay grew and took shape in her mind until she looked with a friendly challenge into Joe Willard's blue eyes.

"I suppose," he said one day, "you're going to put pink apple blossoms into your essay?"

"Don't you think," Betsy returned, "that apple pie would be more in James J's line?"

"An apple in his pocket, I'd say," Joe answered, and they terminated the conversation quickly. Contestants weren't supposed to discuss their subject with one another.

"After we've written our essays," Betsy thought, "I'd like to talk James J. Hill over with Joe."

Phil disliked the subject, and Betsy ruled it out of

their conversation as they bounced, jounced and rattled about the countryside. Apple trees were coming into bloom, and she found herself squinting at them.

"They look pink, but like pink under gray gauze," she remarked to Phil.

"What are you so interested in apple blossoms for?" he asked, and she explained, but he did not vouchsafe an opinion as to their color.

He was interested only in the auto, careening along at twenty miles or so an hour. They went too fast to admire the flowering bushes, the hosts of bright warblers, the brimming streams with violets and strawberry blossoms on their banks. The enchanting scent of May was blotted out by the bitter smell of gasoline.

Yet when they went, it was better than when they stood still. They were constantly getting stuck in the mud, which infuriated Phil. They got stuck going up hills, too; the engine stalled, and they had to pile rocks and pieces of wood behind the wheels. Betsy had always liked hills, but she came to dread the sight of one.

Things happened, too, to a red auto. Tires had to be patched. The insides had to be tinkered with. Farmers had to come and pull it to the nearest blacksmith shop and Phil always thought the blacksmith was an idiot.

A red auto, Betsy decided, was not so nice as a surrey.

The rest of the Crowd was taking picnics out behind Dandy or Alice's Rex. Betsy had loved picnics ever since she and Tacy, at the age of five, started taking their suppers up to the Hill Street bench. But Phil cared no more for picnics than he did for scenery. He talked scornfully of spiders, and sandy sandwiches, and warm lemonade and other inconsequential things. The spring went by, and Betsy hadn't eaten one hard-boiled egg out doors.

The Friday before the Essay Contest, which was always held on Saturday, the Crowd planned a picnic at Page Park. Tacy had had the idea last fall, the day she and Betsy, up on their own Big Hill, had made up the "Dreaming" song. It had never been carried out, but now the Crowd was enthusiastic.

"Don't you think you and Phil could come?" Tacy pleaded. "I know the Essay Contest comes tomorrow, but you must have studied enough."

"I have," Betsy said. "My head wouldn't hold one more fact about James J. Hill. I'd write a better essay if I went out on a picnic today and let the whole thing jell."

"Then you'll come?" Tacy cried joyfully.

"I'll ask Phil."

Phil was reluctant, as Betsy had known he would be. But she was more insistent than usual. Usually, they did without argument whatever Phil wanted to do. But today Betsy so yearned for a picnic, and the Crowd, and Page Park out on the river that she actually teased.

"I can't imagine anything worse," Phil said, but he gave in at last, with bad grace.

Betsy tried to forget about his ill humor. She hurried home after school, took her books to her room, and put out of sight in Uncle Keith's trunk the notebook with her James J. Hill material.

"I'm just going to forget about you," she said closing the lid. She knew she had done a thorough research job, and she would come back from the picnic so full of joy and fresh air that she couldn't help sleeping well, and writing well tomorrow. "I'm going to write the durn best essay in the contest," she remarked to space.

She put on an old blue sailor suit, and dressed her hair in a braid turned up with a big bow. That was the way she had worn it last year; the way Carney still wore hers. She and Anna filled a basket gleefully, and she looked so happy when she greeted Phil at the door that he almost forgave her for making him go on the picnic. They drove around collecting Tacy, Squirrelly, Pin, Winona. The rest were going with Carney and Alice in their surreys.

They drove across the slough and through the high

white gate which admitted one to the glories of Page Park. There was a race track with a grandstand; then a hill with a flagpole, and on the other side a picnic ground with tall swings and a little kitchen. Beyond that the river flowed over its sandy bottom.

The Crowd went to the picnic ground and swung in the big swings. They swung sitting down with someone pushing, and standing, in pairs, pumping up. Tony and Betsy went so high that they could see the river.

They went to the little kitchen, and made coffee in a big pot. They set out on one of the long tables potato salad, potted meat, sandwiches, hard-boiled eggs, a chocolate cake, a cocoanut cake, and a jug of lemonade. It was a marvelous supper, and Betsy ached from laughing at the silly jokes which seasoned it. Everyone was having a very good time. Even Phil was smiling.

When the empty plates had been piled back into the baskets, the Crowd went to the river. The sky was still flushed with sunset. They skipped stones and the boys, to be daring, smoked punk wood. It grew dark and cool and they made a campfire and sat down around it and sang.

They sang the old songs first, "Annie Laurie," "Juanita," "My Wild Irish Rose," and that one about a tavern.

"There is a tavern in the town,
in the town,
And there my true love sits him down,
sits him down."

Tony chimed in expertly in his deep bass. Betsy sat with her arm around Tacy, singing alto and acting as silly as she used to act in the pre-Philip era.

Exhausting the old songs they came up to "Shine Little Glow Worm," "In the Good Old Summer Time," and others of more recent vintage. They sang "Because I'm Married Now," and "I'm Afraid to Go Home in the Dark." When they were almost sung out, Winona sprang up suddenly.

"I know one we ought to sing in honor of Betsy and Phil!"

She started to sing "Dreaming."

Everyone chimed in, and instead of singing the right words they sang the words Betsy had made up. They had learned them the day of her fictitious dream, and had often sung them teasingly since. Winona, Betsy knew, didn't mean any harm. She probably thought that Phil had heard the parody, and that, if he hadn't, it would be a good joke. Tacy turned her head sharply toward Betsy. Her eyes in the darkness seemed to ask whether she should stop it. But it was too late to try to do that now.

The Crowd was singing lustily:

"Dreaming, Dreaming,
Of your red auto I'm dreaming,
Dreaming of days when I got a ride,
Dreaming of hours spent by your side.
Dreaming, dreaming,
Of your red auto I'm dreaming,
Love will not change,
While the auto ree-mains,
Dree-ee-eaming."

Betsy sang merrily along with the rest. Phil had never heard the parody, so far as she knew. But of course he wouldn't mind. Yet she had a queer apprehensive feeling. Phil didn't have a very good sense of humor.

He was not sitting near her and she could not see his expression. Walking back to the picnic ground for the baskets he did not seek her out. They went on to the field where Dandy and Rex were finishing their oats and where Phil had left the auto. Still neither chance nor design brought them together.

Calling jokes and farewells, people took the same seats they had occupied driving out. Betsy sat down on the front seat of the auto. Phil cranked and the car began to shake. He climbed up beside her but he did not speak.

They left Winona and Pin at Winona's house, took Squirrelly to his home and Tacy to Hill Street. Tacy had noticed, Betsy knew, that Phil was very silent. Getting out of the auto, she leaned over and gave Betsy a kiss.

"You write a good essay tomorrow. Do you hear? I'll be saying my prayers for you."

"Thanks," Betsy said, and she and Phil drove on.

Betsy felt terrible. Her apprehension had grown into a premonition of disaster. She felt slightly ill as the car bounced along down Hill Street, down Broad Street, and up the Plum Street hill. Phil had still not spoken. Betsy made one or two timid conversational overtures but he did not respond, so she too was silent.

He got out of the auto, and helped her out. They climbed the two flights of stairs to her porch, but he did not hold her arm as usual. She started to open the door.

"Good night," she said. Then he burst out.

"What do you mean by making a fool of me with that ridiculous song?"

"Phil," said Betsy. "You must believe me. I made up that song . . . or Tacy and I did together . . . way last September, before I even knew you."

"It's about me, isn't it?"

"Yes, but . . ."

"I thought I meant more to you than that."

"But don't you see? I made up that song before I even knew you. Tacy and I were out on a picnic. We were just acting silly. You know how silly we act . . ." But he didn't. She had never acted silly in front of Phil . . . until tonight.

"I thought you acted very silly at the park," he said coldly.

"I suppose you didn't like me that way."

"No, I can't say I did."

All at once they were in the midst of a furious quarrel.

Betsy interrupted desperately. "Phil, listen to me. I tell you again that when I made up that song you were a perfect stranger. But I'm sorry. Do you hear? I'm apologizing. I'm very sorry."

Phil jumped off the porch and ran back to his auto.

Betsy went into the house and up to her room.

"Have fun?" came a voice from her mother's room.

"Wonderful," said Betsy. She started undressing. She didn't wash or put up her hair. She didn't even think of doing it. She got into her night gown, and into bed, and started to cry.

She had lost Phil. She knew she had lost him. The proud dazzling structure of the Betsye-Phil affair had crashed about her head. She had lost Phil. Irma, probably, would get him. She cried for a very long time.

When the gong woke her next morning, she felt numb. Her head was aching. In the mirror she saw that she looked as badly as she felt. She couldn't remember a thing about James J. Hill.

At breakfast everyone noticed how badly she looked. The family knew without being told that she had quarreled with Phil. She took coffee, found a pen, and said good-by. Everyone wished her good luck but with almost frightened glances. They knew, Betsy felt, that no one who looked as she looked this morning could possibly win.

She walked to school and found Miss Clarke and Miss O'Rourke waiting in the upper hall. Just as last year, they directed her into the algebra classroom where the other seven contestants were already gathered. Joe Willard grinned when Betsy came in, but when he saw her expression he looked troubled. A bell rang, and they all started to write.

Betsy's essay was not so bad as she had feared it would be. Everything she knew about James J. Hill came back to her and she knew all there was to be found out about him in the Deep Valley Public Library. Yet even as she wrote her well organized and heavily factual paper, she knew it was not good. Not at one point did she kindle to her subject and bring it to life. Not one bit of the emotion she had felt when she read about the Red River of the North came back to her now and transferred itself to paper.

She wrote until twelve o'clock, then turned in her essay and went out into the hall.

Astonishingly, Joe Willard was waiting for her. It had never happened before. He stood brushing his hands over his yellow hair with a worried expression.

"You didn't feel well; did you, Betsy?"

She managed to smile. "Yes, of course. I have a feeling, though, that the Philomathians have won the sophomore points."

22

Betsye into Betsy

SHE STILL FELT NUMB, but that wore off at last. She
began to be pricklingly conscious of the warm sweet
day pushing in at the windows, the smell of lilacs, the
song of birds. The telephone too grew harder to bear.
It rang and rang, but it was always for Julia, or her
father, or her mother; or if it was for her, it was not
Phil. Her heart would rush up into her throat when

she was called to the 'phone, and her mother and Julia must have sensed this, for they stopped saying just, "Telephone, Betsy." They began to say gently, "It's for you, Betsy, but it isn't Phil."

Late that Sunday afternoon Winona telephoned. She sounded anxious.

"Gee, Betsy, I hope I didn't get you in Dutch starting that song Friday night. I thought Phil had heard it. And anyway, I never thought of it making him mad."

Betsy swallowed. "What makes you think it did?"

"Why . . . er . . . you might as well know. He's called Irma and asked her to go to the track meet. Next Saturday. He wants her to go out in his auto."

So! It had come! But Betsy had known it would come. She had known even before last night when everything toppled. It had always been just a house of cards.

She was silent for so long that Winona spoke again.

"Irma didn't wangle it, Betsy. She doesn't even want to go."

The powerful arm of pride stretched out to steady Betsy.

"Tell Irma for me she's a chump not to go. That auto is fun."

"You ought to know!" Winona gave a relieved giggle.

"Phil and I had a terrible row," Betsy said, "and

we're finished. Tell Irma that if she wants to see the Merry Widow, she can just come up and look at me."

"You don't sound very heartbroken."

"I'll put on my Merry Widow hat for her," Betsy joked. They talked a little longer, and then Betsy rang off.

She went to the closet for a jacket and a tam.

"I'm going for a walk," she called carelessly to the family.

The May evening was poignantly sweet with a moon like a half slice of lemon in the sky. Betsy began to walk, and at the same time she began to cry. She walked and cried for a long time but that was the end of her tears. She found herself at Lincoln Park, that pie-shaped piece of land with a big elm tree and a fountain on it, which stood where Broad Street met Hill. Instinctively, in her trouble, she had headed for Hill Street and Tacy. But she stopped at Lincoln Park. She washed her face and hands in the fountain and dried them on her handkerchief and sat down on a bench and looked up at the sky.

"Well, that's that," she said.

She went back to the thought she had had when Winona told her the news. It couldn't have lasted.

"It couldn't have lasted. It wasn't true from the beginning. It wasn't the real me that Phil liked. No particular compliment in having him crazy about somebody who wasn't even me.

"I'm darned glad I went down to Tom's for that sour cream cake, even though it did make Phil mad, and that was the beginning of everything. I wanted to go.

"And I'm darned glad I did my best on the Essay Contest. The Essay Contest was more important than he was. It belonged to me, not to some person I was pretending to be.

"I'm not even sorry I acted so silly at the picnic. I'm sorry about the song . . . that hurt his feelings. But when I acted silly I was doing what I had a right to do. I was just being myself."

That last phrase brought into her mind something which comforted her. It was the poetry Julia had been reciting around the house last winter.

> *"This above all: to thine own self be true,*
> *And it must follow, as the night the day,*
> *Thou canst not then be false to any man."*

"That's exactly what I'm trying to say!" Betsy cried, and jumped up in her excitement.

"*'To thine own self be true!' 'To thine own self be true!'* That's what I have to do if I'm going to get out and make something of myself. I lost the Essay Contest. But that's all right. I tried. I've done terrible work in school all spring and I have to get busy now if I'm going to pass my exams."

She started walking rapidly toward home. It was hard to go, for she knew her father would be making sandwiches. Julia would have a beau, and there would be singing . . . all the songs she and Phil had danced to. But thinking that, she only walked faster and when she reached home things weren't so hard as she had expected them to be.

For Tacy was there. Tacy had heard from Alice, who had heard it from Carney, who had heard it from Winona, who had heard it from Irma that Phil had asked Irma to go to the track meet. Tacy had had a feeling, probably, that Betsy might like to have her around. Betsy was so glad to see her that she gave her a bear hug. Not that she needed to confide in her now. She had done her confiding to the stars in Lincoln Park. But the loving warmth of Tacy's presence helped.

The family had finished eating but her father made some sandwiches for her, and Betsy and Tacy went out into the kitchen to watch him. They joked about the coming examinations, and stood with their arms about each other acting silly through the singing.

Tacy did not so much as mention Phil. But when Katie and Leo came to call for her, she said good-by to Betsy with a curious and helpful remark.

"Betsy, did it ever occur to you that the better

people know you, the better they like you?"

Betsy thought this over. She thought of Tacy and Tib and Alice and Winona and Carney and Tony and Cab . . . all very old friends now.

"Why, yes," she answered. "I guess they do. What of it?"

"It shows how silly you are ever to act like somebody you aren't," said Tacy, and gave her another hug, and went out.

It all fitted in with what William Shakespeare had said hundreds of years before.

The next day at school Betsy went to Carney. "If you're still looking for members, I'll go into that Girls' Debating Club. I think I'd enjoy it."

A few days later she went to Miss Clarke, "Tacy and I," she said, "have decided that if you still want us to, we'll sing the 'Cat Duet.' We've done it for so many years. It's too bad to break the tradition."

"That's what I thought," Miss Clarke answered eagerly. "I was awfully sorry when you decided against it."

"There's another thing," said Betsy, "I've been wanting to tell you. I really worked on the Essay Contest this year, Miss Clarke. But something happened, and I didn't write a very good essay. I'm sorry."

"Why, that's all right, Betsy."

"I just thought I'd tell you," said Betsy, "so that you wouldn't be building up any false hopes. I'm afraid that next year you'll be choosing someone else to represent our class on the Essay Contest. I wouldn't blame you," she added, "I've let you down for two years running."

Miss Clarke put her arm around Betsy with one of those little girlish gestures she had.

"We'll see about that," she replied.

In the ensuing days Betsy studied. She really studied. She made a game out of seeing how much she could raise her marks, which she knew were bad, by passing good examinations. She wanted to study instead of going to the track meet, but she feared that this was weakness. So she pinned on the school colors and went with the other girls to watch the boys in the hundred yard dash, the two hundred and twenty yard dash, the discus throwing, the high jump, the hurdle races and the pole vault.

She sat beside Carney driving out. Carney had been very nice to her since the quarrel. She hadn't mentioned Phil at all, but she referred to him diffidently now.

"It must be hard," she said, slapping the reins over Dandy's back, "to break off with a boy you've been going around with. It must be something like . . . having him go away."

"I guess it is," said Betsy. After a pause she remarked, "I'm glad you've started going with Al, Carney. He's an awfully nice kid."

"Yes, he is," said Carney. "But I'm going to tell you something, Betsy. Larry has been gone for a whole year now, and I like him as much as I ever did."

"Do you?" Betsy asked.

"I still like him better than anyone," said Carney. Her dimple didn't show at all, and she looked almost stern.

Betsy thought this over at the track meet, for Irma, looking charming, sat in the red auto with Phil and a big box of candy. Betsy didn't like it . . . but she didn't mind it so much as she had thought she would.

"It can't be," she thought, "that I liked Phil anywhere near as much as Carney liked Larry."

She was glad she had seen them together for the first sting was gone. And their appearance at the meet had another good effect. It must have confirmed significant rumors for Tony, Cab and Dennie all appeared as of old the next night for Sunday night lunch.

Everyone was very glad to see them. They went out to watch Mr. Ray buttering bread and slicing onions; they sang around the piano, teased Betsy about her curls. Mr. Gaston came that night for the very first time . . . which made it quite an occasion.

He flushed when he saw the boys, but after a period

of uncertainty he started acting boyish himself. He laughed harder than anyone, made poor jokes. And he must, Betsy thought pityingly, be all of twenty-three! Betsy felt almost sorry for him and hoped that Julia wouldn't really seek revenge.

The next week was filled with examinations, and rehearsals for the commencement exercises. The chorus was singing "Damascus."

"Save the holy sepulchre,
A-a-men."

Betsy and Tacy heard it in their dreams.
Julia was practising her solo.

"A rose in the garden,
Over the way . . ."

"I think it was heartless of you to choose that song," Betsy said.

She and Julia had washed their hair and were drying it out on the lawn at the back of the house. The trees were in full leaf now; the bridal wreath was coming into bloom.

"Why?" Julia asked, shaking her long locks.

"Because of Harry. That's his song. You learned it to please him."

"Oh . . . Harry," said Julia. "I don't feel guilty about turning Harry down. You know, Bettina, I had to be true to myself."

"You what?" Betsy cried. After an incredulous moment she told Julia how those lines from William Shakespeare had fitted into her own life that spring. She said how foolish she thought she had been to try to be different from herself.

Julia listened thoughtfully.

"You're absolutely right," she said when Betsy finished. "Fundamentally, that is. Each one of us has to be true to the deepest thing that is in him. But Bettina . . . a little play-acting has its place . . . with a woman, that is."

"What do you mean?"

"You wanted Phil, and you went out and got him. It took grit. It took determination. It was all right. And you couldn't have done it without a little of what Cab calls 'la de da.'"

"But I didn't keep him."

"Silly! You didn't want to."

Betsy threw down the brush with which she had been conscientiously adding gloss to her hair.

"What do you mean, I didn't want to?"

"You know you didn't. You wanted other things more."

"What?"

"Well, the Essay Contest, for example."

"That's true," Betsy thought, staring at her brush. "And I wanted the picnic more, and not hurting Tom's feelings. I wanted . . . my freedom more."

She did not answer.

"You didn't want to go to the bother of keeping him," Julia continued. "But, Bettina, the whole affair did you a lot of good. You're better groomed, more poised, you have sweeter manners and . . . well . . . more charm than you had before you started it. Don't be scornful of 'la de da,' Bettina. You may want to use it sometime with someone you really like."

"But then," cried Betsy, "surely I wouldn't have to use it! Not with someone who was my own kind!"

"Oh . . . wouldn't you?" asked Julia, and smiled inscrutably, and began to shake her hair again.

This was too confusing! Betsy stretched out on the grass and looked up at the sky, June blue with puff-ball clouds.

"Life," she said, "is complicated . . . for a woman, at least."

"You have to be wise as a serpent and harmless as a dove," Julia agreed, looking anything but harmless.

23
Julia's Graduation

THE FIRST EVENT OF Commencement Week was the joint evening meeting of Philomathians and Zetamathians at which the essay cup would be awarded.

Betsy put on the pink silk dress and the daisy wreath. She wanted to look nice for she would have to sit on the platform with the other contestants, but she well knew, this year, that she would not be asked to stand and bow. Joe Willard who sat opposite her, very blond in a new dark suit, would be the one to rise when the sophomore points were awarded. This year no one would be surprised. Betsy had told not only Miss Clarke but everyone she knew that she could not possibly win.

The assembly room was crowded, even to the bookcases. It was gay with Zetamathian blue and Philomathian orange. Betsy felt festive and untroubled even when, at the end of Miss Bangeter's speech, Joe was announced as the winner.

"That's because I did my best," she thought, applauding.

It was consoling, too, that the Zetamathians won the cup. Competing freshmen, juniors, and seniors had saved the day. The Zetamathians had already won the athletics cup, so now they had two out of three. No loyal Zetamathian could fail to find the evening glorious.

Betsy went up to Joe and offered her congratulations. He smiled.

"This luck can't last forever. It'll be your turn next year."

"Heavens!" cried Betsy. "He's being polite."

"I'm always polite."

"No, it means you're sorry for me. You're hurting my pride."

He grinned. "I do have a few kind emotions. Do you know what I almost did this spring when the apple trees were in bloom up at Butternut Center? I almost 'phoned to tell you not to worry. They were rosy."

"Well, why didn't you?" asked Betsy. She heard her voice growing soft and sweet, the way she had tuned it for Phil. She remembered her conversation with Julia on the lawn, and blushed. Joe Willard laughed.

Betsy looked for him the next night at Class Day exercises. He wasn't there. She looked again at the class play. He wasn't there either. Artfully, late the following afternoon, she went to the library. He was not there.

She asked Miss Sparrow about him. He and Miss Sparrow, she knew, were friends.

"Why, he's left town," Miss Sparrow explained. "He's going to work with a threshing rig this summer. He'll get three dollars a day, he said, and earn all he needs for next year. You know, Betsy, Joe supports himself. Entirely. It's pretty wonderful, I think."

"I think so too," Betsy replied. She heard herself telling Miss Sparrow something of her difficulties with Joe . . . how she had tried to get him into the Crowd, and how he had told her the Crowd bored him.

"I think," Miss Sparrow said, "I can explain that."

They were alone in the library except for some children in the Children's Room. She leaned across the desk, lowered her voice, and made quite a speech about Joe.

"I figure him out this way," she said. "He has no father or mother. He has to work for a living. And being barred from the usual things high school students do, the things requiring money and time, he takes refuge in books. He not only reads them, but he dreams about them. He sees himself as the heroes he admires. He is confident that he could behave as Ivanhoe did, or Marco Polo, or D'Artagnan. Do you know what I mean?"

Betsy said she did.

"He isn't a boy who pities himself. Not at all. He has to work, but he makes that an adventure. He would really like to play football, or baseball after school, but he can't. He has to go to the Creamery. So he just makes plans about playing them in college. It helps that, when he has a spare hour and can play, he is better than average.

"His routine is quite satisfactory to him but only because he puts out of his mind the things he cannot have. And they are the boy and girl pleasures. If he let you draw him into your Crowd, he would be constantly embarrassed. He would be forced to admit that he isn't, perhaps, quite so lucky as he thinks he is. Don't you see, Betsy? Living as he does now, he doesn't mind shabby clothes. But he is a proud boy. He wouldn't like coming to call on you in shabby clothes. When you urge him to come he gets desperate. He just has to be rude. Don't you see?"

"Yes," Betsy answered. "I see."

Walking home she thought over what Miss Sparrow had said. Next year, she resolved, she would find some way to make a friend of Joe . . . and without making things hard for him, either.

Commencement night was drawing very near. The chorus was rehearsing in the Opera House.

> *"Save the holy sepulchre,*
> *A-a-men."*

Presents were flooding in for Julia. She was being fitted to a lace-trimmed, white silk dress with a crushed white satin belt and elbow length sleeves. There was much talk at home about her plans. It had been decided that she was going to go to the state university at Minneapolis. She would take the music course.

"This is the end of something, Bob," Mrs. Ray kept saying. "It's the first break in the family. Next year Julia will be gone."

"Minneapolis isn't very far away," Mr. Ray answered

with his usual optimism. "Besides, she isn't going until fall. We're all going out to the Inn at Murmuring Lake and have one swell-elegant vacation."

"Just the same," Mrs. Ray persisted. "It's the end of something. You know it as well as I do."

He did, and Betsy knew it too. She felt increasingly solemn. Julia was through with high school; next year she would be gone. There wouldn't be any Julia around to play the piano, or to fix her hair, or to tell her to tell boys she had had a dream about them.

Betsy felt tearful at supper, and she could see that her mother did. Mr. Ray acted unusually cheerful, as always when he felt the opposite. Julia put on the white graduating dress.

"You look puny, lovey," Anna said.

"She looks like a bride," Mrs. Ray mourned. "She'll be getting married, the next thing we know."

Mr. Gaston had sent her a gift of pink carnations. Her father had sent her pink roses. Julia mixed them into one superlative bouquet.

They drove down to the Opera House behind Old Mag. Mr. and Mrs. Ray and Margaret and Anna sat together, near the front. Betsy, because of being in the chorus, sat on the stage with the graduates. It was a sweet June night, but inside the Opera House there was only that stuffy opera house smell.

Betsy and Tacy sang with the chorus.

*"Save the holy sepulchre,
A-a-men."*

Julia sang her solo.

*"There's a rose in the garden,
Over the way . . ."*

Betsy, sitting behind her, admired the lovely line of Julia's upswept hair.

The diplomas were handed out. The members of the graduating class marched up one by one to fond applause. Julia went up, and Katie, her cheeks as red as the red carnations she carried.

After it was over Betsy and Tacy started home together.

"I don't see why we had to sing that Holy Sepulchre song," Betsy said. "I felt badly enough already."

"So did I," said Tacy. "It seemed like a funeral at our house tonight. Of course Katie isn't going so far away as Julia is. She'll just be going to the college on the hill. But things won't be the same, Mamma says."

"It's the first break in our family," Betsy answered.

"Remember how we used to fight with them when we were kids?" Tacy asked, smiling.

"Do I! Remember the contest for May Queen?"

"And how we peeked and saw them at their club?

And now they are graduating. Life is funny."

"Life is queer."

They reached the foot of Plum Street Hill where they must part, and had just concluded plans for a picnic the next day when Tacy said:

"Betsy! We've come to the end of your Winding Hall of Fate."

"That's right," Betsy cried. "And what a hall it's been! You sang a solo at school. I went to Milwaukee. We found out that Tib is maybe coming back, and I've had . . . you might say . . . my First Big Love Affair. I'll have to go home and write it all up in my journal."

"Make it sound thrilling."

"I will."

"Of course," Betsy said, "that winding hall keeps right on winding. Only now it takes an even bigger turn. We're practically juniors. Can you realize that?"

"To be frank, no," Tacy said. "Good-by, Betsy. See you in the morning."

"See you in the morning," Betsy said.

Maud Hart Lovelace and Her World

(Adapted from *The Betsy-Tacy Companion: A Biography of Maud Hart Lovelace* by Sharla Scannell Whalen)

Maud Palmer Hart circa 1906
Collection of Sharla Scannell Whalen

MAUD HART LOVELACE was born on April 25, 1892, in Mankato, Minnesota. Shortly after Maud's high school graduation in 1910, the Hart family left Mankato and settled in Minneapolis, where Maud attended the University of Minnesota. In 1917 she married Delos W. Lovelace, a newspaper reporter who later became a popular writer of short stories. The Lovelaces' daughter, Merian, was born in 1931.

Maud would tell her daughter bedtime stories about her childhood in Minnesota, and it was these stories that gave her the idea of writing the Betsy-Tacy books. She did not intend to write an entire series when *Betsy-Tacy*, the first book, was published in 1940, but readers asked for more stories. So Maud took Betsy through high school and beyond college to the "great world" and marriage.

The final book in the series, *Betsy's Wedding*, was published in 1955.

The Betsy-Tacy books are based very closely upon Maud's own life. "I could make it all up, but in these Betsy-Tacy stories, I love to work from real incidents," Maud wrote. This is especially true of the four high school books. We know a lot about her life during this period because Maud kept diaries (one for each high school year, just like Betsy) as well as a scrapbook during high school. As she wrote to a cousin in 1964: "In writing the high school books my diaries were extremely helpful. The family life, customs, jokes, traditions are all true and the general pattern of the years is also accurate."

Almost every character in the high school books, even the most minor, can be matched to an actual person living in Mankato in the early years of the twentieth century. (See page 331 for a list of characters and their real-life counterparts.) But there are exceptions. As Maud wrote: "A small and amusing complication is that while some of the characters are absolutely based on one person—for example Tacy, Tib, Cab, Carney—others were merely suggested by some person and some characters are combinations of two real persons." For example, the character Winona Root is based on two people. In

Betsy and Tacy Go Downtown and *Winona's Pony Cart,* Maud's childhood friend Beulah Hunt was the model for Winona. The Winona Root we encounter in the high school books, however, was based on Maud's high school friend Mary Eleanor Johnson, known as "El."

Another exception is the character Joe Willard, who is based on Maud's husband, Delos Wheeler Lovelace. In real life, Delos did not attend Mankato High School with Maud. He was two years Maud's junior, and the two didn't meet until after high school. But as Maud said, "Delos came into my life much later than Joe Willard came into Betsy's, and yet he is Joe Willard to the life." This is because Maud asked her husband to give her a description of his boyhood. She then gave his history to Joe.

Maud eventually donated her high school scrapbook and many photographs to the Blue Earth County Historical Society in Mankato, where they still reside today. But she destroyed her diaries sometime after she had finished writing the Betsy-Tacy books, in the late 1950s. We can't be sure why, but we do know that, as Maud confessed once in an interview, they "were full of boys, boys, boys." She may not have felt comfortable about bequeathing them to posterity!

Maud Hart Lovelace died on March 11, 1980. But her legacy lives on in the beloved series she created and in her legions of fans, many of whom are members of the Betsy-Tacy Society and the Maud Hart Lovelace Society. For more information, write to:

The Betsy-Tacy Society
c/o BECHS
415 Cherry Street
Mankato, MN 56001

The Maud Hart Lovelace Society
Fifty 94th Circle NW, # 201
Minneapolis, MN 55448

Maud Hart Lovelace Archive

Maud at sixteen

About Betsy in Spite of Herself

MAUD'S SOPHOMORE YEAR at Mankato High School (1907–1908) is fictionalized in *Betsy in Spite of Herself*. Not surprisingly, many of Betsy's experiences were also Maud's. Maud *was* elected to a class office during her sophomore year, but she was elected class treasurer, rather than secretary, as Betsy was. And Maud did write a parody to the song "Same Old Story," which she kept in her high school scrapbook. The lyrics are almost exactly the same as those in the book, with the exception of the last two lines of the chorus. Instead of "For she's Deep Valley's High School Girl, / And she's all right," it reads "Hurrah for 'Kato's High School girl, / For she's alright."

Maud's greatest adventure of the year was probably her Christmas trip to Milwaukee. One thing Maud did that Betsy didn't was stop in St. Paul to visit her friend Connie Davis (Bonnie from *Heaven to Betsy* had moved to Paris, not St. Paul, as her real-life counterpart had). Once she arrived in Milwaukee, Maud undoubtedly met a lot of Midge's family, as Betsy does Tib's family. Midge's maternal grandparents, the Iraseks, were both from Austria, where

Maud's crowd loved to visit Heinze's Ice Cream Parlor, which was owned by Ferdinand Heinze.

High school dances were held here, at Schiller Hall.

Grossmama Irasek did embroidery for the imperial house of Franz Joseph, Emperor of Austria. And Midge's paternal grandparents, the Gerlachs, were from Germany. However, Grosspapa Gerlach had died by the time Maud visited Milwaukee, so she wouldn't have met him or attended a Christmas party at his house. But the Christmas party Betsy attends in the book wasn't purely from Maud's imagination. Her sister Kathleen traveled to Europe in 1909 (as Julia does in a later book) and spent Christmas in Germany. Many of the details are taken from a letter Kathleen sent to her family about her experiences there.

Another fascinating detail about Betsy's Christmas visit that is historically accurate is the introduction of "The Merry Widow Waltz." In fact, "The Merry Widow Waltz" *was* brand-new at Christmas in 1907. *The Mankato Free Press* advertised a New Year's Eve performance of the opera *The Merry Widow* in its December 26, 1907, edition—the first appearance of the waltz in Mankato. And when the Merry Widow hat made its appearance the following spring, it soon became all the rage.

Maud and Midge stayed up all night to ring in the New Year, just like Betsy and Tib do. Maud later recalled a Christmas visit to "Tib" in Milwaukee, where she decided to change her personality. "I was going to be tall, dark, and mysterious." In the book, Betsy decides to inaugurate her new personality by going with Phil Brandish. We don't know if there really was someone like Phil in Maud's life; he seems to be one of the "loose characterizations" and may have been based on more than one boy. However, a yearbook note to Maud from Bick refers to a certain auto and reads, "Love will not change while the auto remains," which was a line in Betsy's version of "Dreaming" about Phil. So perhaps there was a red car–driving boy in Maud's sophomore year.

Like Betsy, Maud did add an "e" to her name. In real life, though, she started spelling her name "Maude" when she was a freshman, or even earlier. Although "Maude" lasted beyond the end of sophomore year, she probably discovered that she was happiest when she was true to herself, like Betsy.

Maud pasted her dance card from the Leap Year Dance into her scrapbook.

Will you dance?

1908

1. Waltz, ...
2. Two Step, Baker
3. Schottishe, Rost.
4. Waltz, Sherman H
5. Circle Two Step, Bratt
6. Waltz, Henry Lee
7. Two Step, Alun F
8. Schottishe, ...
9. Waltz, ... Wood
10. Two Step, ...
11. Schottishe, ...
12. Two Step, C or S
13. Waltz, ...
14. Two Step, Lister P
15. Waltz, Earl Hoon

Maud's lyrics for her "Same Old Story" parody from her high school scrapbook.

Parody on "Same old Story."

(1) I am going to sing a ditty
        Of the little freshman Maid,
    Timid, tearful, and retiring,
        Flirtacious I'm afraid.
    Faithfully she learns her lessons,
        And she never, never, cheats
    Never sticks a pin into her neighbor,
        Or carves initials on the seats.

cho. Same old story, same old High.
    Same old bunch of gigglers,
        As the years pass by
    She's a hummer, shining light,
    Hurrah for "Kato's" High School girl,
        For she's alright

Maud in
her Merry
Widow hat

Mildred Oleson
(Irma) in her Merry
Widow hat

Connie Davis (Bonnie) in
her Merry Widow hat

Fictional Characters and Their Real-Life Counterparts

Betsy Ray	Maud Palmer Hart
Julia Ray	Kathleen Palmer Hart
Margaret Ray	Helen Palmer Hart
Bob Ray	Thomas Walden Hart
Jule Ray	Stella Palmer Hart
Tacy Kelly	Frances Vivian Kenney
Tib Muller	Marjorie Gerlach
Irma Biscay	Florence Mildred Oleson
Phil Brandish	Carl George Hoerr
Dennie Farisy	Paul Gerald Ford
Al Larson	Henry Orlando Lee
Stan Moore	Herman Hayward
Hazel Smith	Hazel Schoelkopf
Joe Willard	Delos Wheeler Lovelace